MW00334858

Thank you for buying this novel. To find more about the story and receive bonus material, sign up for our newsletter by visiting:

themachinemurders.com

ISBN-13: 978-1-7373682-1-2
Editor: Ioli Delivani
Translator: Kalliopy Paleos
Cover design by: Poppy Alexiou
Cover photo: FlorenceD, Pixabay
Author Photo: Maria Markezi
Library of Congress Control Number: 8203893981

For information about this publication, please email info@publisto.com.

 Publisto

Chapters

I. Infinite Datasets of Blue

1.

He thought all waters must ultimately reveal their identity. The cold blue of Cape Cod is nothing like the Indian Ocean's pastels. A Californian could say the same of his steel-grey Pacific, or a Thai contemplating the turquoise Gulf of Thailand. Manos Manu was dreaming of a machine learning system that could pinpoint a location given a single image through a virtually infinite dataset of ocean pics. Their colors and currents, the unmistakable hues of their depths, the breadth of the sun's rays on their surface, the water temperature, the kind of sand. A neural network would even classify the living organisms contained in each and every drop.

Manos Manu was on holiday in Mykonos when the officer from the Cyclades Police precinct asked him to investigate a sunken corpse found in the waters of Ornos there. Manos instantly agreed, mostly to work on his plan. He now found himself on waters of his own origins, its pure, sparkling colors surging as if from a wellspring at the earth's core. His beloved Greece.

The harbor boat sliced through the breezes with a tranquil, self-assured drone.

"Captain Panagiotis here was Director at our local Authority for twenty years, way before I came," Officer Bellas was saying. Manos turned to the captain, who kept his eyes ahead and said nothing. On the opposite deck, an equally silent Coast Guard diver deftly arranged his gear.

"His daughter Lena is a criminologist," continued the officer.

This name got the captain's attention. He gave Manos a smile, sizing him up.

"You're here for the conference too, eh?" he asked.

Manos had seen a large poster at the airport boasting of the criminology symposium. Day one in Greece, and I'm already at a seaside crime scene. Tomorrow, a seaside criminology conference. No country for those with aversion to salt.

"Uh, I'm on vacation."

"Mr. Manu is from the States," explained the officer. "He's with Interpol."

"Interpol in America?" asked the captain.

"Interpol Singapore," Bellas answered again.

"So, there's Interpol in Singapore..." the older man said, as if to himself.

Manos cleared his throat. "Our Global Complex for Innovation is there." His Greek, learned mostly in New York, was halting but correct.

The two natives looked at him, uncomprehending.

"My division is based there," he said.

Manos could see thoughts of pay grades and rank flit across their faces and then vanish. Coolly, the captain asked, "And Interpol sent you here?"

"We were just getting acquainted, and I asked him to come take a look," said Bellas.

Captain Panagiotis gave them a sharp look, then shrugged his shoulders. "Someone goes down every summer," he said.

The officer was staring at the water. "This one's particular."

Manos thought again of the volumes of import packages necessary for a neural system to detect the shoreline of Mykonos. Ornos Bay itself, to be exact. Millions of images. Trillions of pixels. A classifier for the seas. But where to get those image libraries? A bit bashfully, he took out his phone and took a shot of the aqua waves. Have to start somewhere.

Captain Panagiotis cut speed, deftly turning the wheel. The harbor boat obeyed, homing its course around the buoy. Standing in another boat just nearby, a man gave them a nod.

They had reached the corpse.

2.

Particular. That was what the anonymous man on the call had said, panting in horror. *I was diving... over on the left... at Orno... Santa Marina... there's a body... you have to come... he's caught on a buoy... no, not floating... he's at the bottom... he's tangled somehow... it's... particular...*

A mere two hours earlier, within the brilliantly whitewashed walls of the Cycladic Islands Police Directorate, Commanding Officer Yanis Bellas and two older colleagues had been watching closely as their new guest, Manos Manu, helped one of the younger agents navigate a search on his own computer. It was a custom version of Microsoft Dynamics' CRM for Interpol's satellite offices. Way back, a representative had come down from Athens to install it, present it to the twenty-two authorized staff members on the island, and take a dip. No one had even logged in.

"...just as you would any other program," Manos mumbled with gracious forbearance as he clicked. Bellas looked perfectly bewildered.

But Manos' real priority on this, his only vacation of the year, was the Party. The parties. The caravan from beach to restaurant to bar along which Liza Eckerhorn and James Will were going to tow their three hundred wedding guests like an unravelling strand of Greek worry beads. One week from today under the burning July sun, the caravan would gather at the church of Santa Marina for the wedding, champagne streaming along the sands and flowing into the sea.

Manos and James had been roommates at Stanford. Three short months ago, Manos had been in the running for best man. Then, his graduate studies winding down, Manos had made a somewhat random call to Interpol from Palo Alto and shot them an application. A few weeks later, he found himself the rising star of the Innovation Center and a resident of Singapore. James had taken all this in by phone. Hey, good for you, man. But Manos sensed the clique saw it as second-class. A betrayal. Data science would have been one thing - Silicon Valley was paved with gold back then - but who wanted a cop in the bridal party?

Stefan, a friend of the bride who was already a senior partner in a sizeable VC fund, made the cut for best man. Still, they had not lost touch. Manos fought the loneliness of his on-the-job training in Singapore by sending James funny videos over WhatsApp. In return, however, he received grave news: *Liza. It's getting serious. We are thinking of maybe Mykonos for the wedding. You are half-Greek, you speak the language - can you give us a hand? - J...* Manos obliged, suggesting local tourist offices, churches and sites for the reception. However, very soon he found himself outsourced. All that remained for him was a simple invitation.

"Aren't you and your friends staying at Santa Marina?" Bellas suddenly asked him, just finishing up a call and standing up.

"We are."

"Let's go," said Bellas, as the cordial visit suddenly became hands-on fieldwork. "I think one of them just hit bottom."

3.

The bottom in question surged shimmering from the center of the earth; the harbor boat had reached a point just southwest of the golden shores of the Santa Marina Resort. Manos looked past Captain Panagiotis at the man in the waiting boat.

"Plain-clothes officer?" he asked Bellas.

"Owns the speedboat rental by the resort. Never misses a thing," Bellas shrugged.

The man's hair was dried to a crisp around the mask he had pushed up on his forehead. Positioning it back over his face, he said in a muffled voice: "Pretty sure you're going to need some help."

Manos watched the others dive in. *What on earth am I doing here?*

"Let's go see if it's one of your buddies," Bellas called through his mask, sinking down.

The captain handed him a mask. Manos took off his shirt and shoes and dove in after them. About five meters under, the spectacle loomed into view: a sunken buoy above a naked man whose arms were raised, as if just finishing a marathon. A heavy chain wound around his body and led down to an anchor dug deep into the sand. Manos surged forward and reached the others. The chain, about the girth of a man's wrist, rose from the mouth of the dead man and was attached to a rectangular white buoy that did not quite reach the water's surface. Upon it, in unsteady red letters, was spray-painted: FREE.

The victim, possibly thirty years old, did remind him of someone. Wavy blond hair gave him the air of some bemused sun god. But this was a new arrival; the slim, toned form was pale, untouched by the Grecian July sun.

Manos came up for air. *What? Did I just see...?*

He needed a deep breath for the next dive. The victim was like an actor portraying a naked, helpless man. Keen to see the chain again, he bumped up against the diver's tanks. They looked at each other like frightened fish ready to dart, both understanding at the same time. The chain was not holding up the arms of the corpse. It wasn't tangled around his body. It had been swallowed. Manos saw it coming out of the lower torso.

Welcome to Mykonos!

He came up for breath.

"What the fuck?" came muffled from the officer's mask.

Fucking peculiar..., thought Manos. Then he gasped as his memory hit like lightning. He flailed arms and legs just to keep afloat.

That was... Casey...

Bill Casey! He knew that face from Instagram. Everyone did.

...dead ...a chain running through his guts!

They were heading back to the shore now. Manos told them he wasn't well and asked to be let off at the nearest possible point on the shore.

...Bill...!

"It must have happened within the last twenty-four hours, wouldn't you say?" Bellas eyed him, decidedly suspicious. "Is he a guest of your friends?"

""I - I don't think so. Maybe." He could barely speak. Had Casey wormed his way into James' crowd? It was certainly possible.

"Manos, don't breathe a word of this. We'll let you down at Santa Marina. I'll be waiting for you at my office."

Manos stammered something about not getting involved, but Bellas cut in.

"This has nothing to do with Interpol," he said, as he clambered back onto the boat. Out of breath, he said with as much authority as he could muster, "We are calling you in as a witness."

4.

He'd agreed hastily to meet Bellas, but he had to get to James. Within twenty minutes, his hair still damp, he knocked on his old friend's hotel door.

There was no answer.

"Mr. Will's party is at the bar," the room attendant had informed him in Mykonian English, a mix of Victorian accent and Mediterranean dryness.
"Manos! Did you just check in?"

It was the voice of Sandy Voss, a rather bothersome socialite from the bride's inner circle. Her sole current occupation seemed to be mapping out who among the guests had preferential suites and who didn't.
"No - I mean, yes. Seen James? Or Casey?"
"Who?"
"Bill Casey."
Sandy seemed flustered. "Casey the influencer? What's he got to do -" But her mask of surprise transformed to one of coy whimsy: James Will had just come up behind her. "Here comes the groom!" she chimed.
"Hi there..." James murmured mockingly, caressing the small of Manos' back.
"James, I gotta talk to you."
Sandy Voss was no goddess of discretion, but hearing this low growl from Manos, she backed off a bit.
"Hey, now... take it easy!" James smiled. "Here I am in Greece for my wedding and, behold! My favorite Greek God has appeared -"
"Listen," Manos cut in. "Have you seen Bill Casey?"

"Bill Casey's here?" James asked, his eyebrows raised in surprise.

He seemed so surprised that Sandy apparently felt called upon to step up again. "Have you invited Casey, James? ...I didn't know you two were in touch."

"We're not."

"James, it can't wait," said Manos, "sorry, Sandy."

James listened in earnest. He hadn't seen Casey in years, way before his Instagram days took off. Whatever he was up to in Mykonos, he had definitely not come at their invitation. "He really drowned?" James whispered. "How the hell? What a shock! Good thing Liza never met him."

Liza. Of course. And here she was now.

"Hello, Liza." Manos felt a stupid smile spread across his face. "You're looking gorgeous." And after a quick nod - There you are! - at Alexandra Atkinson, an old flirting partner, he tried to get away. It was no more use talking to James right now, much less revealing that Casey was murdered.

"What's got into your friend?" He heard the bride say as he side-stepped a sweaty couple in bathing suits dancing in the entryway.

A minute later, he was in his room. There was no lousier security than hotel Wi-Fi, but his caution vanished beneath the image of Casey's strangled face. He sent three emails: one to Mei, one to a friend with a data brokerage business, and another to his Menlo Park circuit. Each had a different request, but the underlying message was the same: Who has been lurking around Mykonos these days?

5.

"Need to find the craziest whack-jobs? Nuts who can wreak instant havoc? It's either Las Vegas or Mykonos!" It was Captain Panagiotis, who stopped abruptly when Manos arrived.

As he crossed the threshold of Mykonos Town police station, all eyes were on him. Then Officer Bellas barked across the room, "Petro, a cup of coffee for Mr. Manu!" And to Manos he added, "So, was the victim one of the wedding guests?"
"I did know him, but he wasn't invited. Has to be a coincidence."
"This look like a coincidence to you?"

One of the young officers rifled through a pile of papers in front of him, stopping at a single photograph. There was Billy Casey, right there with his 30,000 followers, arms waving and stone dead. Hovering over his head was the buoy. FREE. They're better shots than mine, Manos thought quickly. Casey himself would have posted this one.
"May I...?" he mumbled, taking a picture with his phone, which instantly forwarded to Mei via Signal.
"You're not sending that to anyone, right?" demanded an officer.
"Obviously not," said Manos.
"So, how well did you know him?" Bellas asked.
"Not that well. We hung out sometimes at school, years ago."
"But he wasn't a guest at this wedding of yours?" someone asked.
"What's the name of the groom?" asked another.
"Who do you think would have a motive to do this?" Another voice came from the depths of the office. They waited, as if the entire station were expecting a printout.

Bellas took a step forward. "You haven't worked at homicide before, have you?"

"No." Manos sighed. "Only theory. We've looked at case studies."

"Ok, I get it," said Bellas. "You sure it's him?"

Manos shot another glance at the underwater pictures. A scant hour had passed since that dive at Ornos Beach. "It's him," he nodded.

"Ok, tell us what you know." Bellas made a sign, setting the typist into motion.

"First of all, he was famous. Not like a celebrity but the way people get famous now. He wasn't really anybody, but he had this series of videos of him talking about all kinds of things. He used lots of different platforms, mostly TikTok, and Instagram."

"Talking about things like what?"

Manos had to admit he couldn't really say. "It wasn't exactly... I mean, it was just... silly stuff. He had this one explaining why -"

"Hashtag willcasey," a woman's voice interrupted. Manos thought it was a female officer, but she wasn't in uniform. She was leaning on a white wall, gazing at her phone.

"You boys don't like TikTok, do you?" she asked. The question was for everyone, but she stared at Manos.

The room was plunged into confusion. Two of the officers ran to their screens. One of them noticed his computer wasn't even on. Two more whipped their phones out of their pockets. In a matter of seconds, the entire Mykonos police force was glued to his fast-talking old college buddy making his unpretentious, lighthearted jokes. Manos took advantage and slipped out to the small, whitewashed balcony. Below, scores of tourists scurried to find the best path to the beaches. He took out his airpods and called Mei on Signal.

"Serial killer?" he asked.

"Unlikely to be anything else. He's organized."

"Run down the list for me again."

"Intelligent... male... first or second-born child." Mei was reading in her delicate Mandarin accent. "Adept at impulse control. Charming. Geographically mobile. Up to date on media."

"I talked with Palo Alto."

"Leave that to the office," Mei protested.

"The office can do the processing. I know you still enjoy writing in R!"

"Come on, Manos. Vacationing doesn't mean you break protocol. What if your suspect uses Yandex or Baidu?"

"I'm working on it," he said. But he cut it short. The woman had appeared on the balcony. She was goddamn beautiful, like a bowl of Greek peaches.

"I'll call you back," he said into the mouthpiece. Mei hung up first.

"You don't think they have a chance, do you?" the beautiful girl asked him.

"Oh, not one in hell," Manos murmured.

"I'm Lena," she said.

6.

"William Casey!" barked Officer Bellas. "With a buoy marked FREE snaked through his bowels! Looks like someone wanted to 'Free Willy'! From what, I'd like to know! From who? Himself? His family? His past? Get on it - scour the social videos. George, grab Petro and start off for the hotels. I'll come to some of them too. If we find where he was staying, we'll know who he was with. Simple, right?"

"We don't have enough staff," George mumbled.

"My back is killing me!" Moaned Petro.

But Bellas saw it coming and played deaf.

"We've got pictures," he continued. "Send them to Athens, request a coroner. Or get the hospital to find us one. Now! Chrisanthos, who'd they send last time? He'd be fine. Or anyone. Immediately! Tell them we've got a terrifying crime never seen before on Mykonos. And not a word to Mavrudi!"

"Mavrudi 's gonna want to know."

"We're not talking with the mayor's office!" Bellas insisted. "No politicians, no reporters, no busybody bloggers up in Athens. We will not set people into a panic. It's the 10th of July. If it gets out that people are being murdered off boats with anchors, the season's dead!" Then, as if remembering, he said, "Right, anchors. Like the one down there ...Send the information again--"

"I'm telling you my back is killing me!" Petro whined again.

"Anybody get a look at it? Anybody ask about it? What vessels carry that kind of anchor?"

Someone said, "I don't think it's from here."

"But we have to ask here. Stella, Christo, take a discreet stroll to the marina. See if there are any dinghies missing. With the picture of the anchor and a shot of the victim - not from today! From Instagram. Discreetly! Just pop over and take a look at the anchors. Ask Giorgi, the boat guy - he doesn't miss a thing. And the buoy. Was it swiped from the hotel? What about the chain? Where do you get that kind? Mykonos? Piraeus? They ordered it online? I want to know!" He stopped to draw breath. "Most solved crimes get solved within the first 72 hours, a few days at most. If we don't get him in a week's time, we're in the dark. Discreetly!"

"We have a coroner!" Chrisanthos said with a hand over the mike of his phone.

"Good!"

"He's from Athens, on vacation. I told him to meet us at the hospital in 10 minutes."

"That's it! Let's go." Bellas looked around the room. "Where the hell is Interpol? Where's his pal? Manos!"

Manos heard his name being called and came back in from the balcony. Lena followed.

"Mr. Manu, you'll have to give a deposition about your buddy," said Bellas, with a decidedly more urgent tone.

"Whatever you say, but I'm telling you it's a fluke."

"Is that so?" Bellas scoffed. He had taken back the reins and was not going to let some sniveling techie get in his way.

"The murderer didn't kill Bill just to kill the particular person. He killed him for his own sake."

An icy silence gripped the room. Lena nodded and shrugged her shoulders, making to leave. Manos had trapped himself in a corner, but he refused to stay there.

"The man you are looking for will kill again," he said.

7.

The hospital in Mykonos wasn't far, but the patrol car was quickly deadlocked in traffic.

"No siren," ordered Bellas. He refused to give the slightest hint of anything happening outside the normal summer routine. Manos felt trapped again.

"Can't we just walk?" he asked Bellas and Petro – Lieutenant Petro Xagoraris, his back apparently better – agreed. Moments later, the three of them were at the entrance of the hospital where the director, a colorful local, stood anxiously waiting for them.

"We did everything you said," he stammered, but Bellas brushed past him. Taking Manos out of earshot, he said, "Listen, we're not covering anything up, but don't broadcast your theories unless I ask for them. We can't afford to panic."

"Hey, guess what? I'm on vacation," said Manos.

One of the men withdrew a few steps, but all eyes were soon fixed on someone coming through a doorway.

"Mr Stevias?" asked Bellas.

"Stevis."

"Have you seen the victim?"

"I took a look," he sighed. "Now, listen –"

"Yes, I know," Bellas gave a bitter smile. "You're on vacation."

The body had been transported, but Manos thought he'd seen enough on the dive and in the photos. Bill Casey's body was run through by a heavy chain holding an anchor on one end and, on the other, a buoy that hadn't quite made it to the surface. With eyes still open, his face was one of angelic peace. There were no marks on his wrists, no trace of any struggle. *When a killer is this organized, you only find the ones that want to get caught,* Manos recalled from his Interpol seminars. Casey's lifeless body lay on a gurney that had a large container hanging off it. To one side of the gurney was the chain and the hefty anchor. On the other was the buoy, its spray-painted markings turned towards the wall. There was no blood. Just paint. Mei's team would send the images to graphologists and run them through every handwriting database available to them. The best belonged to a reinsurance outfit. But even there, the findings would be slim.

"I haven't had a chance to do a detailed examination," Stevis was saying. "I don't have my equipment with me. The facilities are somewhat lacking..."

He was a beefy man in his 70s with a broad forehead, leaning over the corpse with the fine concentration of a tattoo artist.

"Doesn't look like he was strangled," Bellas' tone was certain.

Stevis looked up. "Right. Doesn't seem to be the cause of death. But we can't rule it out conclusively."

"Only speculatively."

"We need time, a full autopsy. The lungs show no signs of swelling, but even that wouldn't confirm strangulation."

The lieutenant spoke up. "How did they get the chain in?"

"Again, we're only guessing. Mere conjecture. At this point, I'm little better than a ward nurse."

"Right," mumbled Bellas. "Just guessing."

"I believe he died from a massive collapse of the internal organs."

"Two wounds. First, a gunshot. The second for the chain to get through..."

"But that didn't come first," said Manos. Stevis looked up, eyebrows knitted.

"Mr. Manu is with Interpol," Bellas explained.

"Is that so?" Stevis gave an involuntary glance at the victim's face, wondering if he were looking at someone important.

Manos continued. "How do you get a ship into a bottle?"

"You lower the sails," said Bellas.

"That's exactly what the killer did. His shot wasn't just to kill, but to make an opening. Then he must have used something else - a light spear gun or something. He placed it into the mouth, making sure it would come out the other end. He introduced a small arrow, probably with some light fishing line. He used the line to pull another chain all the way through and out the back..."

"Yes, the exit point is right here," the coroner confirmed, with a probing look into the bucket hanging off Bill's stretcher.

"And then the bigger chain."

"Then he welded the anchor to one end," Bellas was catching on. "And he only needed a simple ring to attach the buoy to the other end."

"And so all his organs collapsed," said the sergeant, standing a little apart. He had gone faintly green. "But the cause of death was the initial wound."

At this point a strong desire for a cigarette surged up in all four men, but since this was a Greek hospital, only the doctor presumed to light up.

"But there was no resistance?" asked Bellas.

"No signs of resistance, no. We have to run a toxicological. He could have been drugged. "Smoke flooded from his nostrils as he whirled around looking for a makeshift ashtray.

"Of course! How could he not be?"

"Anything's possible," Dr. Stevis said pensively. "I've never seen anything like it, but... his teeth and dental work are intact. You'd think dragging a chain through would leave signs of oral friction, even if the victim was dead or drugged. I'm probably getting ahead of myself here, but one explanation could be that... maybe the victim was holding his mouth open. So drugged is our best guess for now."

They all exchanged glances.

"I mean, there's also the ankyloses of the shoulders. The victim's arms were raised high, but there is no evidence he was holding them up because of any molestation. We would have seen something on his wrists."

"What do we know about the time of death?" asked Manos.

"We'll need an incision in the liver to check the temperature," returned Stevis. "You say he was left in the ocean for hours. From the facial muscles I'd estimate anywhere between thirty and forty hours. Mind you, rigor mortis is different underwater."

"And another six hours since he was lifted out. He was probably killed yesterday morning."

"Or the night before."

"We'll have to see." The doctor was hesitant.

"Why on earth would a person spend the night pulling chains through someone's body just to throw them into the ocean?" asked the lieutenant.

Each of them seemed to have a theory, but only Manos spoke.

"You'll need a profiler here," he said.

Bellas looked at him. Clearly, he already knew one.

"And you'll need an invitation," he answered.

8.

All this was too much for the Mykonos Police Department. Too much for a hobbled taskforce of officers on summer assignments, whose primary mission was to assist tax administrators with summer inspections and keep the peace among binge drinkers. Capable of investigating complicated murders they were not. Ideally, they would have run the investigation data, sent out DNA findings for analysis, found not only the scene of the crime but also the boat the victim had taken to the island, held out for the coroner's report while keeping inquiring minds at bay, not to mention notifying the family and interviewing anyone on the radar. Officer Bellas knew that would only be a start, yet he could barely begin. And to add to the fun, Interpol and Manos Manu had just walked away from it and gone to Psarrou Beach for partying. Psarrou was directly opposite the spot where the drowned man had been found. Its undisputed center was Nammos Beach Club. James and Liza's parents had invited over a hundred guests to this seaside jewel for an opulent afternoon of well-wishing, delightful cocktails, and crystalline waters. They had reserved all the best tables at the heart of the club, to which Manos now made a beeline.

"Manna-Manos from heaven!"

Alexandra Atkinson's were the first arms he felt wind themselves around him. She wore a skimpy designer bathing suit, and he found himself wondering why on earth he hadn't married her when he had the chance instead of running off to play rent-a-cop in Singapore.

With her next breath, she herself provided the answer.

"James told us you live in Singapore now. You're, like, a spy or something?"

By her side stood Friedrich or maybe it was Frederick, a perfect specimen of the ultra-wealthy blasé so familiar to Manos: their only passion was the weekly routine of niggling a couple more basis points from their complacent bankers and sticking their upturned noses into some business about which they knew absolutely nothing.

"Oh, you know me, Alexandra."

"What exactly do you do?" asked her escort.

"I use data to make lists. And lists to make predictions. Your basic models guy," said Manos.

"For hedge funds?"

"Interpol."

"Really! The police!" Frederick-Friedrich could barely contain his laughter. "And what models does the police create?"

Manos decided to smile.

"A lot. The more, the better, in fact. Only state resources or law enforcement would allow me to run multiple models on human actors." *Chew on that for a while.*

"Fantastic!" the escort was saying, now without a trace of sarcasm. "And you're a friend of James?"

"He and James are bosom buddies," said Alexandra, bestowing a warm look on Manos.

"And what are you up to?" he asked her.

"Oh, you know me, Manos. " In their private language this indicated, working on my 'Mrs.' Degree.

They both turned a tender gaze towards Frederick.

The second pair of arms to enlace Frederick now slinked delicately around him, accompanied by a gentle air kiss and providing context. Everyone gave a little snicker.

"Why, Manly...!" It was James. Alexandra, Frederick and sundry on-lookers showered him with the usual congratulations before receding little by little. "Have you solved the mystery?" James asked once they were out of earshot.

"It's in the hands of the locals. Not our job. Unless they want to make a formal request, that is - which they won't. It's more red tape than they can handle."

"But did you find out what's going on?"

"To be honest, I think it's just a weird coincidence. Billy was in the wrong place at the wrong time."

"So sick! Strangled!"

Manos recollected Bill's lifeless face drifting underwater but saw no reason to get into gory details with a groom-to-be. They were here to celebrate, and Manos would make sure they did so most heartily. James put his arm around his shoulder, as if understanding. Then Manos felt the familiar Signal vibration in his pocket. Mei. He pulled away with a little smile, putting in his airpods. Time for a stroll on the beach.

9.

"You're with girls, I can feel it. Pretty European girls, with rich daddies and millions in their little signature handbags! Here I am pestering you with measly datasets while you're out fortune-hunting."

"But you're my fortune, Mei. And trust me, the only rendezvous on offer so far is a criminology conference."

"We're getting traction. When I said it was for a murder investigation on Mykonos, I got immediate access. Axciom, Epsilon, Datalogix, Blue Kai - everybody sent me full-access one-time credentials. But I think they like Mykonos better than they like Interpol."

"It's you they like."

All of these companies possessed pre-processed data for the cyber behavior of millions. Although these databases predated the Web, Facebook, Google, and incalculable web services, had added thousands of unique data points. With the help of machine learners, the oldest consumer databases had morphed into enormous psychographic aggregators, setting global marketing spinning on its axis. With turnkey tools like the Big Five, countless personalities were catalogued, and in turn thousands - then millions and billions and trillions - of instantaneous digital decisions were systematically logged. Around the rugged edges of legality, a comprehensive hacker's guide to everyone's inner thoughts was in perpetual operation.

In going to Singapore, Manos was following an instinctual drive to match up classification algorithms with the profiling that had revolutionized the search for suspects in serious crimes. The results of these Graph API queries would return in JSON format like anything else. He detested using the term Big Data - as anyone else who truly understood it. But there you had it. He knew that working with multi-agent intelligent actors would unearth the holy grail of criminal prosecution: a statistical certainty that someone had actually perpetrated a specific crime. If the validation data added up, if the classification algorithms ran properly, if the machine learning models held, then he, Manos Manu, held in his grasp all that he needed to construct the first global Predictive Crime Unit ever. Such was the ambitious dream that had seduced him away from Stanford, away from the family apartment at the lower east side of Manhattan. But every time he needed to run a test, Manos discovered he had to make do with Mei's trusty emails, groveling to download broker datasets and manually run the algorithms he needed. It was a wild goose chase from Amazon servers to the Global Innovation Complex in Singapore, then off to the secure Interpol servers in Lyons and from there to Manos' cellphone, now in Mykonos.

But it worked.

"At the moment, we have geolocation data for approximately one-point-three-three-six million individuals found within a ten-mile radius of Mykonos ten hours before the murder, including cruise ships and other sea craft," Mei was saying. "Among those, just over nine thousand five hundred have serialist characteristics. Nine thousand people just waiting for you to work your magic, Manos. Sending..."

Manos felt the downloading folder vibrate in his hand. Sauntering barefoot on the glistening sands of Psarrou, he enabled the camera on his device and arranged the angle to capture the scenery behind him.

"Take a peek," he said. "Does it look like I'm surrounded by 9,500 psychotic murderers?"

Mei enabled her camera. Ten p.m. on a rainy Singapore night and she was still at work. For him. Her glossy hair, impossibly straight, cascaded on either side of her smooth face. Even in the ugly office light, she was perfect.

"No," she answered, her eyes scanning the seascape behind him. "But what about appearances?"

"Not a thing. Did you get the hospital pics?"

"Yes. And I did what you all forgot - a cop's first duty."

"You Googled the crime, sure. But of course you didn't find anything."

"I ran some other searches too, but barely any correlations," she agreed. "Your man's an outlier, Manos."

"Originality in models is overrated."

"Be careful," Mei sighed again. "We have beaches here too, you know." She hung up at just the moment when he'd have liked to tuck a loose wisp of her hair back into place.

Manos held Mei's face in his mind's eye. They had in fact met barely two weeks earlier. She had just finished reading his proposal for the Lab's general assistant director, and, taking out a permanent marker, had invented the title Multi-agent Analysis of Network Users - MANU - on its cover. *There's a name! His name!* "That's how they'll remember you, really," she said.

In fact, Manos' innovation was that he built social activity models directly into established third party architectures. Data flooded in effortlessly. Every click was tracked, every like, every fraction of a second spent on a ceaseless stream of click-bait. With the interactions remodeled, wholesale assumptions on human character - appearing in publications like *Assessment, Journal of Personality, Journal of Research in Personality* and a boatload of others - could either be verified or chucked in the circular file for good. Not by a peer-reviewing board but by the data itself. Then fresh indicators could be modeled on a layer above. Just as in robotics, a given prediction determines the next feature. The beauty of unsupervised machine learning. When looking for a host of dark traits - egotism, Machiavellianism, moral detachment, narcissism, psychopathy, sadism, superiority complexes, self-interest- the research gave rise to billions of new data points every day. Right here, for instance, Manos saw the crowd in all its glory, everyone posing for their own camera. There were hundreds of ways to say I'm better than the rest without actually designating who the rest were. You just had to know.

Ok, he thought. *Which of you test positive for excessive envy? What's your code?*

Come out, come out, wherever you are...

II. A Profile to Kill For

10.

No one looking at Lena Sideris would give her a day over twenty-one, but at thirty-two, crossing the lobby of the Hotel San Marco overlooking Houlakia Bay, she felt somewhere in her forties. People gazed up instinctively as she passed, less for her youth or her beauty than for her determined step and air of smooth power. Even the seasoned clerk at the reception desk seemed faintly hypnotized.

"Are - uhm - the symposium?" he stammered.

The *secret* Symposium, my friend.
Keeping up her smart pace, she answered, "Yes, all set," in Greek.

Her flowing white palazzo pants were offset by a navy blue blouse and a thin leather belt the same shade of tan as the leather cuff on her left wrist.

"Lena!" A voice called. It was Professor Hansen.
Lena's hand relaxed just as his grip tightened on her palm.

"Time already, is it? I haven't even gone up to change yet," he confessed.

She gave a smile. "That's a summer conference for you, especially on an island. Have to hunt down the presenters!"

They didn't need much chit-chat. Their intense mentor-undergraduate connection had long subsided to an easeful complicity. As Professor of Forensic Psychology, Franz Hansen had heretofore clashed with those he had dismissed as "biologists," who insisted, as Raine did, on mapping the criminal mind in order to explain it. He was equally scathing of the facile "sociologists," who whined over environmental factors. Over the years, however, he'd grown less dogmatic, learning to diplomatically emphasize the same key details and concepts as those increasingly favored by some very enticing grant funders in the US, Canada and Europe. The same had gone for this year's conference location; had he chosen Stockholm, he would likely need help from the Swedish SWAT team to maintain order. Keen to the profound importance of good weather, Lena had seized the moment and suggested Mykonos.

She was in a good position to do so. During her early days as his student at Cambridge, she'd briefly become a click-bait star due to some unfortunate wording in her research: "Cambridge Study: Cannibals Kill 5,000 Annually." BuzzFeed had latched onto this minutely representative group and run with it, attributing cannibalism to all serial killers. Any random Google search soon yielded thousands and thousands of hits linking her name in over a dozen languages to blatant misinformation. A hard lesson to learn.

"No matter, my dear," he'd said consolingly. "People are just bookmarking an idea they will never return to. Nothing to take personally."

She eventually got over it. Franz had been right. It was even something of a triumph, these fake news results. Now all the heavy-hitters in the field had flocked to her breathtaking homeland. At an age when most of her peers were dodging unemployment by taking a second doctorate, perhaps even more superfluous than the first, Lena Sideris had been selected to open the Sixth Annual International Conference on Criminal Psychology and Criminology.

She would make sure it would be one hard to forget.

11.

"Esteemed colleagues," began Lena, settling in with a tug at her shirt-sleeve. "Physicists are passionate in their drive to balance classical with quantum mechanics, hoping to find a unified theory of the cosmos. We too have strived over two hundred fifty years for a unified theory of crime. Many of you have been my teachers. What I have witnessed is a battle between two forces. Biologists and neuro-criminologists hold genetic propensity responsible for crime. On the contrary, social criminologists blame poverty, social disenfranchisement and environmental factors."

A quick glance showed Lena both camps scattered throughout her audience. *Steady now*, she thought. *Their baggage, not mine.*

"The implications of getting to consensus would be remarkable," she continued. "Not only for research and education but for our judicial and penal systems, our police forces and their administration. Imagine a new dawn when the authorities wouldn't have to rely on Netflix for learning how to profile suspects."

The crowd gave a forced laugh.

"In all seriousness, academic consensus is also political, and therefore financial. When neuro-criminology dominates, big pharma receives incentives to eliminate crime. When domestic violence is the accepted driver, social services get stronger. Private sector or public? The individual or the collective? Nothing is as politically and conclusively divisive as crime theory. As scientists, we fall victim to the political dimensions of our research. Yet we are simultaneously perpetrators, feeding into the system."

A sudden silence fell.

"This binary interpretation went on quite well," Lena now said breezily. "Funding vacillated from year to year based on election cycles. Criminologists, psychologists, neurobiologists, sociologists - we all dug our trenches ever deeper, heedless of the cost. After all, we know damn well governmental research budgets work like hedge funds. Place your bets! Just make sure you bet as much on the opposing view. Defund the police! Law and Order! We knew everyone would get paid."

"That's been debatable for some time," protested someone in the crowd.

"My point exactly," she smiled.

Running her two palms along the leather face of the podium, she leaned in for the attack. "What has brought about this change? Politicians? Economic crises? Or has a new challenger, Big Data levelled the battleground?"

She took a breath.

"Models have been running since the seventies. But today they have a couple of things they didn't have then: humongous amounts of social data and great processing power. Stated simply, our static models are now perfectly obsolete."

She gave them another smile.

"And so here we are. Professor Hansen, dear friends, I wish you peaceful reflections and warmly welcome you to our beautiful island for the Sixth Annual International Conference on Criminal Psychology and Criminology."

Five full seconds elapsed. With each one, she felt her heart pumping, her breath still. A chuckle here and there, followed by some sparse, polite claps. Then a few more, and then, as if on cue, there came the steady drone of applause.

12.

Lena felt the crowd's curiosity tingling along her neck. Impossible to turn around. She had showed them not just the elephant in the room, but the acute elephantiasis in the field. Yet as the morning unfolded, nothing more was said on this. Only one professor of clinical psychology, during her presentation, had sneered, "…contrary to what some younger colleagues claim, every profile we currently create for the authorities leverages both the social and the biological."

Lena decided to enjoy the coffee break anyway. Beyond the sumptuous pool lay the tumble-down blue-and-white houses of Mykonos. It was for their sake virtuoso waiters labored for tips, deftly skirting the hungover couples. Of course the shabbiest of all were here for the symposium; economy-class guests in a five-star resort. Law enforcement needs to demand a bloody raise!

"You know, we've used CGT for years," someone nearby addressed her. Criminal Geographic Targeting. Typical software used to localize possible locations of criminal offenses based on research criteria.

"I believe Dr. Sideris was referring to something else." She heard a man's deep voice a few steps away.

It was Manu. Had he been any farther off, she wouldn't have singled him out from the tourists.

"Dr. Manu is the very challenger you warned us about this morning," said Franz Hansen, who'd come up beside her. A few others drifted over.

"You're from the Singapore Criminology Center, aren't you?" someone asked.

"We don't call it that."

"Yes, Global Innovation," said one of the clinical psychologists. "Clever. Has that start-up ring to it."

"Shall we let Dr. Manu tell us all about it during his presentation?" Hansen's decided tone broke up their little group, leaving Lena and Manos to themselves.

"I thought you'd been assigned the Casey investigation," she said.

"I'm not a cop, Lena."

All she had been working toward these months was riding on what he would soon speak about. To her irritation, he was perfectly nonchalant, reeking of his high-tech Asian salary.

"Sets you up nicely to tell them about the murder," she said.

"I'm here for a wedding, actually."

"But you will."

Manos steadied his annoyance with a deep breath. He had dearly missed summers in Greece. The afternoon wore on so gently, as if he were standing in cascades of dawn sunlight.

"Bellas asked me to, when we left the hospital," he said quietly. "I get it. I mean, they're totally lost."

"Sure. He figures, why wait for Athens to cough up a profiler when this kid can mobilize the whole symposium? People will listen to a major client like Interpol."

He didn't answer. From the pocket of his Bermuda shorts he produced a folded up piece of paper and handed it to her.

"You start. Give the first two paragraphs, the background," he said. "You were there. Then me. I'll talk a bit about how the algorithms are built, then you wrap it up. Think you can?"

Lena felt her cheeks redden. *How dare he? How presumptuous, how cocky!* But from sheer habit, her eyes scanned the text he'd given her.

"It's not that. I already... I mean, they know me..." She stopped, not making head or tail of what she was reading. There were mostly mathematical operations, then about twenty first names that seemed encoded into ten full names.

"What - ?" she mumbled.

Manos had been watching her, his face expressionless. Then he said, "Our first list of suspects. Your job is to sell it to the experts. Think you can?"

13.

She couldn't.

She deliberated a moment over his proposition, but her heart was not in it. She clutched the carelessly folded list, her mind going in circles. Yes, the old system was outmoded, but it was founded on research and centuries of tradition. But if you could identify a perpetrator from online activity alone, the entire discussion became... well... useless. Manos' projections were absurd. He had explained all avidly, right up until they took their seats as co-presenters, but now it all sounded like convoluted voices feeding back from a speaker. She wanted to unplug the damn thing. Hansen's voice now flowed through the microphone. "After this enjoyable break," he said, as chairs were shuffled into place and attendees sifted into their seats, "we are itching, I know, to get to the beach".

Lena faltered, staring at Manos a bit too intensely. Even if he were right, if it were possible to generate a list of suspects from their digital tracks, the very insolence of pushing his work at a conference before even fact-checking, of revealing a current investigation without permission from the police, without knowing if it were even legal...

She just couldn't.

Manos, reading her thoughts, gently tugged the paper from her hand and shrugged. Shooting her a friendly smile, he stood as Hansen neared the end of his introduction: "...with us today from Interpol's Global Complex of Innovation in Singapore. Chief Data Scientist in the Digital

Forensics Lab and creator of the Multi-agent Analysis of Network Users web engine which is already," Hansen nodded to Manos, "in beta?"

"Trials are still running, yes," Manos affirmed, crossing the dais to the laptop on the lectern.

"Ladies and gentlemen, Dr. Manos Manu..."

The audience applauded politely while Manos brought up a file. Lena sat, motionless. Even through the air-conditioned seal of this room, she felt the summer sun pulsing through her.

"Thank you, Professor Hansen. Ladies and gentlemen," began Manos, relishing the ease of speaking English. "Thirty-six hours ago, a serial killer drugged his victim, positioned him horizontally and shot him - we believe - through the mouth. He then used a special high-powered spear gun to insert a steel line through the wound and into the internal organs. I share this classified information today with the permission of the Hellenic Police."

Members of the audience leaned forward. Side conversations ceased.

"The killer used the steel line as a guide, so that, pulling it slowly, possibly with mechanical assistance, he could drag a thin chain through the victim's open mouth. Without causing any further damage, this chain then led a medium-gauge chain through. In turn, a significantly heavier anchor chain was pulled into the mouth, then the esophagus, lung cavity and stomach. With just as much precision, it was drawn through the victim's anus. The body was found underwater, off the shore of a nearby beach, the chain attached to a sunken buoy with the word FREE written on it in red spray paint. Here we see an image of the body as the local police found it yesterday."

Manos had to be quick to show the image without letting anyone take a picture of it; some phones were already aimed.

"The victim's name is Will Casey, a prominent blogger with several thousand Instagram followers. His posts represent the significant freedom, in our Internet Age, of a personal channel and real followers. Freedom in the face of the tech giants, in defiance of YouTube's monopoly, an oligarchical society, politicians and their sponsors. The battle he fought was against the profiling used by tech giants and advertising outfits to crush real influencers. Gen Z people here know what I'm talking about. Useful background, in case you get thrown into the sea chained to a buoy with FREE scrawled on it."

The screen had been quickly shifted to a color-coded Excel spreadsheet displaying serial killer traits. The spellbinding image of Billy Casey submerged off the waters of Ornos Beach had made them all go rigid, as though imitating the lifeless body.

"Billy," continued Manos with a nod, "William Casey came to Mykonos with some friends, whom the police are now interrogating. In his murder, we detect a profound sense of ritual. All of you know - especially such specialists as Professor Holmes, who has written books on the subject and whom I had the pleasure of meeting earlier today - this is the case with organized serial murders, whether perpetrated under a contract or by a lone wolf. I leave it to the police to explore the first possibility. From literature, we know that lone serialists like to travel, and they follow social networks. They demonstrate signs of social normalcy and intelligence. It has become impossible for the authorities to find them. As social and biological criminologists, you know the average serialist does not wear Dr. Hannibal Lecter's mask, neither does he enjoy cross-dressing. In reality, he looks very much... like ourselves... so much so, that in fact... he could even be one of us."

Manos paused, a faint smirk on his face. He knew the "organized type" quite capable of returning to the crime scene, perhaps even willing to risk the thrill of slipping into a symposium so conveniently close to where his crime had been executed. Lena understood immediately. Manos' pause was calculated. Everyone looked around, seeking anyone they didn't recognize.

Could the murderer be here?

Furtive glances spread infectiously as guilt itself. Manos pressed on.

"The transport of the victim... the corpse..."

Among the back rows, an odd expression was forming itself on a hostile face.

"...from the crime scene... the beach... his immersion..."

The face now returned Manos' gaze. Then the person shifted just slightly, as if to stand.

"...makes it clear to us that time was needed - much time and planning, which -"

The man sat back down. The expression altered, the mouth twisting to suppress a tight smile, a wave crest that would not break. As if, he were privately enjoying this.

As if enjoying where it all might lead.

14.

"Eight years, my friend."

Officer Bellas had a swift, foolproof routine for forcing someone guilty into a sweat. First, he stared at their shoes. Then he firmly declared the sentence that would be handed down were this a real court trial. Afterwards he looked at his suspects as though they were already condemned. The guilty know they're guilty. They know the punishment is theirs. The confession always trickled out of them in drops of sweat tracing their way down the forehead. Time and time again, he'd seen this basic bodily fluid betray its master, streaming cold as spring rain. *Eight years.*

But the kid before him now was blubbering so hard Bellas couldn't tell the tears from the sweat. Even if he could, he wouldn't know if it was from the guilt or the drugs. All he could do now was get the facts straight.

"Can we please lower the music?" Bellas barked over the choking sobs of the young man and the contrapuntal beats of Mario Biondi pumping from the hotel reception desk. *Damn kids! He wasn't going to get anywhere!*

"You've told me your group, including Billy, left the bar at 3 o'clock, Mr. Skanlon. To go where?"

"I don't remember. We walked around town. Jimmy was there too."

"Mr. Ves--"

"Veksessi."

"Vesseksi. You were in Matogiannia, walking the main street?"

"Where the bars are," said Skanlon.

"Right. Did you go into any?"

"A lot of them. And like I said... I don't remember..."

This was not the Mykonos trip they had planned. They came to have fun going off on @skinnyjew and post shots with @emrata. Not to get killed.

"And at some point you lost, Billy." Bellas kept it up.

"Yes, we lost him."

"He just vanished."

"Vanished. We thought he'd hooked up with a girl." The guy broke down again.

This is going goddamn nowhere! Things went from bad to worse when he saw the face of Stamatis Mavrudis, the mayor of Mykonos, nearing the reception desk.

"Bellas! This guy do it?" he called as he approached.

Mavrudis was tall, slim with longish hair dyed black. Bellas couldn't prove it, but he would've bet anything he dabbled in cocaine. How else could he be everywhere at once? Everybody wondered how he had the energy of a twenty-year-old, around the clock, when he was pushing sixty - not to mention his perpetually runny nose, even in the dead of summer.

"Is this the killer? Tell me!"

"Mr. Mayor now is not the time," Bellas answered drily, unconcerned by Skanlon's desperate attempt to decipher Greek.

"Not the time?" Mavrudis shouted, causing a Japanese family nearby to jump; he lowered his voice to a rough whisper. "Do you realize everybody knows?"

"Who? Knows what?"

"The picture of Casey's dead body is all over the Internet!" said Mavrudis. His hands were shaking.

"Mr. Mayor," Bellas articulated firmly. "Not now."

"You're telling me not now? I have two million tourists here! The damage will be permanent, Officer. This isn't the kind of summer memory they'll forget!"

"I understand."

"People remember Mykonos for partying, for Kardashians - and now?"

Mavrudis had whipped out his phone; the shot of the drowned man was on his Facebook feed. Skanlon started bawling again. And Mario Biondi came pumping from the reception desk.

"Can someone turn off the damn music?" shouted Bellas. This time he was heard.

"You have to issue a statement!" Mavrudis bellowed louder.

"There are protocols--"

"Screw protocols!"

"Stamatis -"

"Because if you don't..."

"Sta- Stam- Stamatis!"

Bellas took two steps from Skanlon and grabbed Mavrudis by the lapels. Shaken, Mavrudis froze.

"I will follow my protocols," asserted Bellas as calmly as he could. "When I need something from your office, you will know."

Mavrudis backed away, wagging an angry finger. He was forcing himself to keep quiet, but halfway across the lobby he gave up, calling out in a mad voice: "Statement!"

15.

Lena was the first to realize something strange was happening. Following where Manos' eyes led, she immediately saw the man. Thirtyish. Sleek sandy hair and a weeks' worth of blond beard. Smack in the center of the back row on the right side of the crowded room. He looked trapped; four people would have to get up if he wanted to leave. At intervals, the light cast shadows around him, creating a momentary scowl on his otherwise bland face; like a holograph, his expression shifted abruptly between hardened criminal and respectable scholar. He looked familiar. How come? Lena wondered.

At the same instant, that she instinctively took her phone out, not even knowing what she would do with it, Manos decided to carry on as though nothing were happening.

"Our last resort for identifying such criminals is therefore also the strongest," he said. "For killers as sophisticated as this one, we interpret digital footprints - since few of them leave real footprints at the crime scene. Our virtual life is actually quite complex, very real and very revealing about who we are. All of us. We unconsciously think being online equals freedom. Thanks to this illusion, our search engine choices tell our truth, even if on social media we post lies. The analysis of both is rewarding, since everyone uses both - all the while thinking we are invisible."

With this, Manos lifted his eyes to the man's silky hair again, and then looked back at Lena. It's him! Lena suddenly realized why she had her phone out. Hands shaking, she found the number for Chrisanthos, the officer from Bellas' office yesterday. Fingertips trembling, she typed:

COME NOW! THE MURDERER IS HERE! CONFERENCE AT SAN MARCO HOTEL HOULAKIA!

"Recent advances in digital forensics," Manos continued, "allow us to find social clues at astonishing speed, almost instantly. No delays. No sending samples to the lab, no waiting half a week to get the DNA analysis back. Now we can customize the system with parameters and, with user data narrowing the field, we run recursive algorithms. We do need data broker access, but we can know which Internet users are more likely to have committed a crime we query with keywords. Immediately. Accurately." He paused, smiling. "When we combine your reliable, wonderful art of profiling with the dry science of cyber-statistics, the results are fascinating," said Manos playfully. With a breath, Lena smiled too.

"Our Multi-agent Analysis of Network Users is configured to analyze millions of terabytes of digital footprints in seconds. The data is cleaned, analyzed and then reclustered, allowing the engine to select the most appropriate models for reprocessing. This is important. As for the models, the system is open-ended. The more, the better. Nevertheless, their use is ultimately determined by forensics..."

Manos sensed the danger of losing his audience. He changed tactics.

"This means they are determined by real events. For example, Billy Casey," he said simply, recapturing his listeners by showing the photo again. The audience froze, breathless, staring at the image of a naked man with a chain running through him. Then Manos went for it: "From this starting point, we craft our queries. Which users were in Mykonos at the time of the crime? Which of them were men? How many of those users have Googled the words 'anchor' or 'buoy' in the past six months? From that subset, who has demonstrated interest in welding products? Who among them knows how to handle a boat? Who - potentially - could do all that? Of these, how many interacted with #willCasey? These, among other elements, are called 'cold digital forensics'. Now for the 'hot' category, such as personality traits, whatever we include in a classic profiling report: gender, educational level, etc. But now we add elements from personality profiling for advertisers - everything. Those new to web-based psychographic profiles are always amazed at their accuracy."

He flashed them another smile. "So, with 'cold' and 'warm' data determined and models developed, adding anything just makes the system smarter. From this point on, it is recursive learning. Math. The initial list of two million visitors ends up with a handful of names. With a prediction in the high-nineties that the culprit will be among them. Crime itself is nothing but a malfunction. A bug. And what the police will do is debugging."

Lena's jaw had dropped. Everyone here must see the possibilities, she thought. But instead of looking around from her front row seat, she looked at Manos. Surprisingly, a flash of disappointment flickered across his face. He slumped for a moment over the podium, as if defeated. Once again, following the direction of his eyes, she turned.

The man in the back row was gone.

16.

Without a thought for the resounding bang of the door behind her, she left the hall. Hansen's intern assistant was lazing over her phone by the hall entrance.

"Excuse me, did anyone just leave?" asked Lena.

Eyes tranquilly caressing her screen, the intern answered, "One or two left early. Need anything?"

Lena rushed to the hotel's main entrance, but there were clusters of new arrivals wrangling huge suitcases. Taxis rolled along. No, she thought. He wouldn't expose himself to the crowd. He's still in the hotel. She ran up the stairs and found a luxuriant veranda shaded by a sky-blue pergola. Upwards of thirty or so people were enjoying their CrossFit training to the beats of an automated playlist. Lena scanned each face, but it was a sea of baseball caps and hoodies. Lena pressed on, since it was a matter of minutes before they came. Manos, Hansen, Chrisanthos and the other cops - anyone.

But no one appeared. She made her way through the cross-trainers, passed a half-naked couple languidly taking selfies, and reached the mouth of an inner hallway. Empty. Just a series of doors. All ajar, some even half open. *He could be behind any one of them,* she thought.

She advanced slowly, breathless. *How would he do it?* He would find a wire, something to go through her throat. He must have it on him already. A length of fishing line as a lead for the heavier chains he stringed through his victims' guts. So easy to find her. To kill her. He would slip out from one of these doors, right up behind her before she could move. He'd loop his line tight around her neck and pull her back into one of these rooms. He'd push the door closed behind him - or even leave it open, just a crack. Just a hair, until he could feel her losing strength, losing all feeling. Until the end.

If she were a cop, Lena would have drawn her weapon. She stole silently down the hall like she'd seen in the movies, but instead of a gun she gripped her iPhone. No time to call anyone. She didn't even think to turn on her camera. The device was now nothing more than a very costly rock she wielded into the emptiness to scare off anyone she saw. But there was no one. Ahead, she saw a spacious corridor leading to the hotel spa and steam baths; the doors right and left were for changing rooms. *I'm an open target. I have to call Chrisanthos.* She looked down at the phone. It was already writhing in her hands.

"Where are you?" It was Manos.
Her voice cracked with embarrassment. "Here," she stuttered. As if the word itself revealed encrypted GPS coordinates. "Here."

Down the hallway, a door opened. Her blood froze. Approaching along the semidarkness, the stranger's form looked like two superimposed shadows. His hair and beard blended into a sheen, now silky, now glossy; as he came closer, the light showed his face. It was him. Eyes flashing, he saw her extend her thumb and point her phone as if it were a gun ready to shoot. He turned. And ran.

It's him!

"Lena? Lena!" Manos called over the phone.
Seconds ticked by. She struggled to come to her senses. What now?
"Yes... He was right here. He saw - me. He's running. I'm at... the spa. The corridor. I'm on him."

She shoved the exit door open with both hands. Through the blinding sunlight, she scanned for his slim form, his crooked smile. Then she saw him, hustling down the path to the beach. There were people everywhere. *Good!* Thought Lena. He wouldn't kill openly in public. But I can't lose him! If there were any words these serial hunters lived by, it was that if a victim couldn't be reached with ease and assurance they shouldn't be reached at all. *Don't blow this arrest...*

She broke into a frantic run, her mind racing with preset techniques to get a confession. *Be direct. Know all the details of the crime. Remember, the murderer only admits what he wants to admit.*

"Wait!" she shouted. Was he on Manos' list? She hadn't memorized the names. Zoran, Leon, Kingston, Victor...

"Wait!" she called, her voice carrying in the summer air.

The man heard her. At the water's edge, he turned and looked at her, clearly shaken. She was closing in. A few feet away from him, a jet ski lay on the sand. He jumped on it and took off.

For the very first time, Lena understood the difference between life and death.

Life was catching this fiend. *Now.*

Anything else was death.

17.

Her next move was a mistake. A big mistake. And it contained many others, multiplying unrelentingly like malignant cells with every move she made. Her move of not calling the police. Of pursuing the suspect on a jet ski. Of leaving the rental attendant her phone so he would let her have the jet-ski. Giving the attendant her code so he could call the police. Her only thought as she fixed her eye on a small, growing dot was that she was about to die, alone, chasing a murderer, while some stranger was going to slowly erase, one by one, the pictures of her life. Most of all, her pictures with Franz Hansen.

Their trip to Iceland. Standing in front of the freezing waterfall of Gullfoss. His eyes as he looked at her.

What had happened to them, really? He was the reason she felt so much older than her thirty-two years. The life they would have shared, children they would have had. But her "mission", or rather her blind determination to "stop crime forever" and do it alone, not with an accompanying professor, turned everything icy as those flowing falls. Yet on this jet ski chasing a paranoid maniac into the waters off Houlakia she wanted the sea to wash over her, to numb all vain ambition. She would take back the decisions she had made, erase having left him, and cry out to the world:
"Wa-it!"

Had anyone heard her?

It was no day for sailing; the winds were calm enough for her to see well over the water's surface. The shoreline was gone; her phone - her only weapon - was in the hands of a jet ski rental guy on the beach of San Marco. He would be the one to answer Manos' next call. They would never find her. The killer was heading directly north towards the light-house, Faro Armenisti. Lena hoped he would avoid the waves whipped by the easterly winds through the strait between Mykonos and Tinos and sail instead toward the villas above Houlakia. But the dot had grown now. It was just below the lighthouse.

Deserted! Only the guilty choose deserted places...

She got as close to shore as possible, cutting speed and thinking fast. *Ok, confrontation. What do I do?* Not many choices. He wasn't big, but he was violent. Keep him away. Testing how quickly she'd be able to get out of there, she spun around. Too fast. She hadn't recovered when a mid-sized wave placidly rolled up and broke over the jet ski. The engine faltered and died. Her hands fumbled to the starter. She tried turning it over. Once... Twice...

Nothing.

"Fuck you!" she screamed.

She tried, again and again. Hopeless. The engine was flooded. *If he comes, I am completely alone, she thought. He won't need a private room. Won't need to drug me. He won't have to perform his killing ritual. He knows I've figured it all out.* She saw him in her mind's eye, shooting a spear gun into his victims with a shiver of delight. *If he comes, it'll be to kill me.*

Lena knew how to get a flooded starter going, but that didn't occur to her now. She could focus only on him, about two hundred meters off.

The man who had murdered Bill Casey was now riding in a loop around himself and, coming full circle, he hovered, the jet ski's bow pointed towards her.

In fractions of a second, her frantic mind tried every option. She could keep trying the engine. Too dangerous to wait here, no.

She looked to the coast; it seemed about a hundred meters off. *I have to get away from him...* She quickly fastened her leather belt on the fourth hole and jumped into the water. Her flowing white pants and blue silk blouse, the leather belt and matching bracelet were already drenched, weighing her down. But with long strokes and strong kicks, she was soon about halfway there. *I'm going to make it!* But a quick glance behind reminded her she'd forgotten to factor in the murder's speed, his jet-ski now fully revved.

The two hundred meters now narrowed to one hundred.

Yet another mistake!

There were coastlines much more beautiful for dying. The parched rocks of northwest Mykonos tumbled a hundred feet into the water with neither drama nor beauty; even after millions of years of rock formation, it still wasn't a tourist site. The lighthouse hunched atop the boulders was a squat hovel, completely abandoned, topped by a watchtower that looked more like a botched minaret. *My God, this is where I'm going to die!* Bracing herself, she took in as much air as she could and then gave it her all. If she could just reach land, she knew exactly what to do. Get through the rocks. Climb that hill as if she were born on it. And scream. She would scream as loud as she could. Plenty of people would be by this time at Armenisti to watch the sunset.

But the coast was barely any closer. His jet ski had advanced, making a circle around the one she had left. Lena, transformed from pursuer into prey, saw the man come to a stop, open the storage hatch and reach inside. He pulled out a chain. Holding it in both hands, he looked directly at her. Unable to reach the shore, she scrambled to grab hold of a nearby buoy.

She had to keep him from getting that chain around her neck!

There was nowhere else to go but down. This buoy! It's got to be attached to something, maybe something sharp I can use! It was half-floating on the surface. The jet ski was now no more than thirty feet away. She took a deep breath, as deep as she could. This was her last chance. Whatever she found down there was her only hope of finding a weapon. The waters were perfectly clear, but she closed her eyes as she carefully touched her fingertips to buoy's chain to guide her as she went under.

The chain must be new. It was completely smooth, had none of the scaly sea bloom she'd been afraid of touching.

She opened her eyes.

A few feet below was a huge mass, almost human in shape, or as though a whale had been caught in a wire net. *Wow, such big fish come this way,* she thought. *I guess because Mykonos and Tinos are so close.* She continued downward. *It's actually not such a big catch. It's small, almost beautiful. You could even say it looks like an angel...*

Then her lungs heaved all at once.

She grasped the chain, climbing up to meet her killer. Anything to get away from what she had just seen: the naked body of a young woman, dead, with her arms raised as if begging for mercy. Swaying with the same peaceful rhythm as Billy Casey, a chain threaded through her naked body, the young woman's dead form now jerked from the impact of Lena's movements. *Oh, I'm sorry!* she thought, unthinkingly. She reached up and grabbed the buoy, steadying herself once her face met the water's surface.

On the buoy she now saw one word, written in raw, red letters:

FREE

The man with the smooth, blond hair had now turned off his engine. He was right over her. In his hands was another thin, light chain... Lena only realized she must have screamed by seeing his own lips moving, and from his grasp as he strained to keep her above water.

"Shshshh..." He was looking down at her with furrowed brows. "Calm down, now..."

Yes, calm down. There's no escape now...

18.

Amidst waves of applause from the seated forms before him, Manos looked for her. He tried to single her out as Franz Hansen and one or two others leaped up, in all the earnesty of academia, to shake hands. With hooded eyes, Manos sifted through the chairs as he passed, heading to the lobby for the break. He searched the crowd during an ardent discussion with an adjunct criminologist: yes, Greeks did like their espresso chilled - an abject felony according to Italians. He lingered idly by the ladies' room, scanning the cheerful summer bustle of the hotel entrance.

But Lena Sideris had disappeared.

He also looked for the bonehead who'd gotten pictures of the slide showing Billy Casey's lifeless body. *It's too late now, anyway!* Maybe he was somehow meant to make sure the image would be copied, forwarded and shared everywhere. Well, no such thing as bad publicity! It can only help the case. His thoughts lit upon Lena again. *Better damn well help mine, too.*

"I'd love to, but I have to attend a wedding," he found himself saying, addressing Hansen, who had invited him to attend the rest of the presentations.
"I'll let you know if any insights come up," said his host, "though I don't suppose you really need our input."
"Oh, on the contrary -"
"I've worked this crowd for years, you know."

They fell silent, sizing each other up. Would it be for a friendly slap on the back or a fight to the death? But with an exhale, they each settled back.

They were both looking for the same woman.

III. A Killer Model

19.

"**N**o, that's not a Pilates position. CrossFit and yoga, sure. Or ab crunches. And massage, of course. But never Pilates, I think." Officer Petro was sharing his wisdom.

"You ever even done Pilates?" Bellas asked him.

"No," answered the young man. Feeling Bellas' stare, he met the older man's eyes. "Massage, I've had." And I could use one right now, he thought.

Officer Bellas had suspended permits and issued search orders for all spas, fitness centers, yoga studios and any businesses of the kind. The discovery of a second victim off the waters of Armenisti now meant he had to act fast or panic would take over. A single post, a single cancellation would be enough. Questions would be asked. Tourists. The Athens Police Authority. Not to mention the mayor's whining. Searches like this would show Mykonos police to have information and to be acting on an organized plan.

The coroner had hinted that before he shot, the killer had aligned the chain perfectly through the pharynx, spine and anus. Under what circumstances would a person willingly and naturally align their body in this way, lying flat with legs open and head thrown back? Sex was one obvious explanation. But it didn't solve everything. A second duplicate body confirmed that the murderer had a system. Drugged or unconscious, somehow the victims assumed this position, such that their last act was to facilitate their death. What if they were not drugged? Were they in a state of ecstasy? In the hands of a massage therapist? Yoga perhaps? Potential victims could find a trainer or masseur as early as 5am. Anything at any time could be found in Mykonos.

"What if they say we're slacking off, Sir? Getting massages," Petro asked. He was behind the wheel of his wife's old Smart car.

"If we were searching boats left and right they would say we were stupid. When they see us looking for Pilates instruct -"

"We've gone over this. No Pilates. We're looking for masseurs."

They parked.

Nearsighted, Bellas now stuck his dark-framed glasses onto his forehead to scan his missed calls. Everyone could wait - except Manos. Turned out the kid was right - they had a serial killer on their hands. Not that he understood a word of the suspect list Manos had given him. That's why he sent him over to the conference in Houlakia. It was a delicate balance. If anything went wrong with Athens, he would need to count on him. *I got it from Interpol.* He called the office and told them to take a look at the list of usernames Manos had so proudly forwarded him.

"Should I bring them in?" Chrisanthos asked, ready for action. He was the only one missing out on the massage hunt.

"No," answered Bellas. "Just locate them. These are usernames, not arrest warrants."

Find them. At your Facebook. That's all you do all day anyway. He hung up, unconvinced. Freedom rolled along the coastline as invisible breezes whipped up the surface in staccato waves. Clothes were strewn, like great flags that had their decorum washed away. Everything was as accessible as the July sea breeze. And those who flocked to Mykonos found whatever they were seeking right here on the golden sands of Panormos. Yanis Bellas and Lieutenant Petro Xagoraris now appeared to speak to mighty George, King of the Sands.

"Officer!" He rushed to greet them with the frank tone of a seasoned insider.

"Hey, George! Does the Mykonos Police need passports to get in?"

"I have just the right hookah for you!"

George was owner of the Principote, the Panormos club.

"How much staff do you have for massages and that kind of thing?" asked Bellas. He was ignoring the perfumed smoke curling up from the clusters of Arab visitors scattered around them.

"Got some aches and pains, Sir?"

"It's Petro's back actually," Bellas returned the banter.

"Hi..." said Petro, rather engrossed in a group of lovely, glossed-up girls all ready to create their Instagram story - live from Mykonos.

"We need to keep our chat quiet, ok?" George now said in a whisper. "Alessandra Ambrosio is here for a private party."

"I need each and every person who does massage," Bellas answered stiffly. *And I have no idea who Alessandra Ambrosio is.*

The other mastered his nerves. "We need to keep our voices d -"

"George... George!" Bellas cut in.

If it weren't for a sudden stop in the music pulsing through the air around them, the King of the Sands might not have grasped the situation.

"We have a problem," said Bellas.

They all looked at each other, thinking, *Right on the beat.*

20.

It looked like a casting call. Three migrant girls from Eastern Europe, another from Ethiopia, and a Bulgarian guy. Selana. Monica. Kendra. Nouma. Sebastian. Wild abandon seemed a global affair where nationality was meaningless; all you needed was a name straight out of a Disney movie. Their IDs bore traces of a forgotten, disease-free world where there used to be nations, complicated numbers, municipal stamps. Stapled-on pictures showing pale, frightened faces.

Finishing up a call, Petro was now all business, ready to take statements. *Good thing the old King of the Sands didn't take me on for the summer after all.* Lured by the prospect of scoring a grand or two per week, he'd considered taking a summers' unpaid leave to try his luck at Nammos or Principote. Now, as news of Billy Casey's murder streamed down the timelines, his instincts searched like antennae for the killer, hidden among the sun-washed masses before him.

"We've acquired a suspect list from Interpol," he said, speaking firmly as the Lieutenant of the Mykonos Police Authority. "We are working in close cooperation."

Bellas knew well there were no secrets among Mykonos locals. Almost instantly, anything they said would be broadcast, from the mayor's office to the businesses and hotel owners, right down to hustlers working the beaches. They're rounding up the massage people. Working with Interpol. They're onto something. *All he needed was a few days*, Bellas thought. With a growl, he turned to the fearful group gathered in the Principote office: "I take it you are all professional massage therapists."

"Y-yes," could be heard in broken Greek.

"And barring actual diplomas, of course you all have documentation
-"

"Yanis..." George cut in, but Bellas stopped him. "Anyone missing
who does massage at Panormos?"

The Bulgarian said heavily, "They do massage up there..."

"Up where?"

"Up the hill. The hotel."

"Er, Officer, no need to see massage staff from Albatross, right?" The
King of the Sands was concerned.

Albatross, barely a mile away. Very exclusive hotel. Petro made to
speak, but Bellas signaled, clutching the papers. He stared at their faces.
It was clear to all that if he stopped short of asking for more documentation, this interrogation was pointless. With a grunt, he went to shove the
papers at Petro, only to find he'd left the room. The prettiest girl of all
suddenly piped up. "Listen, I don't do massage."

"No?" asked the officer.

"No massage," she repeated. "Just sex."

Amid whooping laughter, she insisted, "I'm telling I don't belong in
this line-up. I'm not a masseuse."

Officer Bellas left their papers on the desk for a walk on the hot sand.

21.

The hotel overflowed with people. A night here would cost Lieutenant Petro Xagoraris a month's pay from the perpetually depleted Hellenic State. While most Greeks were drowned in debt and repo auctions, Mykonos was the eternally preferred playground of the wealthy. The cost of living skyrocketed long ago. It was tough, living here. *But someone has to do the job...*

"Mykonos Police. I would like to speak with the owner or the director."

Something about the power to pay so much for even one night gave these people a certain sameness. Their faces were all alike, even the tone of their voices. They had matching haircuts. Matching clothes. An underlying sense of gratification seemed to lash them together in an invisible net of pleasure. It wasn't from the golden sun or its shimmering sands that the Mykonos spirit arose. It wasn't the luscious adornments of the restaurants and spas. The true essence was the delight of swiping a card and charging twenty or thirty thousand with the tap of a code. Without a care in the world. If the rich were not exactly identical, their perfect indifference was universal.

"May I help you?" It was the smooth voice of a petite young woman clothed in what looked like a linen towel with laces.

"Mykonos Police," he repeated.

"Mr Pieridis isn't here," said the girl with the laces. "But I can help you with anything you'd like."

"I need to speak with all massage and yoga personnel," he said, and then added, "but not Pilates."

"That will take some time. May I invite you to wait in the spa?"

He had no other choice. Several seasons ago, the Mykonos Police had agreed to operate quietly wherever tourists roamed, a tacit understanding respected by all. A uniformed officer speaking with a hotel receptionist might incite worry, but a sly local slipping past her into the spa inspired an indulgent smile.

"I might as well have a massage," Petro now heard himself saying. "You know, since I'm waiting."

The seasoned receptionist answered, "You can make an appointment at the spa. You'll have no problem at this hour."

Before he knew it, Petro found himself half-naked in a chic little massage room. It would be at least an hour until the full staff would be assembled from the four corners of the island for him to interrogate, so why not spend it taking care of his back? The wonderful, refreshing scent now filling the air softened the blow of the fee: one hundred fifty euros for forty-five minutes. Wealth isn't so far away after all, it's a feeling, an attitude. You pay a hundred fifty, and you don't worry about it. He was standing in his boxers, the sling of his firearm in hand. Not a care in the world, he thought, till the door slowly opened and a young woman stepped in. High, lovely rounded hips and silky, pin-straight hair. She spoke softly. "Hi. I'm Sonia. Are you ready for your massage?" She hadn't noticed Petro quickly slipping his gun down the sleeve of his white shirt.

"Yeah. My back's bothering me."

"Sure. You can let me know exactly where I should concentrate. Change into this and lie down," she handed him a flimsy bit of cloth. "I'll be back in a minute, and we can get started."

She closed the door behind her. He was alone again, enveloped in the sultry, monotone music. Very soothing. His eyelids felt heavy, and he moved slowly, with weighted arms. Attentive to each movement, he changed and lay face-down on the massage table. *It's like a stretcher. Is this how the murderer positioned them? He would have to get them to toss their head back and open their legs.* Petro tried the pose himself. *I wonder if Sonia will let me touch her. I'll have to be very, very careful.* He sat up on the table, resting his palms on his thighs. She was taking her time. A rush of guilt surged up. What if Bellas found him like this? He wouldn't say a word. It's all just a show anyway, to reassure everybody and have a good season. At this rate, in two months the island would close for the winter, and they could chalk it all up to a paranoid nut who had chosen Greece's most popular vacation destination to pull anchors through people's asses. *I mean, he's not the only wacko we've ever seen.* Honestly, things had gotten more and more extreme over his five years on the force. It was like tourists came to be lab rats, testing who could do more drugs and more booze. And then back they went, boarding the last boat, the last plane, to the world they esteemed normal.

He got up. *She forgot me.* He considered going to ask for her but decided to lay low. After all, he was still officially working. Would Bellas dare to report him? *No way. It's all a show...* But since he was here, he might as well do his job. He could start with Sonia, asking about her work. *What's it like, slathering cream on all those anonymous backs every day? Did she ever develop an emotional bond with them? What if they had zits? Could she wear gloves?* Petro chuckled to himself. *Definitely worse jobs than being a cop on this island!* He started taking a closer look around. On a little console in the corner a luxurious display of scented candles and aromatic sticks spread their magic. Lots of accessories in this business. It seemed like overkill. He reached down to open up the cabinet of the console. *I'm allowed. I'm on duty.* But he saw only machines and such. He closed the cabinet. Whole companies specialized in massage products, mostly junk that didn't even exist a few years ago. Candles and scented sticks, machinery... He opened the cabinet again.

This was not exactly a gadget. It was a winch, bearing the proud name of Smittybilt. *What is a winch doing in a massage room?* He felt an icy spear run down his spine and jumped to the massage table, grabbing his white shirt. He fumbled in the sleeve, and unfastening the holster, he took out his gun.

He cocked the trigger, his aim steady on the door.

He waited.

The whole day seemed to waste away. *Where is she?* He waited. When she finally appeared at the door, she saw his service revolver leveled at her.

"What's this?" he shouted, head jerking towards the open console. The sticks still burned gently. Sonia let out a sudden cry, her eyes wild. Then, as if making to come in, she backed out and ran.

"Freeze!" he shouted, following. "Freeze!"

But she was gone.

Petro screamed FUCK in his head, stumbling over a young couple. "In! Get inside!" It wasn't the gun that made them instantly obey; they hadn't even seen it. It was the sight of this raving, red-faced man wearing nothing but a silk thong. Petro raced to the reception desk.

"Police! Freeze! Now!"

Before long, the whole island was in a stir.

22.

In the taxi from Houlakia to Hora, Manos knew something big was up. There was nothing quiet or discreet about all those sirens howling.

"They caught somebody," mumbled the cabbie from the front seat. Nobody "caught" anyone on Mykonos, unless it was for tax evasion and this only after 2009. But sirens, never.

Lena Sideris. He'd let her chase after the guy who snapped a shot of his slide showing Billy Casey underwater at Ornos beach. He should have told her not to bother. He'd either post it or not. Either way, the case would gain momentum. But why did she insist on stopping him? When Manos called her, she had him right there. Did she take him for the killer?

Was he the killer?

Worried, Manos, reached in his back pocket for the preliminary suspect list he'd worked up from Mei's MySQL files. He'd shared some names with Officer Bellas, but not all. He put on his airpods and called Mei on WeChat. When she saw it, she switched to Signal instead.

"I didn't even see the time over there."

"I'm exhausted! But here I am, all alone and wide awake. For you."

"God, Mei! I'm sorry!"

"I don't believe in God, Manos. Neither do you. Calling about the girl?"

"Uh, about the list." Manos admitted, embarrassed.

"Right," said Mei with a groan. "But new queries mean we have to run everything again. I'm going to bed. I'll check it out with the team tomorrow."

"New queries?" he asked. *What new queries?*
"New victim, new queries," she said.

His heart lurched. He heard a notification come in and clutched his phone tight before unlocking the screen with his face. Mei's message was a photograph. A girl. Underwater. Arms raised high. With a chain rising in a serene curve from her pretty, open lips.
"Fr-free?" he stammered.
"Different location, identical position, identical chain."
"When...?"
"Your friend, the psychologist."

His heart lurched again. "Not her!"
"No, not her," said Mei in a simpering tone. "Her name is Jenna Will. Twenty-two years old, studying law at the University of Strathclyde. Pretty girl. But your friend found the body."
"What? I just... I was with her two hours ago."
"Manos, seen any timelines lately? Someone posted both victims. Your serial killer has officially gone viral."

Tense pause. The cab had reached Mykonos City. Manos wanted to get out and walk, but the cabbie eyed him curiously. He'd wait till they passed the bus station. Manos stared at his Facebook and Instagram Stories. On the street, people looked shell-shocked. A few short years ago, thousands could perish in a civilian massacre with practically no coverage. Today, if a cat broke its leg falling from a tree in the middle of Japan, it caused international alarm. The first posts on his timeline read: "Terrifying murders in Mykonos: Authorities discover mass corpses," and "Mykonos: A State of Horror!" He noticed a family rushing into a bus. Sudden chaos. Hovering silence. Yup. A connected era, alright...
"I'll call the office first thing tomorrow."

"It'll be 3 a.m. over there."

"Mykonos never sleeps," he said into the phone quickly, taking out some money and opening the door. They had reached the police station. On the sidewalk next to the entrance was Lena Sideris, her hands gesticulating, her hair wild and sticking to her face. Beside her was her father, Captain Panagiotis, former Police Director. He motioned Manos over to stay and take over with his daughter.

"Are you...," began Manos, "I mean, did you bring her?" He wanted to ask about the new victim, but he exercised caution. Lena was clearly in shock.

The captain nodded, tight-lipped. He seemed on the verge of saying something like, *Not even in New York, right?* Instead, he turned on his heel without a word, anxious to join the real action. Manos was left standing there looking at Lena. Her face was distorted from the strain. Her ragged clothes were dried and clinging to her body. She threw her arms around him and started to cry.

"Who is it?" She murmured into his ear through her tears. Just then, two officers rushed past them to the entrance. One of them was speaking into his phone, saying, "It's a Greek. They know where he lives..." Lena's body stiffened a moment as she listened. They both had heard, but neither could believe it. They both stood there, but neither loosened the embrace.

"What's happening?" she whispered in his ear.

23.

There was an atmosphere of cautious celebration and pride upstairs at the Mykonos Police Authority, as though they were greeting an unknown new colleague. The boys down at the Coast Guard had called with electrifying news that morning: an identical body was found off Faro Armenisti. Manos was right; it was a paranoid serial killer, smack in the middle of tourist season. Suddenly, being a Mykonos cop meant more than escorting Athens tax agents for restaurant audits, or arresting some drunken Albanian day-laborer. This was history; they felt it. If they could just catch him within a few hours, they'd be heroes. If not, next year's reservations would tank, and reservations were Mykonos cryptocurrency. That number ruled their lives. Two hundred thousand, whether up or down, affected everyone. It had also been discovered that one of the Albatross masseurs hadn't reported to work in several days. At this, smiles dawned, phone calls were made, and delicious cups of frappe coffee were delivered. Their heartfelt relief quickly transformed into certainty, scraps of information into undeniable truth, and suspicions into unanimous proof: the absent worker used his hidden mechanical winch to pull the heaviest chains right through the bodies of his victims. All they needed to practically close the case was to verify their appointment times.

He couldn't escape.

It was only a matter of time.

The juicy details would fuel gossip all winter. Not the least savory was the appearance of their colleague at the reception desk of a busy hotel, wearing no more than a thong and aiming a gun.

"How's our Lieutenant?" Stella and George, a couple of the youngest recruits, laughed till they cried. Only a scandalized local, who kept jerking his head at Stella, could curb the comic relief.

"Hey guys, can I go now?"

It was Haris Theodoru, a tall, gangly young man known by some, but not all in the island as "Happy-Harry." This term of endearment arose from his strange habit of twisting his mouth downward with no apparent reason and his passion for always being at the heart of any happenings. Thanks to this passion - and his cute profile picture - he had three thousand Instagram followers and plenty of unique visitors on themykonian.gr. Two whole hours after finding that poor girl at Armenisti, he was still trying to explain to the police what possessed him to jump on a jet ski and take off for Faro, dragging Lena, who did not recognize him, with him.

"No one else had that picture! It's obvious!"

Not to the guys on the Force, it wasn't. *What was he hoping to do by posting a photo of Billy Casey on his timeline?*

"Readers and followers love an exclusive shot. It's my job."

Couldn't he get it anywhere else? *Why take out his phone and get it off a slide in the Criminology Conference in Houlakia?*

"That's where I found out. I had no idea anyone was killed until that what's-his-name talked about it in his presentation."

And what the hell was Haris doing there to begin with? *Nothing hotter going on than a crime conference?*

"Criminology! I wanted to cover it for The Mykonian. It's not every day the island is crawling with criminology professors, is it?"

So why didn't he just get his shot and beat it?

"That's what I was doing! But then that girl started chasing me down and shouting at me to stop. I thought she was going to make me delete it, and I hadn't had a chance to send it to myself."

And he just happened to wind up at Faro Armenisti. And find another body.

"I didn't find it! She did, by accident. Then she went nuts."

Not a very likely story. Then what?

"I tied up her jet ski with mine and helped her snap out of it. She told you herself. Then I called you, and you brought us down here. Ask her - she's right outside!"

Then he thought, *Actually, don't! She saw me take another shot, of that messed-up baby doll. She was crying while I posted it. But so what? It's viral! In one hour, I'm at ten thousand followers. Ten thousand!*
"Can I go?"
"You're not going anywhere!" Someone barked. Even if he wasn't their man, he was stuck until they got their masseur.

The police were hunting for him right now.

24.

Two hours after Captain Panagiotis called from the Coast Guard boat at Faro, a young woman turned up at the station to make a statement: the dead girl whose image had flickered onto her timeline was one of her friends. Officer Bellas briefly considered taking her down to the morgue with him for a positive identification, then decided against it. In the heat of the moment, the discovery of a second body was all that mattered. Moments later, he found himself at the morgue for the first time in his life, standing, alone, before an angel. Jenna Will was the most beautiful girl Bellas had ever seen. None of the violence that had so quickly and desperately dispatched her from this world could erase the harmony and symmetry of her features. Or the steady certainty of her eyes, brilliant even in death, looking upon her murderer as a long-lost friend, with all the lovingkindness of a mother. A mother that she would never become.

"Just here," Stevis was explaining, absorbed in his work. "No swelling. Seems the vocal cords were active."

"Throat not even forced..." Bellas said vacantly, as if to himself.

Stevis gave a start. "Huh? Er, yes..."

Now Bellas jumped; his phone, forgotten in his pocket, went off. "Yeah?"

"He got wind of us." came Lieutenant Petro Xagorari's voice. "Grabbed his stuff and disappeared."

The officer took a few breaths, thinking. He saw Captain Panagiotis now come through the door.

"Have the guys keep watch at the port," Bellas instructed. "We don't want him leaving on the afternoon boat. Call the ticketing agencies first to see if he booked a seat. What's his last name again?"

"Saroglu."

"He's Greek? That's like..."

"Like what?" Petro asked, realizing he was now somehow among the leading men in this investigation. It felt good. He followed his own train of thought a minute more.

"Ask Chrisanthos if Saroglu is on the list I sent." Bellas said.

"Which one? Everything's upside down here."

"From our Interpol kid."

"Ok, Sir! On it!"

Bellas put his phone in his pocket, turning back to Sideris and Stevis. Both were looking at him intently. He chose to say nothing; Stevis returned to Jenna's lifeless body. He's going to say this is a delicate process, he doesn't have his equipment, he needs time... Captain Panagiotis looked searchingly into the eyes of his former colleague, wanting to know who to blame. Feeling exposed, Bellas asked quickly, "So, how's our girl?"

"Shaken up. She really thought she had the murderer."

"We did too," replied the officer. *But we don't have a clue.* Sideris picked up Bellas' silent message and answered with one of his own, *There's no way it's that guy we pulled in.*

"We have two!" Stevis' voice jarred them to attention. "Not counting the shot! Two openings!"

He had turned the girl's body on its side and brought the knees together to better examine the anus. The now-familiar type of chain was pulled out through the intestinal tract, leading all the way to the floor, where it lay neatly beside a medium-sized anchor. Captain Panagiotis and the port authorities had conveyed everything just as they had found it.

"You see?" asked Stevis, with clinical enthusiasm.

Both men now lowered their heads to get a closer look at the girl's ass. They had to admit, it was a really nice piece. As if the chain had lowered down a mannequin.

"There's another exit point!"

They were silent. Bellas and the Captain stood gaping at the body, not comprehending what the coroner was trying to tell them.

"This might give us some physical evidence," he insisted. "The killer tried to lead the chain through the anus of this Jela girl."

"Jenna...," said the Captain.

"Yes," Bellas confirmed. "I do think it's Jenna."

"Right, Jenna," Stevis quickly continued. "He must have tried a second time, with the shot. We might be able to find something internal." Stevis was now trying to set the body on one buttock. An angel with two anuses? "Do you see the wound?" he continued, clearly relieved to finally be of some use. "He pulled the fishing line through here - a very thin kind. Must have broken. Must have a piece of it still inside her."

"And he had to shoot again, through her mouth."

"Yes. It looks like she must have died instantly on that first shot. And then he put in another line, which actually came out through the natural opening! It came out... here -" He showed them with his fingertip. "That's how the chain got through," Stevis concluded.

"And if you find that scrap of line, you can verify the weapon."

"And the winch," added the Captain.

"And if you're really lucky...," said Stevis.

Bellas understood: "Some DNA."

It was no small matter. The men stood, tallying possibilities.

"How are you going to find the line, you think?" Bellas asked.

Stevis made a simple sign of scissoring.

25.

"Just in case nobody else says it," one of the cops said to Manos, "congratulations!" And another: "A serial killer! How'd you know?"

Two days ago he was updating their computers; now he was the David Caruso of CSI: Mykonos. But Manos really didn't have more to say. He noticed Lena turn her eyes on Haris Theodoru. Haris, who was sitting near her, couldn't apologize enough, and she was still completely mortified by her escapades at the symposium and Faro. Still, they all had a common goal right now: let's catch this bastard!

With a hopeful glance in Lena's direction, Manos answered, "How'd I know? With the assistance of great criminologists."

He'd shot for paternal but only managed awkward. From the moment he saw her again, he carefully treated her with the same easy, professional confidence as before. Yet the light in her eyes faltered, as though her mistakes corroded any former glimmer. Not to worry. He'd stroke her with flattery and reassurance to bring back her sparkle. She'll be fine.

But right now he needed Mei.

"Ok, so you have three criminals," he said to her on the phone. "One of them kills someone once a day. Another kills once a year. The third, once in his whole life. And they're all in the same network of friends. Now, imagine they correlate - differently each time. First, all three of them. Then Once-a-Day with Once-a-Lifetime, then Once-a-Year with Once-a-Lifetime, and so on. Which one offers the most information on that friend network?"

Mei didn't hesitate. "Once-a-Day."

"Wrong!" he chimed. "You need the most meaningful individual of the three, the one who fills in the blanks. Someone who kills every day has little in common with someone who only kills once, ever. If either of them were to communicate with an associate about what they've done or want to do - who would they choose?"

"You mean 'communicate' theoretically, right?"

"Right, they nab the same clickbait."

"Mr. Once-a-Year. The guy who kills every day is a psychopath."

"And the guy who doesn't kill - or tries to do it just once - is a total bore. But Mr. Once-a-Year, with his every scheme, offers the network much more. In theory, the other two seek to connect with him."

"He has a higher Myerson score."

"Of sorts. Now, look again: you get the results of the combined MANU models for the prospective killers here. You single out the top hundred. You run them based on the people in their network with the highest Myerson values - whether they are on Mykonos or not. You get the master list of their own connections. And among them, what percentage kill only once in their lives?"

"Tell me."

"One hundred percent! Which means --"

"That all the other network members are serial killers!" concluded Mei triumphantly. "The network structure itself shows everything! You just have to see the names rotated by the system as members, not murderers."

Some of the oldest sorting criteria, unsupervised classifier algorithms called K means, arranged output data into categories. Mei had worked them on her own. For him, it was a "black box". No way to know what was there. It was what made his work rather like being a weatherman. Given the probability of the data, he could give a five-day forecast of "a 95% chance of rain." That was how he'd tried to explain it to Officer Bellas.

"You have a weather app on your phone, right?"

But Chrisanthos had to answer for him, with his customary, "a God! Oh, a God!"

Looking at the problem through the lens of network models gave Manos even more. Everyone naturally assumed the killer was based in Mykonos, but this was mathematically impossible. The only allowable probability had the killer on Mykonos now. One in a million. The combination of cold and hot overall data with psychographic models yielded "human-lists" that he in turn modelled again from the beginning. It was a series of linear regression models, all leading to the same conclusion:

Your man doesn't operate out of Mykonos. He's here on vacation...

Who else could understand this besides Mei?

He's heterosexual...

But Mei couldn't solve it for him. The rest of the Singapore office was on summer mode. Toying around with two weight parameters on his MacBook for the same degree of certainty to a final list of killers between 116 and 3,673. For just taking out one variable. In a list of thousands of variables. Lena could stay right where she was. He was going to play cop. Someone would get him a nice cup of coffee; he had a screenful of data to explain, a cord to connect and someplace to plug in. But Chrisanthos pulled him into his office. On the bare walls hung an Orthodox icon of the Holy Mother.

"So?" he asked, incredibly serious. "Is it Saroglu?" Manos had not heard the name before.

Your man is not Greek.

"No," he answered. But just then the door opened a crack; Stella's face appeared, flaming red.

"They got him! He boarded the *Superexpress* for Piraeus!"

"Where's Bellas?" asked Chrisanthos, springing from his chair as though he'd sat on a tack.

"Everybody's down there!" Stella and a couple more cops stood at the exit, as if waiting for a signal to run. Chrisanthos grabbed his gun in its holster-strap.

"Scientists!" he scoffed, running for the door. "I ask for a simple yes or no, and you're lost at sea!"

He slammed the door behind him, leaving Manos alone in the office.

"No..." Manos said, this time into the emptiness.

26.

Amidst the jubilant chaos of a Greek port, with honking cars crawling up the ferry ramps and pedestrians navigating the cement pier on their seasoned vacation sea-legs, Officer Bellas stood like a general, the mastermind behind a great military invasion. In reality, his invasion consisted of only four personnel assigned to board the loosely tied up ship: Petro, Stella, George and Chrisanthos. Their mission: to find a Greek man, approximately 35-years-old, responsible for the deaths of Billy Casey and Jenna Will. His name was Makis Saroglu, sometime masseur at Albatross Hotel of Panormos Beach, and living just outside of Mykonos Town. Under interrogation, Sonia and the hotel owner revealed that somebody hadn't shown up to work in a few days. Authorities found his residence, but his personal items were gone and the suspect nowhere to be found. Albatross, regrettably, had kept no records of him, but the landlord of his rented room happened to have a photocopy of his ID, which was dispatched to the Athens Cyber Unit. The suspect's telecommunications provider was duly contacted, and his account verified, as well as the UDID of his device and its exact location. All this, with unprecedented speed. And so, half the Mykonos Police Department was mobilized on the port to trace this flashing dot - pulsating right now - from a passenger cell phone somewhere within the Golden Star Ferries Super Express.

A matter of time.

Officer Bellas was on the line with Athens, trying to figure out if the suspect was at the front of the vessel: "...he's heading towards the back... I - I think... I lost the signal..." Time was running out. He gave the team a moment to try to identify anyone on Facebook with the name Makis

Saroglu, or Gerasimos Saroglu, Gerasimakis Saroglu, Prodromos Saroglu, P. Saroglu, M. Saroglou... Nothing. He had the office cross-check
the name on Manos' list. Nothing. Their last resort was the grainy thumb-
nail from his ID card; and now, it was time for plain-clothes officers
Petro Xagoraris, Chrisanthos - and the Stella-George duo - to board the
ferry.

Under normal circumstances, the ferry needed no more than a scant
hour while newcomers disembarked and those bound for Piraeus
boarded. If Saroglu was not apprehended, the ferry would be held in port
and all his electronic transactions frozen. Meantime, there was to be
strictly no panic.

"Eyes open! Look for a wig, a hat!" Bellas hissed into their wireless
radios. "You start at the back and plough through. Radio silence!"

From the corner of his eye, he spied Mayor Mavroudis's familiar silhouette, heading for the pier with the two young guys from the munici-
pality's video channel.

No time to waste!

The four police officers had divided into pairs at the ship's main desk,
ready to case the boat from opposite sides. As they went, Stella noticed
George's hand was trembling. Taking it, she murmured, "Hey, now..."
to steady him. She always tended to snuggle up to him, but now there
was real reason to; she felt just as unsteady, and there was no going back.
They both imagined the suspect to be armed, even though Manos had
explained to them that this species of killer didn't work that way. Better
be safe than sorry.

Mid-July. With a thousand people getting off this ferry and another thousand boarding, one group rushing to remember all their luggage and the other scrambling for a good seat, Stella and George had only one chance to glimpse those high cheekbones, the bulging forehead, that dark hair, now possibly curled around the temples if it had grown out. On the other side, Petro and Chrisanthos started out posing as a couple of partners in crime, saying goodbye to Mykonos after having scored plenty of pretty girls, but they hadn't taken twenty paces before transforming back into plain old cops. Xagoraris discreetly swapped his wireless police radio for Bluetooth earbuds.

Officer Bellas was coaching from the pier: "He's traveling alone. He knows we're on to him, knows we've found the bodies. He's got our number now. And when we went to Panormos, he saw us put all those massage people in a lineup. He knew he had to beat it. While you were off getting a massage..."

"I was not getting a massage," Petro snapped, unconvincingly.

Chrisanthos gave him a look. *Get over it.* Their man would be chubby around the middle. The ID was only a headshot, but he had that pudgy kind of face. The economy class lounge and corridors were packed. At the snack bar, people were lined up practically on top of one another for iced coffee and cheese pies. As if star of the show, a fat dude with a wacky print shirt and dyed beard struck a campy pose, yelling: "We're like sardines in here! We'd be better off as refugees, swimming to Piraeus! Sar-deeeeens!" Everybody broke out laughing. It was the last summer before COVID.

"Sar-deeeeen-ies!"

Chrisanthos moved towards the bow while Petro hung back. Stella and George appeared from the other side. Normally Petro would have noticed them, but instead he suddenly stopped, motionless as a statue, staring right at the murderer. He was utterly paralyzed; it was Chrisan-thos who drew his weapon.

"Saroglu! Freeze!"

Cries of panic were heard. Petro heard Bellas in his headphones: "What's going on?" George and Stella also recognized the wacky shirt guy as their suspect, instantly drawing their guns.

"Freeze!" Stella warned.

"Makis Saroglu?"growled Petro.

"I- It's me!" blubbered Wacky-Shirt.

A protest came from the crowd. "What's he done?"

"DON'T MOVE!" George shouted with all his might.

"I - I'm ...not moving!" cried the suspect.

But he was trembling in fright, confused between the stillness of sub-mission and that of shock.

"Maaaaki!" Someone called, another chubby man rushing up from the crowd. He fell with a flip of dyed hair into his partner's arms.

"What do you want from us?"

"Don't move, both of you!" Stella barked.

"We're not ...moving," they said in unison. But their bodies were still fluttering, though now it was as though they were just bursting with meg-awatts of happiness and terror. The four police officers sensed a release of tension around them as the onlookers started smiling.

Out on the pier, one person was not smiling. Officer Bellas. The *Super Express* had untied and was drifting away. The suspects were being driven, handcuffed, to the station. In the distance, Mavrudis gave him a triumphant thumbs' up.

"These two couldn't have killed a spider", Petro was mouthing.

Bellas didn't need telling.

The ferry sounded its horn far and wide: something big had gotten away.

IV. Free

CJ ABAZIS

27.

S itting side by side in an old -fashioned taxi headed for Paraga Beach, Manos Manu and Lena Sideris barely spoke. The driver whipped through the maze of the afternoon rush; pedestrians were jostling around cars and buses, high-powered motorcycles, and 'gurunes', those chunky three-wheeler beach buggies with monster tires. Everyone was on their way from the beach to the hotels: *Let's get ready for tonight!* Manos and Lena had just reached one of these hallowed places. Past the airport, past Psarrou and Platis Gialos, lay an isolated bay shaped like a metal clamp. In the old days, the local people contemplated this beach and called it the Shanty. When a couple of Germans stumbled upon it, they saw claws and proceeded to found a community called Scorpios, consisting mostly of a restaurant overlooking two coves, two sandy beaches and a peninsula jutting out like the long neck of an electric guitar. And like smooth venom, seductive music gently tainted every person seated at the tables; one by one, everyone so self-assured, everyone posing, everyone available.

"I grew up here," murmured Lena. "For me, murderers were for other places. Places with grey skies, poverty, subsidized housing. Not here."

"That's why you chose criminology? A longing for cloudy skies and ghettos?" Manos asked.

"What about you?" she countered. They smiled at each other as their glasses were being filled.

"It's not so much crime," Manos answered. "It's more. Missing numbers, the data loss. Like looking for a street number. House number 24 should be right next to 22 - but it's gone! That's what I'm after. That disconnect."

"And do you find what you're after?"

"So far. But then, every time I do, someone's died."

Theoretically, they had gone to catch up with James and Liza, whose parents had complemented the pre-wedding festivities of the groom's parents with an evening of their own. But upon arrival, they saw they were underdressed. Manos strategically chose a secluded table with a view of Platis Gialos beach.

"And what's the disconnect now?" Lena asked gravely. Manos rotated his glass like a three-dimensional model, as though she'd asked his opinion of the wine.

"Look at the data we have on hand."

"Is it too much or too little?"

"Over 95% of other murders say the same thing. It's a foreigner."

"How?"

"The suspects in our system all have foreign profiles, with over 90% of their interactions localized as non-Greek. An interaction, you know - a post, a like, a comment, even the scrolling itself, or using a third-party application. Collected over a range of months. We can assume this correlation also applies to our killer. He gets his victim alone, brings them to a state of ecstasy and kills them. He meticulously pulls a wide chain through their body with a winch. Then welds on a heavy anchor. Then he gets everything onto a boat: the corpse, the chain, the anchor, and a buoy with his scrawl on it. Without being seen! And down it all goes, underwater. He's done it twice."

"Hopefully twice. The coast guard boys are combing the water. They're diving even now."

"At least twice. It's like he's saying 'Catch me if you can!' The anchor, the winch, the boat. He has welding tools... buoys, spray-paint. Just one of those could betray him. The searches he's done for machines, his online purchases. But beyond this psychological information, the data falls mute. That's the disconnect driving me crazy."

"Isn't there a Dark Web?"

"Sure! Online, offline, dark, open - everyone has a digital profile. People want the same things. They do the same things. They react the same way. But when they stop - even a short while - the system can interpret their silence. Disconnect!"

"No," she shook her head. "People want different things."

"Really? Look around."

More people were gathering in the club. Regal, easeful, confident. It was going to be one of those nights. Sunburnt men with dilated pupils and billowing shirts, like monkeys ready to pounce. Clinging to them, delicate she-giraffes, their personal devices dangling from their fingertips. Together they plucked their way into this, the very pinnacle of Aegean watering holes.

"I can't argue that. Mykonos celebrates diversity, but of course it has none."

"Except in some rare cases."

She raised and eyebrow. "Such as?"

He smiled. "Some wild girl who abandons an academic conference to chase a murderer on a jet ski!"

He instantly wanted to delete the words. Like cleansing a data set.

Lena shot back, saying, "Has it crossed your mind that our friend might be offline completely?"

"That alone would uncover him. One hundred percent probability."

For offline suspects, the system had working access to speech-to-text files instantly generated by telecommunications providers. Yet even that - zero correlation.

"You might need a little help from traditional criminologists. Come with me tomorrow. We'll close the conference together."

"I'm not a criminologist!"

"Oh - yes you are!" She laughed. "You just don't know it."

Alexandra Atkinson and Sandy Vos soon appeared, ready to offer their hearts to Manos. Behind them, James Will, the groom, looked eager to introduce himself to Lena. But Manos felt far, far away from them all. Far from Silicon Valley and Menlo Park and the Department of Statistics next to Memorial Court. It seemed decades since their endless discussions - bursting with passion and confidence - at Palo Alto Pizza. Centuries since their mad antics in the dorms, the rush of affection he'd felt for his classmates. The years had pitched them, rolling fast, as if into separate bowling lanes. Manos knew that these faces, this hot afternoon breeze, the crisp fabric of this moment, lighthearted and carefree as only Mykonos could weave it, were nothing more than a quantum lapse; their past selves coming together for a blip in time. Then Alexandra would be off to her next delicious flirtation, Sandy her next juicy story, James to his lavish wedding - and Lena and himself to the most heinous serial crimes he had ever seen.

He had turned into a criminologist.

28.

Officer Bellas was no mathematician. But he was staring at a wall of numbers. In his hand was a confidential set of findings dated from the previous day, marked "For Official Use." It bore the Interpol logo and below it, in elegant typeface: Global Complex for Innovation. Most mysterious of all was the code "DFL Case Number 1189108, Singapore." In the margin, apparently an afterthought, someone had jotted: MYKONOS ISLAND/BUOY MURDERS. Everything about the document cried out the importance of its content. But the content was a pyramid of numbers.

And what the hell is a DFL? He wondered.

This kid was really something!

Seeing Bellas' dismissive attitude towards his first stab at a suspect list, Manos Manu had resorted to the official channels. Authorizations procured, the whole Singapore team set to work, a report drawn up. The report had bounced quickly to Athens, through the airport police office printer, landing in Bellas' hands within the hour. From what he could make of the phrase "Live Acquisition" printed below the columns of numbers, these guys went into various servers, directly accessing "dataflows," and apparently ran them through something called Multiagent Analysis of Network Units. "Units" - this means people? There was a ray of hope on page four, where the words "...our Digital Forensics Lab" caught his eye.

DFL - got it!

Athens was no stranger to digital analyses, either. But their Intelligence Agency and police only accessed data - emails, images, log files and Internet browsing histories - on computers and personal devices held in their possession. This document had a full analysis of all devices within an entire area, like a cloud would. Just like Edward Snowden's system, he thought. He drew breath, wanting to tell someone and lifting his eyes to Chrisanthos and Petro. But they were busy.

Saroglu, hunched up in a corner, red-faced and innocent as a lamb, was still in custody. Next to him was Jenna Will's friend, in tears since the moment she'd crossed the threshold.

He looked back down at his report.

For Official Use.

Sure! I'm the official - but how do I use it? He had seen plenty of reports over the years. He was comfortable with words like allegedly, likely, possibly. But everything here involved a 100% degree of certainty, as steadfast and obvious as one plus one make two. Any profiling reports previously gracing his desk included the usual crap: "serial murderer typology," and "psychosocial" or "psychosexual history". This was different. This murderer didn't have a psychological profile; he had actions, clicks, screen taps... And numbers, dozens of numbers. Acronym upon acronym. Bellas couldn't make head or tail of it. He picked up the phone and dialed Headquarters. He needed this kid on his official team, and Athens would know what to do. But phones didn't get answered very quickly in July. He covered the mouthpiece with him palm, calling out to the whole office for all he was worth:

"Anybody know where the hell to find Manos Manu?"

29.

Lena, dancing. Sinuous, mesmerizing.

Manos stared with a slack jaw, as if stopped at a rail crossing watching car after car glide past with no end. Her body was just right for this ceaseless, repeating train of movement. He had only to wait. Wait for her eyes to meet his. But her eyes were turned away; he realized his own stillness was uninviting. So he revved up like a kiddie car in first gear, mechanically moving back and forth a few steps. Yet his mind was not on the scene around him - not on James or Stanford, or even the killer. He wasn't thinking of Mykonos, or music, or Lena's moves.

His mind's eye was focused on the two victims.

When the police went to find Saroglu, Manos found Jenna Will's timelines. Truly gorgeous girl. There she was, making a silly duck face. And again, caught off guard, smiling. Such a sweet light about her. She was captivating in every single shot. Ok, but where's the connection with Billy Casey? In none of Mei's findings was there a social media correlation. They were more than thirteen friend requests apart, which was about average. With no common ground between the victims, the killer may have chosen them simply because they were available. In the wrong place at the wrong time. The murderer compensated for this random sampling through his meticulous ritual of the killing itself. However refined he might seem, he was in fact rather banal.

C'mon! Lena seemed to be saying, *time to charge up your little motorcar, my little crime genius.*

He took broader steps now - two forward, one back.

"Tell me about the corpse," he leaned down to whisper into her ear. Lena stopped still, just as the throng jumped into a new beat.

"Excuse me...," she said and tried to go.

"How can anyone keep their eyes open with a shotgun on their mouths?"

"You never stop, do you?"

"You're the one who saw her!" he insisted. "You saw them lift her out of the water. I saw Bill Casey. You saw Jenna. Both with eyes wide open. With eyes open, how do you not see that someone is aiming for your mouth with a gun? Where's the look of terror?"

"I need a drink," she said, gently nudging past him to get to the bar.

Left to himself, Manos checked his messages. Nothing from Mei. He checked his Greek Google News timeline, all the blogs, and his I-24/7 - a closed Interpol network accessing new datasets directly from their Lyon servers. Both murders were the main attraction. He sat on a low wall, forfeiting the sunset which set everyone else dancing in favor of the numbers which gave his work meaning. James, even through his mad joy, noticed the change in his friend. He sat down next to him.

"Pretty friend you have there."

"Huh? Oh, yeah. She's a ...criminologist."

"I've never seen you so serious," said James. He wiped the sweat dripping from his darkened forehead with his white shirttails.

"Because I'm scared."

James laughed. "I'm the one who should be scared! I'm getting married!"

"You shouldn't be scared, my friend," said Manos. "You should be terrified!"

They each gave a chuckle. A spark of their past closeness flickered between them.

"What's to be scared of? Your friend is getting married!"

Manos sighed. "I became a quant in a domain that doesn't pay. Now I have to make up for it by morphing into another quant!"

"What a quaint quant you are, my dear!" Manos laughed. He spotted Lena flirting hard with a very stylish twenty-something. His hands in the air, hers around his waist. He waved his arms higher, demanding the barman's attention. "It's time to transcend your fears," James advised.

"My greatest fear can't be transcended."

"Which is...?"

Disconnect, thought Manos. But said nothing.

The sun was sinking. Dozens of unstructured datasets started to clash with thousands of invisible models. Disconnect was all around him. The positioning of the table he and Lena had chosen, rather far away from James' in-laws-to-be. Disconnect. No logical order to the different kinds of drinks he was consuming. Disconnect. The buddies who had come to distract James from their monomaniacal imbibing of alcohol and data varied both in gender and motive. No corresponding model of human actors to support any conclusion. Disconnect. The holograph of Lena's expression, now inviting, then distant, now hopeful, then hollow with regret. Disconnect. On top of everything, some of his psychographic models hadn't run as planned. People were so scattered, so different. They react to their social environment. They make mistakes. They set goals. They learn. He had included each of these expanded features in the MANU models. But there was something else. People have power. They have that driving connection of initiative, determined by their private internal volition. People want to be who they were before datasets made them what they are. Often, you can pinpoint this with sheer speculation. Other times it's the one missing detail: an inaccurately weighted parameter, one mistaken criterion, or a third choice. He was left with the murky dance of data all around him. Without truth. Without delineation. Without meaning… He was dying to tell all this to Mei. But he'd missed her; his Signal calls had got no answer. He would have to wait until three in the morning. He heard a voice beside him.

"Mr. Manu."

"Yes?" He recognized Chrisanthos from the Mykonos Police Department.

"You'll have to come with us."

"Are ...are you ...arresting me?"

"Officer Bellas would like to show you something."

30.

They had taken the same road for Ano Mera, the same side street with its low houses leading to the hospital. Only now, in the middle of the night, no one greeted them at the entrance. Chrisanthos, deep shadows under his eyes, walked heavily beside Manos, wanting only to carry out his orders and be done. As predicted, chasing down massage therapists had proven an utter fiasco neither wanted to discuss. A male nurse on night duty led them through a waiting room to a surgical room, full of instruments and equipment. In the blaring light, Manos perceived Officer Bellas, motioning him over with a jerk of his head.

"Ma-nos!" he called breezily, "Drinking's off limits in China?"

"I live in Singapore," answered Manos. "Everything's off limits."

Manos dimly registered Stevis, the coroner, engaged in some procedure on a woman lying unconscious on her back. He barely looked in that direction until hearing him blurt out: "What the fu-?"

The woman lay sliced open in half, like filleted trout on ice at the fish market. The cross-section started at the larynx, running along the chest and belly to the hairless pubis, where the lips were parted like oysters swimming in white wine. The heavy chain had been removed, except where it remained embedded, through the neck to the mouth. Stevis' carefully moved his hands in the thoracic cavity, as if trying to further open it without collapsing the ribcage.

"You may not remember this when you wake up tomorrow," Bellas began, "but you are hereby officially working with the Greek Police Force. Meaning - among other things - that everything you see and hear is confidential."

"I don't work for the police," mumbled Manos. He was staring, entranced, into Jenna Will's glassy, dead eyes. His were only torn away by his phone vibrating. It was Lena. *Come to Cavo.*

"You're based in Singapore, but you work for Interpol," continued Bellas, unruffled. "The Greek Police Force has been an Interpol member since 1956. We're the ones paying for your sushi boats and Peking duck."

"Ramen."

"Huh?"

"I'm into ramen."

Bellas opened his mouth to speak but then closed it again.

"Listen, my department has already issued three separate directives for both bodies," said Manos.

"Think I don't know that? We want background on the victims, we're issuing a warning about the murderer. We need information and methodology. We made the requests in every classification!"

"Yeah, well I still don't work for you." Manos had spoken with steady confidence. But just then he looked up to see Stevis, cupping Jenna's delicate heart in both hands, looking for a place to set it down.

"For God's sake!" shouted Bellas, turning white. At the last possible second, Manos grabbed a trash receptacle and puked his guts up. The acrid smell of alcohol and mint rose up from the plastic. What the hell did Scorpio put in those drinks?

"I'm so sorry!" cried Stevis. "I think I have something."

"Just... just give us a second here..." sighed Bellas. He gave a quick nod to Chrisanthos, who had hung back all this time in a corner. Going out for a moment, he returned with a glass of cold water for Manos. The Officer took another deep breath, signaling to Stevis to pull up the green surgical cover. They'd seen enough. Knew Jenna inside and out.

"Considering the significance and nature of these killings," Bellas went on, "I contacted Athens, asking them to request Interpol assistance in the form of an IRT. I've been struggling a bit with acronyms lately. But you know that one already."

Of course, he did. *Incident Response Team*. What it really spelled out was YVIO - Your Vacation is Over. Jenna's body now covered, Chrisanthos came closer, looking like a zombie.

"Athens further requested the team be led by someone particularly familiar with the island. No briefing required. I don't need Miguel or Choi Cho. I need Manos Manu."

"I'm no operations manager! I'm a..." Manos groaned, clutching the trash can, fighting the urge to puke again, "...data scientist."

"All the better! And tomorrow your division will inform you that your leave is terminated. You are chief administrator and coordinator of the Response Team for two serial murders. Starting tomorrow, you essentially become our boss."

"I'll block it..." But Manos' voice was weak.

"You know, you have a lot to learn," said the officer in an insinuating voice. "Tomorrow, your new team and the entire Mykonos Police Force will be awaiting you at the San Marco, in Houlakia. Along with those criminology professors and the other nutty quacks. You will present your plan for catching this fucking wacko who gets his rocks off on anchors! Does 9 a.m. suit you?"

It was a sucker punch. *Why did I send that damn report to Singapore?*

Bellas wore a poorly disguised look of triumph. "But enough formalities for the time being," he said, finally turning towards the corpse. "What's up, Doc?"

In Stevis' gloved hand, held high for all to see, was a fine bit of thread.

31.

The air buzzed with anticipation. Two million travelers were flocking to the restaurants and bars between Platis Gialos and Agios Stefanos. Anybody who wasn't could be found at Cavo Paradiso, outside of Mykonos Town on the other side of the island. Below the able hands of a young Siberian woman, dance music was pulsating through the few thousand half-dressed revelers, a good number of whom were tripping hard on acid for the first time. Somewhere among them danced a woman who, just yesterday, had opened the Sixth Annual International Conference on Criminal Psychology. *Where is she?* Someone handed him a drink. *Anchor.* He chugged it. *Boat.* He called for another. *Winch.* They asked him to pay. *Welding.* He paid. *Buoy.* He was pushed. *Spray paint.* He pushed back.

He could very well be here...
"Chill, my friend!" Someone murmured into his ear. "Chiiiiiill..."

Human flesh surrounded him. Bare shoulders, exposed midriffs, sweat-bathed backs. Belly chains and dainty anklets. Flesh. The whirl of nose rings, belly rings, tongue piercings, tattoos - wherever he looked, he only saw Jenna. Her body open on the table, split in half.

Are you FREE?

As the sun started to rise, someone would track a new victim, just like Billy and Jenna. At the perfect time, he would drag them away with just a scrap of wet rope. They would sleep until the very last, when the harpoon gun poised at their mouth sent the lead chain through. But how did they look so serene? Stevis had suspected ketamine. Had sent to the lab tissues to check for other substances.

The beat intensified. The cool bass reverb sizzled in the heat. *Where is she?* Two skinny girls in sports bras pumped their arms, elbows flailing as if fighting off a giant. *Come to Cavo.* The scene was like a crazy dispersal chart, points jostling with no axis. If you have already murdered two people, where would you go to feel the rhythm? The music grew louder and louder. Lena Sideris was nowhere to be found.

He spotted her. Completely alone, despite the wild crowd. She too was looking for someone who recognized patterns. She motioned with her head, calling out to him:

"There's your killer!"

Above them, a girl was swinging high on a swing hanging from above. It was an Instagram moment: her bare feet, her long hair streaming as she offered up her nakedness to the adoring crowd. Manos went to speak, but then he noticed the chains of the swing. Childhood... freedom... Get it. The murderer associated innocence with chains. Are you FREE? He purified his victims with chains. But they had already run correlations for chains, one parameter among thousands.

He smiled. Lena had a few things to learn about MANU. But lessons could wait.

This was the time to dance.

32.

Manos and Lena danced from one end of the club to the other through a series of wide, open verandas. About sixty feet down, the crowd throbbed as one. A post-apocalyptic world elite, spectacular in its artful nakedness. Arms undulated in great waves, hands pulsating in unison, everyone penetrated by some electric hum, saying: "Surrender ...is the only truth ..." But the hum itself surrendered nothing, not in the face of such an uncertain future! Tonight, there was no need to rush into decisions. Except for Manos Manu. He was out of time. Already in the taxi heading to the club, Greek blogs were abuzz: Greek Defense Ministry helicopters had transported members of the Athens Homicide Task Force to Mykonos, bringing special geolocation equipment to "sweep the island and search the phones of the two victims." Their own coroner as well, no doubt. According to Bellas, dozens of police officers, homicide experts, conference criminologists, and sundry busybodies would be waiting for him tomorrow morning at San Marco. Each with their own theory, backed up with their own data. Bellas' move was no surprise; with so many cooks in the kitchen, there was no one left to point fingers at the Mykonos Police Force, or Bellas himself.

They each started the race from a different point. If Bellas wasn't bluffing and Central had really assigned Manos to the IRT, then with even a partial list he'd focus on who, among all those on the island, would commit such crimes. Police traditionally started with how it happened, then searched for evidence. The criminologists were capable of anything, but ultimately, they concerned themselves with why. Manos had to be ready for all of them. Thanks to the system he had created – for the who and the why, he had better data than anyone. What remained was how. The police work. That's what he needed to know. By tomorrow morning.

Lena was contemplating the crowd with wonder: "They are amazing!" Maybe, Manos thought, but they're still mortal, leaking data all around. Lost in his thoughts, he said, "Could you just lie down on the ledge here?"

She stared at him, wide-eyed. The evening meltemi winds pressed her linen clothes to her slim frame. *That's it,* he thought. *A body.* Behind her, the Siberian DJ had made her appearance from the decks. The crowd rose up in one great roaring cheer.

"Everything happening down there is linear," he said. A wave of confusion swept over them. They really had drunk much more than either wanted to admit. It was hitting them now. What he meant was, *They're all dancing, shouting - it doesn't lead anywhere, there's no conclusion.* But then he saw her lie down on the ledge without a word.

"It has to be ...aligned," she said. "The head ...has to fall ...back."

"True. Can you go over there - where the ledge ends?" he asked.

As she moved away, he said, "I'll be right there," swiping a stray lighter as he went. Might as well put it to use. He burned off a long section of cord hanging off a beach umbrella. Lena was already lying down, letting her head hang freely off the ledge's end.

"Gimme," she teased, taking one of the ends of the cord. "I would swallow it to help you out, but I'm not sure how I'd get it out again."

"Cut it out," he laughed too. Giggled, actually.

Now they were close enough to take in each others' scent. *This is nice...* Without realizing it, Manos was stroking her cheek while trying to keep the rope straight. She smiled.

"It depends on the body shape," he tried to sound clinical.

"I'm Jenna," she interrupted, keeping him going.

"You're more beautiful," he heard himself say.

They fell silent. At least one of them should just get up now. The string was now pulled tight, but he had to draw it downward. *I have to simulate the shot...* His face was right between her legs. *So beautiful, so beautiful...* So beautiful he barely noticed he was practically straddling her.

"He had... to..." he mumbled, trying to get Stevis out of his head. "...drug them...."

He felt her arms wind around his hips.

He inhaled her smell, then let himself fall onto her, breathing her in more deeply. He slid his hands around her and lifted her hips, plunging his face into her pussy. The music completely enveloped them. Her hands reached from behind, twirling closer as if from another world, unbuckling his belt and opening the first two buttons of his Bermudas. The music pulled them in. *Perfect synchronicity.*

When each of them were spent, he thought, *I should really kiss her.* But at that moment he felt the heat of a spotlight on them, from a light fixture on one of the club's scaffolds. He realized it wasn't the first time.

Ugh, I'm a jackass...

A bunch of half-naked partiers were waving at them. Just like old friends.

33.

Manos checked his email and saw the message. His department director, a good-natured Czech, formally informed him of the Incident Response Team, led by Manos himself. A protocol normally reserved for
terrorist attacks was now in place almost instantly. Everyone wanted immediate victory. When it came to communication, global police smart-
weapons had no data-lags. Or jetlag: with lightning speed, every tourist's
timeline showed Interpol's presence on the scene: lurking, recording, policing. Greek agencies also protected tourism with grave authority:
*We've coordinated every step of the way. Interpol sent us their wonder-
child - a computer expert. A Greek, no less!*

What would the murderer do with all this coverage? Like most serial
killers, regardless of language or culture, their man would likely follow
the investigation of his crimes with perverse curiosity. Pictures, like the
ones Happy-Harris Haris had taken at Houlakia, would turn this curiosity
towards Manos. *Would he stop there? Or race to the end?* He set his
watch timer for 17 hours; a time benchmark always helped when things
got cloudy. In seven hours, he would publicly appear in his new official
role. Including the photo-op, of course. The perpetrator would get wind
of this in about another ten hours. Leaving Lena at the club and his shoes
on the pure white sand, he wandered off to call Mei on Signal. It was
now 3:00 a.m., Greek time; Mei would be on the train by now. He'd just
had sex with another woman, but he felt closer to Mei than ever. A part
of him - the utterly exhausted part - craved the sobering reassurance of
routine.

"Are you there?"

"Jesus, Manos! You're no cop!"

"Trust me, I told them," he almost whined. "It's politics. It's temporary!"

"You're not doing anyone - or yourself - any favors here. Pull yourself together!"

"Mei, I need you to run a few things for me."

Silence. An intercontinental flash of feminine intuition. He felt her wanting to hang up in his face. *Please, just... trust me,* he mentally begged her. *I was only leaning over her. She started first.*

Mei spoke, her voice dark. "Listen, I have information for you too. I'll call you from the office."

Then she was gone.

Along the shore, lost in trance, couples were dancing. In their intoxication, this felt like the summit of personal freedom. But they were wrong. From a tiny, faraway Asian country, thousands of crawlers were already combing through every nuance of their personality. The dancers were transformed into arrays of data, the arrays into forecasts. Manos took out the folded piece of paper that he'd transferred from pocket to pocket for the last two days:

@solanzalexander
@borinok
@55godlessgod
@caribou6
@louiseandphilippee
@manoliadry
@ashramw
@jeronim5657
@pauldistrur
@018poweroflove

Each alias was an umbrella profile for a number of social networks and corresponded to a number of other arrays. The match-up for any of them could be automatically pulled from the system upon request (some, like @pauldistrur, had been pulled already). For now, correlations interested him more than real faces. In the scholarly literature, some two hundred psychologists had created serial killer psychographics, scoring them low on altruism, kindness, respect, and trust. *Great! But what will you say to my four thousand classifications?* How could altruism be one category, when he had 150 situational strains of it, shaped by thousands of contexts? After all, a serial killer could commit murder one minute and put out milk for little stray kittens the next. They could kill, and still bequeath all their possessions to the church. He was thinking hard. That's what computers do! Pinpoint behavioral data, piecing together scraps of bias. Take this delusional crowd; when people were locked in each other's arms, they thought the world was moving together towards an everlasting embrace. *Clustering Illusion.* Someone kissed a stranger, just as he had kissed Lena. They thought this opportunity would never come again, they could mess up just this once. *Gambler's Fallacy.* Individual freedom was an ephemeral dream. They fell victim, time and again, to their own preconceptions.

Not Manos. Or the murderer. They met on a level playing field. Both were cold: one towards the neutral data, the other towards human beings. From outside, it looked the same:

Data has no bias. Neither do you.

@kingstonbay768
@stupk08236
@leonardan8

@jkorry_xx
@lamdapor
@michaelhutchisonn
@angelof_
@mm56540x
@amazingvic008
@martin_hu

Each alias had handwritten notes. Forecasts, weights, potential model errors. MANU had only been used experimentally for verification, not research - and never in cases like this. But it was their best chance of finding the truth.

He put the list back in its pocket. In the other, he felt his phone vibrate - the code he had set for Mei's calls on Signal.

34.

Manos had left the mad scene behind, but he could still barely hear her. Crouching down on a boulder, he clasped his left hand against his ear, gripping the speaker of his phone as close as he could to the other ear. He knew Mei's workspace well. She operated like a fleet of V-8 engines: earbuds and cellphone for Signal and three screens. One for the Multiagent dashboard, another interfacing with Lyon's servers, the third for some IDE since she was forever coding or debugging a feature or two, even if it wasn't her job. He imagined her with three big cups: one for coffee and the other two for water because she hated wasting precious seconds of work time going to the office fridge.

"Most of what you're doing out there is not so bright," her tone was insinuating. "But some things are downright brilliant. Not MANU - somebody else could have invented that. And MANU or not, the guys here won't forgive your rent-a-cop nonsense."

"I told you, it's just for now. Public relations. And it's..." he sighed, "Well, it's... Greece."

"You know what? You love every minute of this, playing policeman with your countrymen. Before you know it, you'll be requesting a weapon."

"Never! You know that, Mei. I'd wind up shooting some tourist."

"So do you want to hear the most brilliant thing you've done?"

"Why not? We're on cell signal - let's go!"

"Brussels is picking up the bill. The miracle is that you took so many models and put in values that mitigate all cognitive biases. Not one or two, but everything ever outlined in all the literature. Anything referenced even two or three times on Google Scholar. Bam! From IKEA bias to the bizarreness effect. It's built in. Absolute, neutral AI!"

"Not more than thirty - and stop with the AI. You're not a journo."

"No one's ever done it before, Manos. Ever. Take finance, all the hedge funds - they talk about it all day, but then they fall back on good old regression analysis. Not you! You've taken it farther. Few systems have ever worked as efficiently as yours."

"Ours."

The silence between them was peaceful. Manos could hear the pumping rhythm from Cavo. *Where's Lena? Is she still there?*

"But you know," said Mei, "My balancers kept giving me problems, hogging up resources."

"Did you take them out?"

"That's the issue. The logic is fine. I've alternately muted them."

"The model cross-checks that automatically, Mei. Are you guys cleaning the data properly?"

"Please - don't underestimate your underlings! I didn't simply mute them, I ran each similarity in the database separately for each balancer."

"Get anything?"

"The murders indicate one constant. Only result. Anyway," Mei said. "You wanted me to run something?"

She stopped, waiting for instructions. That was Mei style; her finger gingerly alighting on a detonated grenade launcher, she'd suddenly ask, Gee, I've forgotten how you like your coffee. One lump or two?

"What the fuck! Tell me what -"

"You mean the balancers? But I interrupted you. What should I run?"

"Nothing."

As she drew breath to speak, Manos screamed, "Mei!" into the phone.

"I don' think ...the guy is an ordinary psycho. I think he's trying to make a statement."

"A statement?"

"This might be totally stupid, but the only constant coming up when the balancers are muted are the names of the victims themselves."

Billy Casey? Jenna Will?

Free Jen... Billy... William... Will-iam Casey. Jenna Will...

"They both have *will* in their name," Mei's voice was a hoarse whisper. "I feel like... I feel like some sort of social commentary being made."

Free. Will.

Manos clapped his phone between his hands. Turning, he scanned the party grinding in the distance. Every individual there, pulsating in unison, was controlled by the choices made by a girl from Siberia perched high above them. *Damn! I can't believe I didn't see that!* FREE scribbled on the buoys! It made sense. It didn't refer to the victims. It referred to their will.

He said, "You have to try it with the Myers-Briggs parameters."
"They're running."
"And send me an updated list of handles."
"Give me about forty-five minutes."
"And if the murderer is choosing victims because they have *will* in their name, then I need a list..."
"I need refreshed data from our sponsors, but I'm on it."
"A list of -"
"Right, anyone there with *will* in their name."

Manos stopped dead. Remembering why he himself was in Mykonos.

Remembering James.

35.

Just after daybreak, Manos' fatigue gave way like a bracing, revivifying breeze blowing faster and faster. As they did every August, the faithful meltemi winds arrived, combing the Cycladic islands. Manos wouldn't sleep a wink. Unable to find Lena anywhere at Cavo, he'd run to Scorpios to find James and warn him. Then it took some time for James to understand Manos' urgency about being careful. James needed someone with him at all times - until the murderer was caught. James told Manos he loved him like a brother but was so disappointed about him joining the police. Manos tried to get it through James' head, once and for all that he hadn't - and never would.

"They just have the best data," he said, for the umpteenth time. But they had little time for true confessions. All Manos could really do for James was to sympathize with him, reassure him, warn him, encourage him, and - finally - say goodbye. Day had dawned. The wind was growing wild. His audience was expecting him at Houlakia within the hour. He had to run to his hotel for a shower and shave, to change clothes and, above all, download the new sets Mei had sent.

At the Hotel San Marco, the high-speed winds had swept staff members into action, gathering towels and folding chairs, moving pretty plants in their pots - anything that wasn't bolted down. Impossible to stay out for long. Everyone was jammed into the lobby as if lining up to check out of some impending disaster. Still, today was the very last day of the Annual Conference on Criminal Psychology and Criminology; even though there were precious few of them up at this hour, an ordinary person would have thought there were additional guests just for the occasion. But these delegates were special: they wore uniforms, spoke discreetly into wireless radios, and carried weapons. Thanks to an article posted on a major news website, the serial murders had already made their rounds, kilobyte by kilobyte, on timelines around the world. The murderer and his buoys had become global news, and God help them if they couldn't handle it.

"Anybody go out?"

"Did they go out?"

"No one went out!" Bellas told them. "Go where, in all this wind?" He had been in touch with the Coast Guard earlier; there was no sense looking for new buoys during the meltemi. For now, there were just two murders, but this was no reassurance. The article had set Athens on edge; now his officers were thinking like journalists, watching the weather, when they should be thinking like cops and getting out in front of this crisis. Things only got worse when he saw their Interpol connection - their main line of defense in this investigation - stumbling aimlessly, stinking from ten feet away.

"Ma-nos! I was just wondering if you would show up, or if we would find you out there hugging a buoy, too..."

"I'm not the murderer's type."

"Maybe not, but you were seen taking a swim last night, fully clothed."

"No laundry service at the hotel," Manos smirked, giving his damp shirt a playful tug. Despite his efforts, he smelled of alcohol and looked sleep-deprived. Someone got a shot of him with a professional camera. Another, on a cell phone. A criminology instructor from the FBI Behavioral Crime Unit handed Manos his card, inviting him to reach out for anything he might need. Professor Franz Hansen informed him that since his introductory presentation the other day, a number of colleagues had come forward to offer their help.

"You and I should really discuss all this," he said.

Further off he spied Lena Sideris, observing him without any expression at all. *Like she barely knows me.* Their common fear was that hundreds of partygoers had seen them at Cavo last night. Their common hope was that this crowd wasn't exactly the Cavo Paradiso type. As if on cue, an agent with a military air appeared, along with a couple of almost identical men close behind, from the Athens Homicide Division. The man declared himself ready to serve and seemed affronted upon learning that Manos, not being a police officer, had no instructions for him.

"You're leading this investigation, aren't you?"

Manos was busy unveiling the true source of his power - his trusty MacBook - as he mumbled, "I'm a data -" But he got no further, because just as he was yanking it from its case, the laptop went flying. He popped up to catch it but lost his balance. The other man couldn't break his fall; Manos landed flat on the big glass table in the center of the lobby, launching an ashtray that smashed on the marble floor. Two or three people rushed to help him stand - except Bellas, who didn't need a second whiff of his breath. Manos, his face burning, tried to catch Lena's eye again, but she had turned away. Manos felt everyone in that jam-packed lobby had seen him fall and knew exactly why. One person, however, stepped forward to formally introduce himself.

"Mr. Manos," he said, completely unfazed and fresh as a daisy, "so very pleased to meet you. I am Stamatis Mavrudis, Mayor of Mykonos."

"I believe the police will need all the support your office can give," he said, trying to steady himself on two feet. Officer Bellas approached, now holding out an iced coffee to Manos.

"Let's talk in private," he said.

They retreated to the empty bar next to the reception desk, closing the door behind them. An artfully placed billiards table commanded a view of Houlakia that stretched all the way to Mykonos Town. Bellas introduced Officer Tsardis, "from Homicide," to Manos and Mavrudis. On the other side of the door milled the cream of the criminology doctoral world, in a meeting of their own. The murderer himself, with his buoys, had stolen the show, and each had their brilliant theories to present. But only Manos had something tangible to show: the latest MANU summary overview, complete with names of both suspects and potential victims.

"The police have about thirty people who need close monitoring," he said.

"If I had that many, I'd be running the CIA, not Mykonos Police!" growled Bellas.

"That's our list - including potential victims," said Manos quickly, ready for inevitable pushback.

Mavrudis was impressed. "We know that much?"

"The suspect may have a preference for victims with any form of the word 'will' in their name. Last name, first name, even a variant. Vill, Bill, Billy, William. It's the one constant thread in all our psycho-graphics. Right now, there are 14 of them on the island, and 16 very likely suspects."

"We don't have the manpower," Bellas insisted. "As it is, I'm getting complaints that I don't let anyone go anywhere."

"You asked for my help," said Manos, breaking out into a coughing fit.

"And I do want help, Mr. Manos," said Mavrudis, his arm out as if offering Manos some refreshment. "Frankly, as long as I don't wind up with an anchor in my ass, I personally don't care whether you find him or not. I need people to know we're handling this situation so they can enjoy their nice, little vacation with us."

"The suspect is male. Not Greek, but somehow connected with Greece," Manos' voice was steady and detached. "Very advanced level of education. All you need to do is monitor them."

Tsardis, handing the list to Bellas asked, "And can your models make a projection for the next murder?"

Running one model on top of another is easy, thought Manos. *The problem is having them learn.*

"It's not about predicting the next murder," he said, weighing his words. "It's about foreseeing when the next murder can be predicted."

No one spoke. The meltemi winds were like a tropical storm in the thickening silence. The two police officers exchanged glances, Bellas handing the piece of paper back to Tsardis as they walked out together to the lobby. Mavrudis stared at Manos, stunned. Then he suddenly drew a deep, inexplicable sniff through his nostrils, made a funny kind of about-face and headed for the lobby just as Bellas came back in. Now it was just the two of them. Bellas lay a cloth shopping bag onto the felt of the billiard table.

"Your bio file says you did some training."

"I won't touch it," snapped Manos.

"Those sixteen are going to be whittled down to one. You can bet he's going to come after you."

"I said, I'm a data -" Manos hissed.

"Great -"

"- scientist!"

" - just tell him that when he finds your friend the bridegroom. Then you can bop him over the head with your laptop!"

The officer walked away with a scoff, leaving the cloth bag on the green felt. Manos stepped to the corner of the table and took the gun out for a minute, looking it over. *I've got to clear this brain fog,* he thought, wandering away with the gun. *I have to find a place where I can sleep. Just to close my eyes for a few minutes.* He was soon at the edge of the hotel's main veranda, where a few dozen early risers diligently followed the orders of a CrossFit trainer.

"Plank!" barked the trainer to his obedient group. "Arms long! One, two, three - GO!" They instantly broke into coordinated movements. Manos laughed out loud, an imaginary silhouette of the murderer surging up in his mind. Staring at that inner image, he pulled the gun from the cloth bag without realizing it and put it into his pocket. The cold metal gave him a taste of unexpected freedom; he wanted to feel it with his bare hands. Hearing a bustle, he looked up. The trainer had turned white, his devoted athletes now stopped dead, staring in horror at Manos' hands. Like fallen dominos. Disconnect! He fumbled, trying to put the weapon back into the bag. *I need some damn sleep!* Chrisanthos from the Mykonos force came up beside him.

"Hey, boss! Mr. Manu ...Manos!" Chrisanthos helped him find the cloth bag and put the pistol away. The CrossFit session seemed to be breaking up.

"Listen," he said to him quietly, "We're going to have to fill in some paperwork for this. Ok?"

"Uh, sure. Yeah...," said Manos, letting Chrisanthos lead him to a chaise longue.

Beyond exhaustion, his dry mouth still reeking booze, Manos could sense the curiosity of a few people watching him from a safe distance; he saw Chrisanthos signaling to someone. It felt good to stretch out on the chaise longue. The Aegean glittered in the morning sun, transforming into an immense, sky-blue dashboard with dozens of white indicator lights blinking before his eyes. *If I can't see the patterns, who else will?*

It was his very last thought before falling into a deep, deep slumber.

V. Winch. Welder. Anchor.

36.

"**H**ey, Fischer! Fiiiii-scheeeeeer!"

He was floating face-down among the waves, arms wide, the strap of his speargun alongside him. He seemed lifeless except for his snorkel, completely engrossed, aware of even the tiniest pebble beneath the waters. The surf didn't rouse him, only the voice that came again: "Fischer, time to go!"

Night was falling. It was a full six miles back from the Ktapodia Islet, out at Lia. When Fischer had reached the sand, the Greek fisherman couldn't tear his eyes away from the Riffe Bluewater Elite. Custom-built. He'd never seen anything like it.

Yes, feast your eyes. The spear can penetrate a two-meter, 300-kilos tuna from ten meters. Like sinking a carving knife into a pot of sweet cream.
"Fine instrument," said the Greek.
"Yes."
"Fischer means fisherman in German, right? In Greek, it's psaras."
"I'm not German."
"I know, I know," the Greek said. "You're Russian. Ari, is it?"
"Fischer."
"Sure," repeated the Greek with a chuckle. "Fish-er..."

No answer.

Why did I bring him out? Thought the Greek, punishing for his own mistake the larger octopus they'd caught, slamming it against a boulder with all his might. Then, out of nowhere, he asked, "Hear about the murders?" The octopus weighed about five pounds. Fischer took it and turned it upside down. With his fingertips, he scooped out the flesh inside the bulb of its head and made as if to gobble it down.

"It was a couple, both of them killed," the Greek went on, not getting the joke.

"Is that so?"

"Found them underwater - but in two different places. The guy, they found by Armenisti, I think. The girl got thrown in by Ornos. In front of everyone. Or maybe it was the other way around... And he tied them up with a chain, to make sure they sank. That's what I read online. Crazy world, huh?"

The two men felt silent, trudging toward the boat. In this wind, the waves hitting from the side, they would steer towards Delos on their way back, reaching Kalafatis.

"You come every summer, huh?" asked the Greek, rummaging in the little hatch of the inflatable dinghy for ropes.

"First time."

"Really? How'd you find out about Ktapodia? First-timers only make it to Rhenia, or at most Tragonisi - never this far down."

Knowing the other was looking for the cooler, Fischer contemplated him digging around without a word. All he found were ropes and a can of spray paint, which he gave a light shake before putting down.

"What's this for?"

Fischer watched. Silently.

"It's like those kids who do graffiti up in Athens! Or the guy who buried those two bodies at sea, I read it in the -"

The Greek shut his mouth. *Too late!*

Fischer made no reaction. He gathered up their face masks and swim fins, clutching his Riffe close to his side.

The Greek carefully replaced the spray paint. "Have you seen the... uh -"

The cooler was forgotten on the beach. With slow steps, Fischer went to fetch it, handing it to the Greek with a piercing stare. It was a mere flash, but it was enough. The two octopi went into the cooler. This was normally the most satisfying part of a fisherman's day out, but an ominous cloud now loomed overhead.

Es muss sein! It must be!

For a fraction of a second, either outcome was possible. The Greek gathered up the ropes with a nervous smile, trying to stay calm. Fischer stood over him, ready to push the boat into the water. The seconds ticked by. Nothing happened.

"I use the spray paint for the buoys," said Fischer. The outcome was sealed.

"Really..."

"I want whoever finds them to know why they died."

The Greek went white. *Ok, just talk.* He thought. *About something else, anything else!* But only the murders came to mind, not pleasantries. It was just the two of them, late in the day, all alone on a remote islet. His opponent was the one with the weapon. Knew how to use it. But he clung to hope.

"Who? Who do you mean?"

Fischer smiled. The time for innocent queries had passed. The fisherman inwardly cursed himself. *Why did I talk about the murders? It's none of my business!*

"I won't say a word!" He spoke so sincerely only a madman would not have been convinced.

Fischer wasn't. He merely gazed at him, clutching the Riffe, assessing the parameters of the hunt: he had the boat keys on him; the Greek had not yet lowered the oars; right and left of them the rocks rose sharply; within them to the left, there may have been an opening in the rock, a chance of escape. He looked in that direction, as if silently directing the Greek there now. The Greek, who had also been calculating every possibility, sprang from the boat and ran towards it.

Fischer was in no hurry. He knew his opponent had just committed his greatest error: abandoning the boat. Plenty of time. Today's catch: two octopi and one man. He placed his custom spear carefully in its track, rigging each of the power bands one by one on the reinforcement plate at the muzzle. At the top of a hill nearby stood a small hovel, where the fisherman would certainly try to hide.

Three minutes later, the fisherman felt something hit him. It was inconceivable that the spear had punctured the flesh and bone of his tibia, coming out the other side, intact. It's just a wasp, a sting. Sliding his foot, he felt something tugging. Not until he saw the steel wire of the fishing spear did he let out a first, brief cry. Behind him, Fischer watched him with wide, steady eyes, the speargun like a toy in his big, beefy hands.
"I won't talk! Please! Don't kill me! I won't say anything! I know nothing! I won't say a word! Let me live! I can keep a secret! I beg you! Let me live!"

The wind rampaged in the dying light, drowning out the words. As if conceding to his plea, Fischer released the line of the spear, letting his prey off.

Relief washed over the Greek.

His leg was burning. He knew he shouldn't run. But he did.

Without a thought of thanks or apology, he wanted only to escape the line of fire. But Fischer had already reloaded. This time, the three-milli-meter gauge spear was launched without a line. The shot hit him in the back muscles, the sting much sharper this time, the pain searing. Turning, he saw the spear had left a thin trace of blood on a parched Cycladic boulder just beyond.

My God, it went right through me! How many more does he have? As if answering this unspoken question, Fischer slowly placed another spear on the gun's track.

"Don't! Don't. There's no reason. You don't have to do this!"

Now the Greek ran with all his might. The third shot nailed him just below the waist from fifteen yards away; this time it got stuck, the tip lodged in his navel. The hunted man clutched his flesh, trying to endure the pain.

"Perhaps..." said Fischer, but his voice trailed off.

He advanced, taking up the two spears that had fallen onto the rocks. He might have meant any number of things. Perhaps... it would be sad to see him die now. It would deprive him the pleasure of seeing how his body would react to all the shots. The next one, from eight yards away, went right through the belly and disappeared. The Greek felt the pain like a silencer, turning his mouth into a wet scrap of cotton, allowing only a helpless yelp:

"Why are you doing this?"

These were his final words. Fischer had already bound each of his wrists with rope, yanking him hard, as if he thought the soul had to be manually ripped out. No one would find the blood traces, at least not before the early rains.

Back on the beach, he bound the victim's feet with another heavy rope, strung the heavy anchor on the rail, and took off. The Greek man's body was pulled and jerked like a fallen water skier tangled up in the lines. The sky was completely dark. In this swell, even from close by, no one would see him. No one would remember him.

A mile offshore, the water was about as deep as a steep hillside, sloping into darkness. Unwinding the rope and the anchor from the rail, he hurled them into the water, watching the man's face sink down, down, down. *Could be a whole minute before he reaches bottom*, he thought.

He did nothing for this entire minute than staying still and thinking of the welcoming sediments below.

37.

It was already ten o'clock when Fischer tied the boat to the dock below his house. The meltemi was now silent. On this side, from Lia to Vathia Lagkada and around to Agios Nikolaos, there were dozens of abandoned moorings. Mykonos became like any other Aegean island, an elaborate sculpture of steep coves and hidden anchors, a mosaic of offshore boats. Nobody knew or cared whose they were. But the previous afternoon, a gray boat had appeared in the anchorage and the port authorities had begun asking questions. They would return with more. Fischer took the spray paint from the cabinet and loaded in his fishing bag. He would get rid of it in the landfill in Metallia. But first, he had to use it.

He closed the outside door of the small, secluded villa behind him, took out his earbuds, and put on some music. From the spacious kitchen, he got some cooking parchment, which he lay down on the smooth floor, fixing it in place with tape. From the bedroom closet, he took out the remaining four rectangular buoys he'd bought from Piraeus. One by one, he lay them on the parchment and slowly wrote in water-resistant letters:

FREE

When he finished, he absently gave it a last shake to check how much paint was left. He set the buoys to dry on the wide, low marble table in the living room and stuffed the parchment in a garbage bag. Then he grabbed his phone and visited her Instagram profile. For a while, he scanned her most recent posts, from just earlier at Ornos Beach. #Mykonos #perfectsummer #will. In one of the shots, her hair flapped like a great flag, her torso like a mast he wanted to enfold in his arms. In another, the turbulent sea. In the third picture, she wasn't alone. It was the age when having a boyfriend was almost a conquest in itself. On the beach in Agrari, 8:08 p.m. It wouldn't be that hard. He made sure he was using his secure VPN, logged-in his fake profile and soon found her boyfriend's WhatsApp:

Yo are you in Mykonossssss? We just arrived from NYC xxx me and my friend thinking of ♟in town, have any tips? Hohoho ♥Stef.

The reply was almost immediate:

Eating at Caprice Bar with my gf tonite guys! Sorry abt that! Perhaps another time, Kev.

That's right, Kevin. Another time. Fischer stripped and took his clothes onto the veranda to wash them. The wind would die down. He pounded and hung each octopus to dry when the morning sun came, then dismantled the spear gun, rinsing it thoroughly until all the salt was flushed away.

Not a breath of wind. The night air would be calm. Perfect for hunting.

A dazzling array of colors and people flowed along they tiny streets of Mykonos Town, around Matogiannia. Wealthy Greeks jostled up against backpackers. Tourists, locals, Russians with their bodyguards. Young Arabs, the girls without burkas. Eastern European girls - Svetlanas, the locals called them - all ready for Stories, Groups and Moments. A few Americans, easily spotted, rented mega-yachts, their every pleasure catered to by multinational crews. The French favored catamarans for sailing. Albanians stretching out on their rented chaise longues. The Lebanese offering a hairy-chested embrace through their low-buttoned shirts - and the Israelis who imitated them. Out-of-work actors and clothing peddlers... Everyone converged at Mykonos, the great meeting place. After all their other summers, they could whisper to themselves - and any else who happened to care, *I'm here. I've really made it.*

Fischer, pace steady and lips closed, had nothing to say. Not even when a group of drunken Italians tumbled onto him with force. The expensively dressed women, the men with their Swiss timepieces, everyone instinctively shifted out of his way as they went. He went straight to his destination. Little Venice. This was the very seat of Mykonos' fame. The fright provoked by the raging waves smashing so close to the tourists was the primal feeling from which all else arose; the clubs, the beaches, the stargazing - all that came later. In the beginning, it was just this little bar, just this wild sea.

How can they stand it?

He glimpsed Willa Kendall strolling along, holding hands with her boyfriend. The silent radiance in her eyes. *I'm here. I've really made it.*

His heart skipped a beat.

From a seat at the bar across the way, he kept watch on them.

Beautiful, invincible, triumphant. No buddies, no parents. Even the people poring over her posts the day before were far away. Kevin and Willa. All alone, finally. They gazed, face to face, over a bottle with an exotic label. In a vase, flowers they had never seen before. A pair of immaculate glass plates and a rustic Greek salad in a cleverly designed bowl. Such fresh tomatoes, succulent onions, tangy feta and tender olives. And in the air between them, the very victory of being here, on this Greek island, blessed by their unshakable conviction: this is love.

38.

Though Manos Manu had tried to avoid it, the morning's presentation led to an evening meeting. Originally supposed to be dinner with "the team," the team turned out to be Bellas and Chrisanthos; every other available member of the Mykonos Police were tracking suspects. Bellas and Chrisanthos were to follow, after finishing their souvlaki in Matogiannia.

After sleeping all afternoon, Manos was now ravenous.

"Enjoyed your day?" asked Bellas, without touching his food. "Hate to disturb you."

Chrisanthos smiled broadly.

"You guys can't hang out, right?" asked Manos.

"Just a quick bite."

"Trouble finding any of them?"

The two cops stared, dumb, at a little glob of tzatziki on Manos' lower lip. The guy must be starving.

"You know, from the sixteen. Any issues?"

Chrisanthos hesitated, looking to Bellas for a cue.

"Ten of them," Bellas answered. "I told you kid, we don't have the manpower. We selected six from your list and had a couple names of our own. Aside from the guy we're going to meet after dinner, everyone's out there tracking them."

"Following suspects, not victims? Who made that decision?"

"All we have for the victims is your Will-Willy business. For the suspects, it's different," explained the officer. "We got an email from Interpol."

"How -" Manos spluttered, almost choking. He chugged his beer. "How did you pick from them?"

"Ten of them wouldn't hurt anyone," said Chrisanthos, not without some pride in his voice. "We have our methods, too."

"What the hell kind of methods?" Manos was irritated.

The officer tried to calm him down. "Boss, you're here as a consultant."

"So why not listen to my consulting? Victims aside, how did you select six suspects from a list of sixteen? I just don't get it!"

"Why don't you tell us about your system?" Bellas said, taking back the reins of the conversation.

"The system? It manages data. Ego graphs. They become the logical centers and are connected to other nodes. The nodes generate probabilities. The system ends up with sixteen suspects. We haven't processed their information yet, meaning your choice among them is totally random! Like drawing names from a hat! Any name you didn't draw has the same probability of being the killer as all the others. He could be wandering the streets now. The next victim he chooses could wind up dead - tonight!"

"Boss. Let's stay calm."

Bellas took a deep breath; he was boiling inside. How he would like to wring this brat's neck, here, for everyone to see! But no sense picking a fight. Not yet.

"Just tell us about your research," he said, with a calming sigh.

"Jesus!" Manos took his head in his hands, beside himself.

A waiter came and placed a family-style platter on their table. A rustic Greek salad.

"Yeah," said Chrisanthos. "That stuff you do." Seeing Bellas give him a withering look, the younger cop wished he hadn't spoken. But his words had worked some magic. Manos shifted immediately. *Scientists, totally whack!*

"We get data - media graphs. Social, web, phones. Call it 'bag-of-words,' since we don't really know what we're looking for."

"The police -"

"Yes, the police know everything. Interpol's just a pack of idiots, I know... So, we get all this jumbled data. Like... take this salad, for instance. We get tomatoes, we get olives. Slices of feta, cucumbers, onions. All mixed up. So, we have to prep them, spruce them up before we put them into the models - or...," he said, pointing, "- into the bowl."

"You wash them," said Chrisanthos.

"Exactly! Only instead of water, we wash our ingredients with algo... let's just call it math. Algebra."

"Fine," said Bellas, finally calmer. "Even I can get that much."

"Now, since it's all washed, we put everything into the salad bowl, our model. If it's a platter with sections, we put tomatoes in one, onions in another, see? That's a supervised model. If not, we tell the bowl itself to recognize the ingredients."

"The bowl... recognizes..."

"That's it! We call these bowls convex functions because they're bowl-shaped. And the fruit falls in them. With gradient descent. That's 'training'. We can teach the bowls to tell tomatoes from cucumbers."

"And," Bellas speared a tomato wedge from the platter in front of them, "then we eat them."

Chrisanthos twiddled a crust of bread.

"Thing is, we need different sets of tomatoes, cucumbers and olives to make sure the model works. Tomatoes for teaching, tomatoes for testing and tomatoes for validation."

"Lots of tomatoes..." Bellas' attention fell for a moment to his cell phone.

"If you don't, you run the risk of false results. The tomato you thought was a tomato turns out to be a... a yam."

"Definitely not good in a Greek salad."

"And when all your tomatoes turn out to be tomatoes?" asked Chrisanthos.

Bellas scoffed. "You get a tomato salad."

"You've got it!" cheered Manos. "You are data scientists now! If everything works, you have a tomato salad consisting of exactly sixteen tomatoes."

This statement drew the attention of a nearby waiter taking orders.

Manos continued. "So, where's the guilty party? It's one of those sixteen - how do you pick the right one?"

His two dinner companions stared at him, unblinking. Manos had gotten so riled up, tables around them could hear them. Bellas explained to the waiter they didn't need any tomato salads, much less sixteen of them.

Manos answered his own question: "You start the whole process all over again. With refined data. It's called 'machine learning'! You clean the tomatoes again, you put them in a new platter, with custom dividers for sorting tomatoes. You have to keep the design simple, otherwise they all turn out the same."

"Hold on," said Chrisanthos. "There are sweet tomatoes, others you can tell are rotten from a mile away."

"We picked the rotten ones to chase," said Bellas, taking a hearty swig of beer.

Just as they were beginning to enjoy themselves, it was time to go. Bellas, speaking discreetly into his phone. Even in civilian clothes, the locals knew him. *The check... I'll pay you later.* With a nod, he arranged it with the waiter, who was now approaching with a tomato salad on his arm, bright as a cluster of rubies stolen off a pirate ship.

"That was delicious," said Manos, stroking his tummy. "I owe you guys dinner."

"You can pay us back now, actually," said Bellas, in a low growl. "You're coming with us. A guy on your list came to Mykonos alone. The boys think he's on the prowl a few streets down."

Manos felt a surge of fear. *I'm unarmed...*

"I..." he stammered, "...a wedding, I'm..."

"We've got your pal surrounded," Chrisanthos told him. "You're part of this team."

"I'm not an... investigator," insisted Manos.

"Maybe not," said Bellas. "But you sure know your veggies."

39.

They had finished dinner. From the bar's platform right on the water, careful in case anyone brushed against them and spilled their cocktails, they gazed at the tranquil sea. So young, so cute in their post-teenage slouch. Barely twenty-five. Their attire was entirely typical: Kevin in beige Bermudas with a button-down shirt that said, *I'm from the City in London, I'm downtown Wall Street.* A slim brown bracelet, matching his cloth espadrilles, gave him a summer look to match Willa's. She, in a pale, backless summer dress, was clearly not on her way to the office. She wore a similar but more intricate bracelet on her left wrist and a thin silver ankle chain. The music bathed the place in a crescendo of bliss.

She was leaning close to him, trying to be heard.

For Kevin had been unable to tear his eyes away from a pair of girls dancing close together on a raised bench just near them.

"They're not even pretty!"

But he didn't catch it. "Wha...?"

"Kev, they are not even pretty," she shouted.

This time he heard, as did one of the girls. Piqued, she turned to face them. For an instant, her eyes and Kev's met in a flash of mutual pleasure. Willa stared, in utter shock, but Kevin took her waist, dancing with her as if nothing had happened. The girl turned back to her friend.

Some girls might put up with this kind of thing, or - even worse - some would put with anything at all. Not Willa Kendall. She stiffened, just like in plank pose. Kevin didn't even notice. Completely tense, she put her glass down and turned away.

The crowd was so thick she had to push, winding through tightly packed groups, getting nudged in turn, struggling to catch her breath. *He totally betrayed me! But had he?* She wondered. *What had he really done? Stared at two girls who weren't exactly ugly - and they were prac-tically making out. I mean, I'm, like totally fine if they're gay. It's just... I mean, don't flaunt it and cut in on someone else's guy!*

She left the bar. Time to just teach him a little lesson.

And in fact it was a glorious moment, to be all alone in this wonder-land. She didn't realize what a high it was, how sweet it was to be by herself, away from Kevin, until she felt an admiring gaze upon her. How nice, to be stared at by a stranger... Instinctively, she stood tall, her ele-gant neck drawn. *See? I can do it too. I'll stand by this doorway and give him a chance to catch up with me. It's easy...* By the time she thought of Kevin again, why she was mad at him, it was already late.

"Hey," said the stranger, his voice like a mysterious, low rumble from an old speaker.

"Hey," she answered.

"I'm Ari."

40.

Officer Bellas left Interpol's Boy Wonder sleep all day because his job was done: show up at the conference with the nutcases and let the world know action had been taken. It was all he needed, a little time. The first twenty-four hours to pass, without it looking like Mykonos Police were off getting a tan. The murders would fall a few inches down on the blog scrolling, and he could do the real work: comb through inflatables, dinghies and boats. Sort through anchors, ropes, line and buoys. While the hotshot snored the hours away, Bellas had also taken the two agents from Athens Homicide out for some day fishing.

Good to have them on his side.

As for Manos Manu's lists, an email from Interpol headquarters in Athens confirmed the link between certain suspicious social media accounts and the verified information of their real users. But where was the manpower he needed? Captain Panagiotis had asked about it, strictly off the record, but quickly regretted it. "Not under the goddamn General Data Protection Regulation!" Bellas had thundered, then added, simpering, "Greece is a law-abiding country! If goddamn Athens issued a goddamn warrant we could actually catch the killer!"

Athens did send a couple men down, but left list-making in Bellas' lap. He included a couple of Manos' names, just for appearances. In an effort to overcome the fiasco with Petro, the masseur, and Saroglu, he had got wind of some information about another two or three people.

Among these, Bellas was now ready to stake it all on one.

"Over here!" he said, just ending a call on his cellphone.

Chrisanthos, followed by Manos, fell in line behind him. Twenty yards down the street, a man was swaying all by himself in the happy throng, drink in hand. Definitely something funny about him and his strange dance. Bellas took his phone out again and showed a picture of the man.

"I found it on Facebook," he mouthed.

"But that's not my sample," Manos said, brows knitted.

Who gives a fuck about your sample? "He was in Piraeus a few days ago, and bought some machinery from a nautical supply shop," whispered Bellas importantly. "Then he came here, alone. We've been watching his room a couple of days."

"Oh, it's not him," said Manos, the tension in his body slackening.

A girl had now appeared; the man went to talk to her. The hand of each policeman flew instinctively to their weapon.

"Not a crime to hit on someone," said Manos, observing nonetheless.

They talked for a while. The girl made a show of looking at her watch, pretending to look for someone. Then she and the suspect started to walk towards the port.

"Rooms are scarce," snickered Chrisanthos.

Manos felt his stomach turn over. *What if I'm wrong?* With an elegant sidestep, Bellas and Chrisanthos avoided a pair of drunk guys. Manos ran to catch up, his mind churning with everything that could possibly go wrong with the system.

His list of sixteen. He had just run it offhandedly, identifying names with social accounts through the Lab. He was certain this was the definitive data set, even though he had to manually remove one that had popped up from the criminology conference because of a snag in the psychometrics. But the mistake could have come from a thousand other points. Something mixed up in the original data. The Asian data was still out. Mei had promised to get it - Yandex from the Russians, WeChat from the Chinese - but they were still waiting. The K algorithm sequences may have mistakenly assigned files as corrupt, leading supervised regression into undetected errors. The squashing functions which led to the usernames could be invalid. Same with the random forest tests, which ran verifications. Anything could go wrong. Perhaps Mei had made a mistake, or Yan, their colleague who did math so fine-tuned that no one understood it - possibly, it was often suspected, not even Yan. Or maybe those infamous weights they'd given to rational biases were just... well, off. In this work of his, a million elements needed to function perfectly; even if only one didn't, nothing worked at all.

"Over here!"
The suspect and the girl had now left the bright little streets and chic boutiques for a dark, secluded alley. It was the moment Officer Bellas was waiting for. He drew his gun. Without checking if Chrisanthos was covering or Manos was following, he rushed into the side street, barrel straight in his outstretched hand.

Manos caught up just in time to see the suspect white as a ghost, the girl trying to tug her little undies up from around her knees. With a face flaming red from fear, she stared at the armed policemen, whose faces were flaming red from embarrassment.

Illicit sex, maybe. Not murder.
Bellas couldn't back down. "Police! We have questions! We need answers!" he barked.

Chrisanthos utterly faltered, seeing their terrified faces trying to comprehend the sight: himself, the weapons, the authorities. He turned his own despairing eyes to Manos, who stood there, hands on his hips.
"Wrong tomato....," murmured Manos.

41.

After the breathless hush of the wind, the sea transformed into a luminous black mirror. Like an eager set of nostrils snorting froth, his motorboat reached forty knots, rounding the islet of Baos. Willa lay on the cushions behind him. She couldn't weigh more than 120 pounds; the ketamine and xylazine cocktail should keep her surgically unconscious until they got home. Then the MDMA would take over. But that didn't give him much time. His fingers gripped the leather steering wheel, while hers were limp as a lifeless doll's over the speedboat's couch. An electronica version of *La Vie en Rose* streamed from the boat's speakers; Fischer felt more powerful with each rhythmic pulsation. Power surrounded him; around him were seacraft costing twenty, thirty, even a hundred million - but their owners had never tasted this potency. Their life consisted of pending lawsuits and bored wives. Sons and daughters on drugs. Customers defecting to other suppliers. Bankers and lawyers silently siphoning as much as they dared. Fischer had one responsibility: to set this girl free.

A Filipino was leaning on the railing of a huge boat, smoking. Fischer waved to him, and he returned the greeting. *He thinks I have it made, with a girlfriend drunk out of her mind, ready to go home and do it. Moron.*

Willa's voice came like a puppy's whimper. "Where... what's happening...?"

He lowered his speed. Twenty minutes before they could drop anchor.

"Everything's cool. We're going to a party. The best party you've ever seen."

"W- will... Kevin be... there?" she asked.

"Of course," he smiled. "All your friends are going."

It was enough to reassure her. Her fingertips stirred, making sure her dress was in place, and she went back under, aware of nothing. Unaware of Fischer cutting speed, tying up the boat and turning off the engine. Unaware of flopping over his shoulder as he climbed up to the house. Of his palm running along her pussy as he drank in her scent, of being lain out onto the wide, marble table of his living room. She felt nothing. It wasn't until he played an old Greek song, *To Minore tis Avgis*, crackling through the speakers, that she stretched like a kitten on the table, entranced by the dream she was having.

"Where am I...?"

So many colors in the night! Darkness danced with minuscule shapes and little plaster angels! Waves of black marble broke, becoming bouzoukis - rows and rows of them! Behind them, she saw an inverted face, with a kindhearted mouth on his forehead, and eyes where his mouth would be, and a short beard like a wig.
She heard someone.
"Feeling tired? I bet you are."
"I ...tired."
"You're in a dream, that's why you're here. I'm your dream."
"What... what should I do?"
"I want you to open your mouth and suck on this fat straw. And when I tell you, I want you to just let go of your whole body so you can taste the flavor I'm going to give you."
"Will it... be chocolate?"
"Oh, I mustn't tell! You'll have to tell me."
"I suck on the straw..."
"See how big it is? Did you see where it's drawing from?"

"Suck..."

"It draws right down from the sky, you see? Sucking on life itself. You can even catch it. Lift your arms, catch it!"

"I can ca..."

"Catch it. Take it in your arms. Turn your body, that's it! Nice and high. I'm going to pour some life into you - ready?"

"Ye -"

Fischer drew an imaginary line from the barrel along the trajectory of his shot and pulled the trigger. The spear made a sound inside her body. Had it broken? He might need to tug it back out from her open mouth. Might have to try again. But no, it had cleared the throat, chest, stomach, and pelvis; he'd managed to lodge the tip just right. *Or did I?* He ran to check. A perfect shot was a delicate matter, requiring dedicated practice. He saw, with every reason to be satisfied, that perfection was near. The spear had killed her instantly, pierced her very being. The tip was no more than five centimeters from her asshole; lodged deeply enough to prevent him from pulling it back, but not so far through that he could grab it. *It's enough,* he thought with a deep sigh. He saw the blood flowing from both ends, the blood from her chest oozing out of the pharynx into the mouth. He lifted the head from its reclined position and repositioned her on the marble table. He was not as concerned for the bleeding at the spear's end as for the face. He didn't want it stained with blood. He turned her face-down and placed a bucket below her to catch the fluids and solids that would be emptying from her body. He then turned his attention to the spear, trying to tug it backward along the wound. It had wedged against a bone in the pelvis, but the tip was now out. *Yes, it's enough.* He tied a fine metal cable wire to it, winding it around several times, and then attaching it to the pulley block of the electric winch. The music was on repeat.

The hardest part was over. Only the sweat of good, clean work remained. Purifying. He turned on the winch, but the cable wire had loosened, falling off. *No problem.* The essential thing was to be calm, to breathe steadily. There isn't a problem that can't be solved by a deep inhale through the nose and a mindful exhale through the mouth. He reattached the wire to the spear tip and pressed the start button again. The winch sprang to life. *It's working.* When the spear's tail appeared, Fischer once again marveled at the strength of the fine metal cable, this one detail that made everything run properly. People always admired the wrong things, like their little YouTube videos. They did not understand. Man's greatest miracles are performed with his own materials. *Man is his materials.* This thin spear and this wire were the real material from which dreams were made. His dreams. Dreams of a perfect liberation.

Fischer now attached the wire directly to the winch drum. Two manual turns on this end, and it was ready. At the other, something else altogether awaited: Patience. Not skipping chain gauges. *Patience.* Using the very smallest possible diameter of well-made, durable chain. Just as he was doing now. He painstakingly attached the wire rising from Willa's mouth to a chain almost just as fine. He turned the winch back on. The girl swallowed it easily. If he were to rush in any way, he would have the same problem that happened with Jenna. The chain - maybe even the wire - would break. *Patience.* Gauge by gauge. We go slowly. Always. We'll take all the time we need. Willa had all the time in the world. She deserved to be liberated properly. When the chain had been completely threaded through, he attached a new one, going up only one degree in diameter, and turned the winch back on. At its very lowest setting. He listened anxiously, hoping it would not get stuck as it dug into the girl's bowels, widen the bone passage and, finally, wend its way out.

When that was done, after ten minutes of angst and sweat, Fischer had only to keep repeating to himself: *Patience... don't rush...* He went into the other room and found the next size chain. Color didn't matter, only width and resistance. In another two hours, when everything was finished, each of these guide chains would be meticulously washed and rewound, ready for use another time, on another body - for the same reason. The only ones he would lose forever were the heavy, three-centimeter chains. On one end, below the ass, he would weld a new anchor. On the other end, the painted buoy would rise from the mouth announcing their final cry of liberation.

It was hard labor. At some points the winch struggled; he felt like Leonardo trying to get a light touch from a thick, dried-out brush. But he managed. Fischer's great moment had come, and it was time for a break. He headed to the bathroom to splash his face with water. He looked at himself in the mirror, fingers stroking his cheeks. He rolled out his wide tongue. *No one can do this better.* He began to rub his cheeks again, this time with all his strength. It shouldn't be. This shouldn't be happening. But there was something... *To take out my eyes... to gobble them down...* He was suddenly certain he would see more clearly. *Ok, just get out of here...* He eventually forced himself to flush his face with as much water as he could, wiping his tears away with a towel. There was work to do. Work came first. Always. And there wasn't much time. Dawn was approaching and he still had another chain to pass. He felt drained, his legs trembling. He found himself before her, seeing his own reflection in the intestines and blood and shit and mucus pouring out of her mouth, from the anus, and the opening the spear had made.
"I'll make you beautiful! I will! Forgive me!"

He secured the three-centimeter chain to the winch. Made sure Willa's mouth was wide open and stable, so as to not break her teeth. He wanted to start it off by hand, but the chain was caught in the sternum. *Impossible without the winch.* He turned it on. Despite its 300 watts of power, it started bucking as it broke through bone. Pieces of flesh were dragged out with the chain as it came out of the anus. There was so much to do. Get the chain passed through. The anchor soldered on. The buoy tied on its other end. The body washed. Everything placed just right so he would be able to close the windsurf bag. The marble table scrubbed with water and bleach. Get on the boat, hurl the body into the sea.

She would be waiting for him when he got back. And day would soon be breaking.

What if he didn't make it?

Fischer crouched down on the floor, thinking. Everything around him swimming in floods of blood. His legs were shaking. He was famished. But he must keep on. As we all must. There was nothing, nothing aside from a simple runway for take-off, a few friendly smiles in the sky. That is why we are here.

To be free.

42.

Ten in the morning. The hour when Mykonos enjoys as much light per square yard as the brightest points of our solar system. The wind is picking up. But before the meltemi takes hold, the island fills with sharp shadows. Fischer stares down at his own, drinking his fourth coffee of the morning. Exhausted, but happy. His boat is docked. His house is spotless. Willa is free. The tranquility in his blissful soul is absolute.

Happy. And waiting for a woman.

Happy, because she doesn't let him down. She's right on time, in her high-end clothes and broken-down car. She parks, gets out, flashes a smile. At this distance, she can't see his eyes, can't detect last night's work. When she gets closer, Fischer takes her quickly in his arms - to hide it.

"Are you awake?" her voice comes through her soft, wavy hair.

It's the same question she asked as his student. Just after waking up, in the bed they shared.

"Lay-nuh Sid-erees," he teases, admonishing.

He loves saying her name in a phony Greek accent.

"Not just awake," he says. "I'm in love."

THE MACHINE MURDERS

VI. The Mei Day Parade

43.

If good data was a mixture of science and art, then Mei Ni was the scientist and Manos Manu the artist. On their first date in a restaurant over in Little India, she systematically devoured any visual cue as though processing a data stream. Meanwhile, Manos, telling her she looked just like the actress Sun Li, put her into an unexpected mental model. Afterwards, he took her hand, as if waiting for a signal. Like a computer from the '80s, Mei was slow to process the information streaming from his gaze. It wasn't until they'd parted that she came up with her results: *I think he wanted to kiss me! I'm definitely short on RAM!*

The opportunity was fleeting. From then on, they had an unspoken agreement: Mei would focus on processing power, Manos on algorithmic models. If each could improve their work, they could arrive at the desired result: redeeming that lost kiss. In an afternoon, they even coded a side project, a web dating aggregator service they named "our Mei-Nu". To prove that redemption in love is very real and possible.

But these days, Mei wasn't sure if that kiss was ever going to happen. Every time she spoke with Manos on Signal, she struggled to contain her worst fear: that she'd fallen into unrequited love. He was in his homeland, where wealth was strewn upon the sands. He was off fighting crime, speaking his native tongue with his old friends, his tribe. But she didn't belong anywhere. She was Chinese from Shanghai, not Singapore. She wasn't a Stanford mathematician, and her friends were far away. Like now, for instance; she was with Dr. Daniel Novak, a Czech, who, as Team Leader for ICGI could make the simplest things complicated and make complicated things vanish altogether. But, as Manos said, that's what politicians were for.

"Miss Ni, capacity-building doesn't mean we can do whatever we want."

"I never asked to do whatever I want, Dr. Novak. But we need the Russians, and we need TenCent."

"To catch a killer?" he asked in a hushed voice.

"A serial killer," Mei reminded him.

"The system…"

"Dr. Novak. Daniel."

Her voice was steady. No one in the building messed with Mei. One look from her, and the guys would make sure that next time the system needed an advanced algorithm, something would go wrong. *Fucking prick,* she thought. *Have you ever even tried to find out what a clairvoyant algorithm is, much less what it actually does?*

"So far system results indicate someone who isn't Greek," she explained. Again. "There are roughly 200,000 Russians and Chinese on Mykonos right now."

"Quite a crowd! I'd love to go," Novak said. "Can you believe I've never been?"

He had the jovial look of a high-ranking European bureaucrat, his face always flushed from a good glass of wine. He may have spent some time with Statistics, but they must not have taken notice of him, except to show him the best restaurant ratings in Brussels, and Strasbourg and of course, Singapore. Why not add Mykonos to the list?

"This is our first real-world attempt to use the Multi-agent Analysis system," she said. "Not simulations, or anti-terrorism."

"In Europe, terrorism is the real world."

"Where should Interpol hold its next conference?" Mei asked, disgusted. "Damascus or Mykonos?"

Dr. Novak, after apparently musing for a moment or two on the prospect of being a keynote speaker at such a conference, answered, "Ms. Ni, lately you've been getting far too... political."

Mei left his office, preferring a different landscape: dozens of screens, the tops of familiar heads - heads filled with so much talent they had no need for politics. She breathed in as deeply as she could. This was the breath of freedom: screens and power banks, whirring fans, wafting take-out boxes and stale energy drinks. *This is why I'm in Singapore.*
"Mei, should we deploy the latest build?"

It was Yan, a tall, gangly, kid with a baby face. He always aimed higher than anyone she'd met, solving the unsolvable. The travelling salesman problem, kernel methods, the best gradient descent algorithms. He'd go without sleep for two or three days, then come into the office on the fourth, falling on his face and hoping Mei would cover for him. She always did. Then he'd work for a week straight without a wink, to make it up to her. It didn't bother Mei; he did amazing work with the MANU - as long as he could remember what day of the cycle he was on before falling on his face again on the Unsolvable: Nearest Neighbor. Or wipe out the ramp loss. Optimize the information bottleneck. *Damn!* She thought. *We won't see him again till October!*
"Hold on!" she said, but she knew it was hard for him.
"Nothing's going to change," he said moodily, following her along the narrow, crowded offices.
"When we Asians get into a sample, Yan, everything changes."
"Oh, we're good people," said Yan with a smile. "Name one Chinese serial killer."

But Mei just smiled. She had done enough politics for one day.

44.

For Professor Novak, the problem was not the Russian-Chinese datasets or the algorithms of his employees. It was how far down a failure would plunge him. It was risky business for the ICGI, raising such a bold hand in an auditorium full of listeners ill-prepared to accept reality. Probabilities could identify crimes, but not pinpoint criminals - not definitively. Politicians in charge could grasp this, but they weren't alone. And these top-notch ivy league graduates expected to stroll into jobs in some state-of-the-art temple out of *Minority Report*: whole-brain simulations, quantum mechanics, highly classified algorithms running millions of rules - only to run up against Miss Ni, who completely ignored them, and Miss Li, his Malaysian secretary in her eternally soiled dresses, who issued their Windows pin number and wished them good luck. And for what? The system Manu created, with his Chinese girlfriend and a couple of others, had groundbreaking architecture, but in the information world, data makes the difference. Even that, you had to beg for, and it always came in the wrong format. When someone in the Commission, after much effort, finally convinced Menlo Park to create new, non-public endpoints drawing directly from their APIs, all hell broke loose. *Privacy! The Right to be Forgotten! The GDPR!* Because Interpol as an organization was controlled by Europe. Novak spent endless energy convincing his superiors that their data was secure.

"All those guys are interested in is probabilities," he'd say.

Probability is a dangerous thing; they could have responded. In England, Durham police had used data from the credit scoring company Experian, publicizing its system as "predictive policing." And this after Chicago had tried something similar. It was a media bloodbath! Both were a total fiasco. The results demonstrated only that individuals of lower socio-economic status were more likely to commit a crime. Which of course was entirely misleading.

"A classic case of overfitting," Mei Ni had tried to explain. "They took the original data, ran it as usual, and when new data came in, nothing worked. They resorted to the lowest common denominator because they had already gotten all that attention on the forums. They said whatever nonsense they could think of."

"What should they have done, Ms. Ni?"

"Changed jobs, fast."

The human mind is not built to be a mechanism of truth, but a clustering machine. A category. A second category. A Durham category. Who had time for anything else? Look at the engineers, Novak thought. You're a fool when they get hold of you and a jackass when they're done. They like clustering, all right. Afterwards there's just the conference, a touch of Mykonos, some local interviews, and a good meal.

But Mei and Manos, obsessed with these murders, threatened to change everything. Blogs across the globe insinuated that Interpol, despite an apparently advisory role in Mykonos, was leading the investigation. The departments in France were becoming curious about Manos. Novak had two choices: he could either embrace this shit with a smile on his face or let the shit splash down on him - and annihilate his career. He preferred the first option. In cooperation with Lyons, he dubbed Manos Head of the Counteraction Team and just prayed the local police would find the killer. Now, engineers were clamoring for data and international media were calling for statements; cheap influencers wanted to see the perpetrator, and his own superiors demanded results. But absolutely no one understood it was just good old, plain old cops-and-robbers. Dolled up with a few statistics, sure. Run on computers, alright. But still.

Damn it! He grabbed his intercom.

"Ms. Li, get me Dr. Zhong on the phone."

45.

Mei was running late. She entered the conference room, automatically heading toward the front, where Michaela Saab from Cyber stood explaining her division's methodology to a group of visitors. Her singsong Italian accent was a lovely contrast to the dissonant English web security terms. Mei knew the presentation by heart. She considered Michaela a pal and had helped her understand various pseudo-anonymization methods. In this pre-Zoom era, the mesmerized audience devoured the slides one by one, like the coffee cakes sitting at the welcome desk next to the fancy name badges and complimentary Interpol notepads. She passed with a thumbs-up: *Go, Michaela!* Michaela continuing her mellifluous speech seamlessly, waved discreetly. *Thanks!*

Mei slipped through a side door giving onto a wide corridor with a tall, futuristic glass façade. It looked like a spaceship bridge, with a view on inhabited planets rather than headquarter buildings. Daniel Novak, briefly entrusting the command center to another, rose to greet her.

"Mei," he chimed. "Have you met Professor Zao Zhong?"

"I haven't," she said. "But you haven't written anything that I didn't completely devour." A spark from her eyes plunged into the constellations of his own.

"I'm honored," he said. "Daniel has told me much about you. It's your team that developed NARCISSUS?"

"We call it MANU, but yes," she replied. "I am on Dr. Manu's team."

"She *is* Manos' team," Novak declared. He wanted to make it clear that this beautiful, high-strung girl was the future of police investigation.

"Well, that is much more interesting than our work in Beijing," Zhong said.

"Nothing can be more important than your work, Professor Zhong," Mei said dazzled. "You are changing the world."

"The world doesn't change, Mei," he said. "It only reveals itself."

The three of them strolled upon the thick pile of the futuristic passageway. For the first time in her life, Mei Ni, this headstrong farm girl from Wushan, felt the utter intoxication of success. Zao Zhong was a demigod in machine learning and, rumor had it, behind the most crucial architectures of China's social credits system. At 46, he was a restless pioneer, a piece of the country's global history and also published the most insightful research on solving the control problem in AI. Mei also noticed, with a shy glance, that he was rather handsome.

"Dr. Novak and I go far back," Zhong began.

"The first time the European Union and China collaborated on networks," added Daniel.

"He has asked me to take a look at your program," said Zhong.

Mei, holding back something that sounded like a gasp, said, "Of course. Dr. Manu -"

"Dr. Manu always gives us free access," said Novak, "but he's not in Singapore."

"Would you do me the honor of a personal walkthrough on the central nodes?" Zhong asked, in an encouraging tone.

Under any other circumstances, Mei Ni would downplay the importance of the experimental program, kindly offering to inform her immediate superior, away in Greece at this time. For Zao Zhong, she said only:

"I'm at your service."

They spent two hours side-by-side at her workstation, where, at Novak's urging, she explained the software architecture of the Multi-agent Analysis of Network Units in detail. Zhong listened intently, with few interruptions, asking questions about key choices of the architecture and occasionally asking for a demo. Afterwards, still having much to discuss, they agreed to go to the laboratory's cafeteria. As if in a dream, Mei now watched as this celebrated man recounted his own work, including the Chinese government's architecture with TenCent, Baidu, Alibaba and other big companies.

"There, we work towards a common goal," he was saying.

"I wish we did as much," Mei confessed. "Sometimes we literally beg. Others, we have to run data manually."

"True," Zhong smiled. "Our problem is not data."

He told her to call him Zao. His official title was Head of the Center for Statistical Science and Machine Learning at Tsinghua University in Beijing, but rumor had it that for drawing up five-year plans, the Party much preferred Zao to Mao.

"Politicians are the problem," he told her. "What they understand, what they don't understand, what they think they understand, yes, quite problematic. But this is true in all countries. With or without data."

Mei found herself blurting, "The division of the Internet into East and West is a crime!"

He didn't answer but nodded in silent agreement.

"We have the power to solve a lot of problems," she expounded. "All our models lack is endpoints."

"Epidemiology. Illness. Who knows what happens in the future?" He agreed. "And what do you do in this world, Mei?"

"I ...," she sighed, throwing her hands up in an answer.

"Never give up, Mei. Go where you find the best data."

She smiled. "Are you offering me a job, Professor Zhong?"

"Not yet! But I get the feeling you will soon be asking me for data access."

"I won't be returning to China," said Mei. "Our work here has great significance."

"Great, significance," he agreed, leaning back and taking a breath. "As long as you do it right."

Her eyes were instantly ablaze, ready to consume everything.

"The sixteen murder suspects you showed me for Mykonos...," he began gently.

"Yes?" said Mei, not breathing.

"That's high."

"Why?" It was as though the world, all that was and all that would ever be, awaited this judgement.

"Oh, that... I can't tell you that, Ms. Ni."

Ni looked at him questioningly, but he only sat back in his armchair, a playful glint in his eye.

"If I were to tell you now, you would have no good reason to show me around Singapore," he said.

46.

Avoiding Marina Sands and the business district, Mei booked a table for two on the open-air tram that wound through the many acres of Singapore's Zoo's Night Safari. There was something surreal about the scene; below the huge full moon, young couples and families on overnight adventures bathed in African music watched the animals' nocturnal excursions. Zao Zhong looked even younger, freed from Tanglin and the glass tower of Interpol. Each having taken a moment to freshen up before meeting, Mei appeared in a simple button-down blouse and dark v-neck sweater, looking ready for a job interview instead of a night out. She knew they guys at work called it Mei's parade uniform, since she looked the same every day, but it suited her nicely. She launched the conversation. "Do you come often to Singapore?"

"A number of times," he confessed with a smile, "Singapore isn't all banks and tankers. Submarine cables come through as well."

"Not to mention elephants," she said, nodding to a herd taking an evening stroll.

"Of course!"

"Ok Zao," she jumped in. "What's our mistake?"

"What you've done is very clever," he began. "You took behavioral insights and gave them values. And you mainly configured messages pulled from social -"

"Web, too" she added quickly.

"Web, too. So as to match them with characteristics of people capable of murder, and - if I understand you correctly - a particular category of murder."

"We used a lot of dark traits with keywords, tags -"

"Right, keyword filters, sentiment analysis and tags from the actual crimes. You run them without human logic biases, and with social post historicity in regression analysis. Stop me if I'm wrong..."

"No, you're right."

But Mei was tired of feeling like a schoolgirl whose project was being graded. She ordered another gin and tonic from the waiter. Not losing the pace of Mei, Zao also ordered another with a nod. The tram had slowed; they were approaching the Malaysian tigers, and the sightseers were breathless with anticipation.

"Here's the problem: Getting someone who looks for buoys - as in the Mykonos murders - to be in the same cluster as someone who receives ads for spearfishing. You haven't looked for the vortex."

"The vortex?"

"That's what the fluid dynamics guys at the university call it. You're assuming that the perpetrators receive the same number of posts based on their characteristics or the details of the crime. But sometimes people get a lot more because they fall into an algorithmic vortex. Each advertising provider notifies the other of a specific profile." Zhong looked around. "Take these tigers. That's how advertisers are when they find fresh meat. Your system is missing an important parameter, which makes it too neutral. Remember, ours is an opinionated world."

"And your conclusion..."

"Obviously, we have the same problem. But we have direct access to their algorithms. Chinese programmers in ads are required to upload everything on GitCafé. So we know, we see, and we configure them.

"We receive frequency files, too."

"Sure, from one or two of the giants. But there are thousands of microproviders in your system. A programmatic agency in the UK. A web ad broker in the Emirates. It becomes chaotic, you lose all grasp of its operation. You only get outputs. The data. We get everything."

Mei spoke quietly, taking this in. "I see it."

Their drinks arrived. It dawned on Mei with a surge of unspeakable sadness and apprehension that her homeland was much more advanced in what they were trying to do. She had uprooted herself and come to Singapore for the cutting-edge technology; but her past had slinked past her like a Malaysian tiger in the night. Leaving her behind. Zao, watching her face, saw it all.

"Of course, the uncertainty can be reduced somewhat," he said, interrupting her thoughts. She saw a wet gleam of gin on his lip.

"How?"

"Contrary to popular perception, WeChat and Facebook are not the same all over the world. They don't run the same everywhere. In fact, they are our most local tools."

"True," Mei said. "It would be impossible - too expensive, I mean - to run that amount of code centrally."

"And what would this mean for their systems architecture?"

"That they're... that they're more... vulnerable."

Zao watched her closely as she followed her thoughts.

"In what way?" he asked.

She looked up suddenly. "In... every way."

Professor Zhong smiled. Mei felt more like a schoolgirl than ever.

47.

Manos could hear the tension in Mei's voice. He pictured her slinking furtively along a muffled street, whispering furiously into the mikes of her airpods as though gasping under a big pillow, taking aim behind a long silencer. Everything around her, seemingly silent and obedient, was ready to rage like a wild animal. But not yet.

"Manos, forget advertising servers using Google and Facebook algorithms," she gushed over Signal, standing at the exit of the zoo. "We couldn't get through them if we had a thousand years! But Zao's right - local platforms, how they run, that will yield insights!"

Zao! He's all mine!

He pictured her right in front of him. Mei Ni, puffed up by attention from the famous Dr. Zhong! He couldn't help feeling a pang of jealousy.

"That's what he says," Manos sighed, stalling. The sun was setting in Mykonos. Thousands had flocked along the unpaved path to the edge of town, among the windmills, to watch the defeated, crimson sun of the Aegean - and to score the best selfies. Manos gently nudged through the throng, straining to hear her.

"Where are you going now?" he asked.

"The office. I have to rerun sixteen models with configurations."

"Where are you going to find them?'

"Novak will find me the Greek Facebook source code."

"At one in the morning? He's gone by five in the afternoon!"

Mei hadn't thought of that. The line went silent; Manos was afraid she'd hung up. But Mei was staring at a t-shirt on display in the Zoo's gift shop. A pair of large, searching eyes. Printed in intriguing patterns.

Symmetrical rhombuses. Night Safari, Singapore. Mei had never been interested in clothes, but she had always been obsessed by patterns. Patterns were a comfortable habitat.

"Mei," she heard his voice. Manos, far away in Mykonos. "Your friend might want the source code for any number of reasons. What do you do when you don't have enough data?"

"Quit?"

"You learn to use your imagination. I'll send you another solution to run. Sure you're going to the office?"

"Sure you're not going to find a new body tomorrow morning?"

Manos wasn't sure. Earlier that day, rumor had it that the police were searching for two new missing persons, a boy and a girl.

"You're a good girl. Even if you've got a crush on Grandpa over there."

"I do not! And Zao -"

Manos saw the tourists watching the majestic Mediterranean sunset by the white windmills. It's like the dance of the bees. Hundreds of people doing exactly the same thing, as if by some invisible contract. They strolled, enchanted by the spectacle. Then they stopped a while, bewitched by their cell phones. Soon after, they sought their partner and the best pose. Identical hugs. Identical smiles. Identical devices: #summertime. But... does the companion matter? He got an idea.

"I need you to do one more thing," he said to Mei. "Political criteria. We haven't factored in the political nuances of the killings themselves."

"Free Will..." Mei caught on. "He believes none of us have it. That he alone can free his victims from digital slavery. Their death sets them free."

"Leftist. He's into Assange, Snowden, Yuval Harari, I don't know whom else. Follow where he leads. Run related terms. Determinism. We might not have time for your pal's hacks."

"I got you. Imagination."

48.

The tourists in Matogianni inspired neither annoyance nor fascination in Lena Sideris. She was savoring her sense of freedom. Free from the shackles of Professor Franz Hansen and the love that had tormented her since her student days at Cambridge. Their last caress that morning was a farewell. She sensed it.

They had met - supposedly - to discuss the conference. Franz said he'd be returning to England in a day or two to publish his findings. He wouldn't admit it, but his guilty look and nervous trembling betrayed him; times had changed, a new era dawned - and he was out of a job. The lofty battle between neuro-criminology and socio-criminology was reduced to squabbling chit-chat. Manos' speech was clear; for real murders, it no longer mattered whether someone was born a killer or turned into one. It mattered that he killed. The time was near when digital activity would predict criminal tendencies. A social worker could intervene before the crime. Or the police. Thousands would be spared the devastation of senseless loss of a family member. A daughter. A son. It meant the end of crime.

"How nice," she mumbled to herself, stroking the fabric of a pareo wrap with her fingertips.

"That one has a pretty print." A salesgirl had come over.

But unlike Mei, Lena wasn't concerned with patterns. For her, it was lovely to feel the cloth against her skin. So nice to the touch.

She had read hundreds of academic studies, now obsolete. She was young enough to change. Have a career.

But others reacted differently. Some conference delegates had already left Mykonos, dejected. And Franz's face that morning. On his lips, the trace of a smile that never quite formed had given him a somehow despairing look. She sensed his hatred for Manos Manu. Deep hatred. He must have been thinking, *Is this it? Some programming bugger barges in and gets everyone's attention? What about their exhaustive studies? What of the thoroughgoing psychographics determining how someone, in the fraction of a second, picks up a knife, pulls a trigger, crushes someone's throat? What about Lombroso, Enrico Ferri, Hans Eysenck, or Robert Hare - would their accomplishments become one more software command among millions of others? Does the human spirit convert to just this? Is the ultimate human ambition reduced to... surviving as a line of code?*

49.

Mei was driving fast, a rare occurrence in Singapore. She should have been thinking of a story for the police just in case, but even with her airpods, she was straining to hear Manos over the engine.

"Novak's going to get us Tencent and the Russians," she told him.

"Great, but I doubt it'll make any difference," he was saying. "Listen, the only way to handle your friend's vortex interference... is to find the unique interaction grids for all sixteen." *UIIDs!* she thought. *How could we have forgotten?* They were like scatter charts directly pairing the type of posts and which users had interacted with them, like an ID showing response behavior and frequency based on the content an individual was served.

"Let's be careful, Mei. If we can match one of the graphs with a similar one from anywhere in the world, we -"

"We'll find others?"

"We will find similar crimes in their countries of origin. They're all foreigners. The pattern will have started in their country and reproduced in Mykonos. They didn't just take up murdering in Mykonos."

"They will have practiced somewhere else..."

"Without anyone finding the bodies."

This was going to take all night. Mei parked haphazardly and ran towards the entrance. The security staff at the Interpol Global Complex for Innovation looked like Playmobil figures in a stop-motion movie.

"Wouldn't they have shown up on Interpol's crime list?" she asked.

"Mei, the bodies were found by chance. The first sunken off one side of the island, the second below a lighthouse on the other. No one was notified."

"Ok. And why not sink them deeper?"

Manos mulled this over. "He didn't want to hide them. We should adjust his risk tolerance - our man is a gambler."

She swiped her identity card through the reader; the guards mechanically greeted her with their usual "Good evening Ms. Ni."

Manos pictured the office. "Give it to Yan to formalize it. Yan there?"

"Want to bet he is?"

"I don't know where he is in his cycle."

"He's been here since last night."

Should have made that bet, she thought. There he was, just as the elevator doors opened.

"Time to work," she said to him curtly, before turning back to her conversation.

But Yan knew who was on the line. "Hel-loooo, Dr. Manu," he called cheerfully, following Mei.

"How do we get all those graphs? Novak?"

"Not a chance," said Manos.

She was starting to panic. "Then what?"

"I just cc-ed you. Jack's an old buddy."

"Jack?"

"That's what he goes by. He'll get you the graphs in JSON, but to uncover the pattern from the rest of the timelines, you have to run them pretty fast. You need your own computer."

"Yan," Mei nodded, "To your Slack. Sorting additions."

"Got it," said Yan, at his keyboard.

"With egoism and psychological entitlement as core criteria."

"Querying MySQL columns."

"Anything you can correlate with free will."

"Free will? Anyone ever had it to lose?"

"Risk, too."

It was one in the morning. Yan was true to form, playing his keyboard like a concert pianist.

"I hope I can manage all the validation sets."

"You will," she affirmed.

"Who's d'Holbach?"

"Not now," mumbled Mei, watching.

"And probability?" Manos asked. He had scaled the ridge of the windmills. From whatever direction she approached, he would see her. But there was still a crowd. Everyone searching: Perfect pose. Perfect partner. Perfect hashtag. The sun had left just a sliver of his regal disk floating on the horizon. Opportunities were dwindling.

"Ninety-one?" Manos asked now. "Ninety-one percent?"

Mei supervised Yan running the models with the new configurations, knowing Manos was less concerned with reducing the number of suspects than with increasing the likelihood of their link with the crime. Whether six, sixteen, or twenty-six, it was up to the police to trace them. But if the probability of guilt fell to 80 or even 70 percent, it was unreliable. *We'd need new assumptions...* Mei's eyes were riveted to the dashboard.

"Where'd you get ninety-one?" she gushed happily directly into her phone, leaving her airpods on Yan's desk.

It's moments like this we work so hard for! thought Mei.

Manos had reached the windmills, standing between two of them as the sun disappeared.

"Ninety two? Ninety three? Ninety four?" He was calling to his airpods.

"Stop counting," said a smiling face, openhearted and light as an apricot. She put a finger to his lips, pulled it away and kissed him with utter tenderness. Manos fell into her arms like a child. He let her pull out his little earbuds; she held them in her hands.

"Ninety-six percent! We're down to eight suspects!" came Mei's voice.

But there was no answer on the line. Only the sound of fabrics swishing together, the winding breezes billowing out the sails of the windmills.

A whirling hint of desire.

"What's he saying?" said Yan. "He's nuts!" He came over and tried to listen in on Mei's phone too. He couldn't. Mei was clutching it tight, as if it weren't an iPhone at all but her own heart. She wanted to squeeze it tighter, to crush it. Instead, she pretended Manos Manu didn't matter anymore. Not one bit. She slammed the phone down on the desk.

Yan jumped out of his skin.

"It's UIIDs, Yan," she cried, beside herself. "How could we ever forget?"

50.

Daniel Novak understood the paranoia of Western politicians. But he believed, like anyone at the forefront of machine learning, whether at Google or Baidu, that progress in artificial intelligence was not achieved with flags, clichés or hammer-and-sickles. Sharing highly classified files with researchers who didn't have relevant clearance was a necessary evil. Giving Chinese nationals access to Lyon servers to run some optimization - quite logical. Bringing a legend like Zao Zhong to Singapore for a few days to validate his team's architecture and code - why, he was glad to do it. Nothing to do with politics, and everything to do with confidence. And if Washington or Brussels raised an eyebrow, his answer was simple: First of all, getting help from the Chinese to catch serial killers is collaboration, and second of all, they could kindly fuck off.

But right now, on the other side of his desk, Mei was asking the impossible.

"You want to run the source code for Greek Facebook... Would that be on a CD or should I get you a flash drive?"

"Not just Greece. I need to run a lot of local versions. For eight specific patterns. That's all. But I need a supercomputer."

Mei struggled to seem wide awake, but she hadn't slept all night. Novak could sense she already had an in somewhere. Without his help.

"You have local versions..." he said.

"I have some connections. But I need CERN."

"They're physicists, Mei. Highly unlikely they will hand over their computing resources so we can monkey with profile updates!"

"So issue a warrant, Daniel!"

"To arrest... the physicists?"

"I need a supercomputer. The Grid - just two days. Starting now."

"You are aware of the waiting list, I trust."

"You're the Police, Daniel! The World Police Innovation Center. One hundred and ninety-four countries - just waiting for your innovation! For global security! And don't they give you even half a computer to do your job?

"Can't you run them from Lyon?"

"And collapse the network? It's not enough."

"Mei Ni."

"I need RAM for petabytes."

"Mei..."

"And petaflops for speed."

"Mei!"

"What?"

He had never seen her this way. Her eyes were sunken in their sockets. Her normally impeccable collar was crumpled, one side in her sweater and the other poking out askew. Her hands trembled so badly Novak expected her arms would come off their shoulders any minute.

"I can send an email," Novak said calmly. "We have some friends at CORDIS and in Switzerland. But for this level of computing power, exascale infrastructure, there is bureaucracy. That's how it is, Mei. It'll be three days - at least."

"I don't have three days!"

Mei turned on her heel.

Novak's office closed with a bang; he didn't know whether she made him want to laugh or cry.

Better watch out for her, he thought.

51.

"A supercomputer..." She pushed his lips open again with her own. "I need one."

He broke out laughing. "That's why you're here?"

"I'm here because... everything hurts..."

"Mei... so young, so talented, so lovely. You'll get over him. Just find some data! Where there's data, there can be no pain."

"I have that already! It's the supercomputer that's missing."

She fell into his arms, seeking more subtle ratios. This time he lifted her, lightly, sweetly, and they turned together, around and around, until Zao found his way through her pants and they started making love.

Mei felt like she'd slept for days. She woke abruptly, full of worries. Full of Manos. Stupid Manos Manu! Fucking stupid, stupid, stupid! And your stupid fucking Greek women! She could only chase away his image by thinking of the victims. Submerged below buoys at Mykonos, just as she had seen them in the crime scene pictures. *Justice,* she thought. *This is my 'free will'.*

@55godlessgod
@018poweroflove
@angelof_
@mm56540x
@leonardan8
@amazingvic008
@caribou6
@kingstonbay768

Dr. Zhong leaned against the window, smoking and taking a careful sip from his coffee cup.

"Zao, this isn't China!" she cried, grabbing the cigarette from him and rushing to throw it into the toilet.

"I asked for a smoking room."

"There's no such thing in Singapore!"

They laughed, each a bit bashful.

"Still want your supercomputer?" he asked softly.

"Yes," she whispered.

"You know whatever you give me becomes property of the People's Republic, correct?"

"I do."

"That poses no problem?"

She thought about it. Doubtless, they already possessed any data she would be giving them. What she didn't want to give them was a sense of possessing her. Not Manos or Zao - they understood she held the life of one, perhaps two other girls in her hands. Who knew when he would strike again? Or even when some other criminal would appear? Blood and data, they unite humanity. They belong to everyone.

"Politics doesn't matter," she declared. "I care about the victims."

Zao saw her the way she'd looked only hours ago, as though he were captain of a space station. Only now the space station was a hotel room, with all of Singapore behind her in panorama.

"I've contacted our center in Wuxi," he said. "I work there as well."

For the first time in her life Mei felt like a princess. Her knight had come with glass slippers and fastened the finest diamonds around her throat. *Wuxi!* It was like he opened a magical chest to reveal a magnificent gown within. *The National Supercomputer Center of Wuxi!*

Zao spoke simply: "What do you want to run?"

52.

Surprisingly, Yan showed up at the office for a sixth day in a row. But the surprise was on him: his seat already was occupied. By his Director.

"Dr. Novak!" he said, tugging off his backpack and setting it down.

Mei was coming out of the ladies' room. Yan had walked into a trap - a trap that had snared someone else.

"As I was explaining to Ms. Ni," began the Czech, "we can play this either way. Either explain to me what you're up to, or else face disciplinary consequences."

"I spoke ...with Dr. Zhong," confessed Mei, looking down at her shoes.

Yan's eyes popped. "Wait! We got it?" He was thrilled, but Mei turned her attention to Novak, this short, pudgy man who called the shots.

"Well?" Novak asked.

"Yan," she said, "print me a dozen QR codes, one per page."

"Which QR codes?" He asked.

"Any QR codes!"   ,

Most of the work terminals were closed; the three of them were alone. Yan took out his phone.

"Daniel," she continued. "As you know, using mostly MANU's psychometrics, we're down to eight people - thanks to our system, which includes web, social, searches, and phone calls."

Novak looked suspicious. "You mean the Mykonos murders."

"Exactly," she nodded.

Yan fired up his computer as Novak rose to let him sit; a nearby printer was already chugging.

"Each of us has a unique digital footprint," she sighed. "When we connect to a site, how frequently we post, how long we linger over a particular item on our timeline, our typing speed. The industry calls it the UIID, the unique interaction identification. For example, someone has the habit, a 91% probability, of accessing the Internet with Chrome at 7:30. Or spends four seconds on one type of post, but sixty-two seconds on another - all with 95% probability. Analyzing billions of data points, you conclude that for an average day, this person's unique interaction id is at a probability of 99.6%. That's the idea..."

She grabbed one of the printed A4-sized pages, quickly setting it on the rectangular conference table in the room. She pointed to it proudly:

Yan took in a breath, watching.

"Ours isn't exactly a QR," Mei went on, seizing the moment, "we use 3D visualizations, but just imagine it like this. The point is, this traces the same path, your social ID, for a set period of time. The last five years, say. That's you. Your online behavior."

"Ok. Go on," Novak said.

"Now for the murderer. The system gave us eight candidates, right here."

Yan was already remotely connected with the computer in Wuxi; Mei lay eight freshly printed A4 sheets of paper in order:

"Let's suppose," Mei was actually smiling now, "The probability sets of their parameters give us a unique interaction ID. That becomes a benchmark." She lay one more down next to the eight sheets:

"Wait! It's not the murderer..."

"Reference values, I get it," said Novak.

"Right. The benchmark we needed." she answered. "Now we need to run it on all the networks for any correlation with a probability of over 99%. But! Every network has regional markets, meaning we need to run everything in key markets. Greek Facebook, or German Twitter. Impossible without a supercomputer."

Yan called out: "I'm IN!"

Mei stopped for breath. Novak connected the dots.

"And you... already have... the regional builds?" he asked.

She didn't bother to answer this. "We run them locally, we find all their little pals - meaning UIIDs with similarities above 99%. So we get a list of five, ten, a hundred people having a 99% similarity to the benchmark made for the killer in Mykonos. We run a statistical analysis on their network - quality and degree network, robustness, the lot - quite simple."

"Couldn't be simpler," quipped Novak, completely confused. "What's the end-result?"

"The similarities within the networks boil down to a common UIID, which we can compare with the UIIDs of our eight MANU suspects. We compare them to the kind of networks of people like them. Which leads us to -"

Yan piped up: "Ninety-nine! I've got six!"

"- to 96% of the initial probability that the murderer is one of the eight," May said excitedly. "At 99%, it means the killer is one of these six:

Mei set aside two of the pages, looking at Novak in triumph.

"So you..." Novak began. But he stopped, not knowing where to begin.

"Down to six!" she sang. "From eight!"

"Three!" shouted Yan, ready for a heart attack. "Three, from a hundred!"

But he quickly fell silent, mesmerized by the movement on his three LCD screens, as though following tennis matches on three different courts.

"All this, to clear two suspects? Why not have Mykonos police arrest them all? You got source codes, where'd you run them?"

"Doesn't matter," Mei snapped. "Nothing's really hidden! And we didn't run eight or six. We did..." her attention turned to the probability calculation of these being the perpetrators. She mumbled, "ninety-six, ninety-nine..."

Even Novak could grasp that this had never been done before; the question was whether or not to show it.

"And the computer where you've just run it -?" he asked.

But Yan interrupted, groaning, "Something's wrong."

Mei turned from Novak, eyes glued to Yan's screens. "What's up?" she asked.

"It's... showing... two more at 100 percent," he stammered.

"Impossible!"

"You ran this on some supercomputer, right? Can you tell me..."

"With validation data?" her voice was tense. "Any other errors?"

"I'm running it again... this thing... whew! Fast as quantum!"

Novak lost patience. "Mei Ni! Can you please tell me what's happening?"

Yan turned, nodding. Mei drew a long breath.

"Here it doesn't say we have one killer," she said. "It says we have three."

VII. Dark Traits

53.

L ena stood naked by the window. Manos stared, admiring how the pelvic bone traced a graceful contour below her slim belly. Light reflecting from the street illuminated her tender flesh. Hundreds of people wandered below, not one of them looking up. She didn't make the slightest move to put anything on.

"My father always said that if you treat people like numbers, sooner or later they will commit a crime," she said. "Before becoming general director here, he served with Santorini Police. He was one of the officers who caught that famous killer. The guy stabbed his wife seven times. With five different knives. Cut off their dog's head, then his wife's. He was carrying it in his arms, strolling along the cliff, the most romantic place on earth. He got about 800 yards or so, till my father took him down with a bullet. For years, they never told me the story, but they couldn't keep it from me forever."

The room overlooked the windmills; in the darkness beyond the town they looked like oversized sheep. Inside the house, books covered every wall, filled every corner. Books about psychology, about love, about crime.

"These made me a criminologist. That's what I am, and what I remain. It's the only way to see the people beyond the crime."

"If you want to catch a criminal," Manos lifted his phone, "you look here."

"No. To catch him, you have to start here." She brought her right hand to her heart as she spoke. "Before I met you, I spoke with Jenna Will's friend. Yesterday, I saw Joe Skanlon and Tibby Vesseksi - Billy Casey's friends. And my father; he's miserable. Murder takes a human toll, Manos. It's not just a game of numbers."

"You're letting it affect you."

"I-am-not-a-ro-bot," she said robotically, checking off an imaginary box in the air. She turned looking into his eyes; the colored lights from the street now illuminated the smooth skin of her beautiful, bare pubis. This moment felt a lifetime away from the lonely view out his fire escape in Alphabet City. He left the bed, stepping towards her; she was perfectly still. Manos ran his hands gently along the lifeless titles of the books on the shelves.

"Ask any child why the wind blows," he said. "What'll he say? Because the leaves sway on the trees, the leaves make the wind blow. He sees, but he has it backwards--"

"You can't run a model for everything!"

Six individuals; he wished he could show her:
@55godlessgod
@018poweroflove
@angelof_
@leonardan8
@amazingvic008
@caribou6

But he couldn't. Not until it's validated. He'd shared the social handles with the local police. Chrisanthos had already sent messages for one or two they'd located. But they still had to check with Facebook - via Singapore - which accounts were fake and which were real. From there, their IP access addresses needed to be found. Interpol would receive the real-time name, email, address, phone number and location from Internet Service Providers. Singapore would take these updates and run them on the system, updating the database with new correlations - hoping they hadn't been accessed via a VPN or a Tor browser.

None of this works automatically.

"I need time," he said, as if to himself. "The data needs to be clean, fresh. To reveal things you have to sleep with it."

"Really?" she asked with a raised eyebrow. "Call me old-fashioned, but I don't sleep with data."

He grunted and then kissed her. She answered, coming into his arms.

An hour later, the sounds of the city woke them; rejoicing in the everyday, intercontinental celebration that was a Mykonos summers' night. Manos contemplated Lena's sleeping body lying next to him, but Jenna Will rose in his mind's eye; he could virtually feel the chain running through her now shoved through Lena's flesh. He jumped up. Lena shifted a bit in her sleep, with half a sigh. He gazed at her, thinking. Now that people have discovered data, they'll be at each others' throats, teeth bared. Everybody wants to stick their little drinking straw through your skull, suck you out neuron by neuron. What will preserve your humanity then?

Mathematics. Its integrity. Its impartiality. Its beauty.

Mei understands. With a little smile, he grabbed his phone to check if she'd sent anything, but then remembered it was 5 a.m. Singapore time. Plenty of other messages, though. The Athens Homicide agent: one missed call. Happy-Harri, the Mykonian blogger: a WhatsApp message. Chrisanthos: two missed calls and a message. Daniel Novak: one voice message on Signal. Officer Bellas: a text from his local number, in Greek with a jumble of Greek and English letters, *Everything ok with the accounts. Moving forward as discussed. Call Chrisanthos.* Daniel Novak again, wanting to know "how Mei Ni received source codes from the majors." He would have to fess up about his friends at Stanford Persuasive Technology Lab, but he preferred to speak with an attorney first.

And from James, on WhatsApp: Hey man, don't forget, tonight is UDN - Unchained Debauchery Night! Starting at Salt Baaeee! Expecting you.

The bachelor party...

He reopened Haris' WhatsApp message. One link, and one word: "Copycat?"

The link was to keynews.com, a local Florida paper. The headline read: *Submerged Murder Victim Raises Questions for Key West Police.* Some similarities, ok. A buoy, but no writing; possibly an anchor. Probably random, Manos thought; the paywall popup blocked him. Typing a question mark, he forwarded it to Mei, then wrote to Influenza: "Likely nothing, but we're inspecting everything thoroughly. Don't post till Central checks it out. Thanks - I'll pay you back BIG, man! 🙏" Send. Slimeball journalists! No matter what corner of the globe they crawl out from, they're the same master bullshitters. "Copycat?" Fucking know-it-all!

He called Chrisanthos, who sounded very tense over the phone.
"I'm watching @Leonardan8. Not sure how you found him, but he's a fright. He's by Gucci, the boutique in Psarrou."
"Wait for me! We're coming."
"Where...?" Lena, beside him, was wide awake now.
Manos gave her a wink. "Party's gettin' started!"

54.

Rumors about two missing people were taken up faster than sun loungers along Ornos beach on an August morning. After Lieutenant Xagoraris' fiasco at Hotel Albatross, Makis Saroglu's mistaken arrest on the *Golden Star Superexpress* to Piraeus, and the trampling of a simple back alley liaison the day before, Mykonos Police desperately needed a win. Interpol's suspect list and social media accounts falling from sixteen to six, Officer Bellas had no choice but to focus all efforts there.

Five of the six had uploaded photos of themselves, including one for @leonardan8: a somewhat blurry image showing a bald man somewhere in his sixties; he held a German shepherd in a headlock, smiling into the distance. Chrisanthos identified him from this image alone, having seen him by chance a couple of days earlier at the Ornos supermarket. Definitely not a face you would forget, especially now with thousands of people wondering if a homicidal maniac was wandering among them. Leo A., from his profile picture, seemed the perfect candidate. The hate in his eyes was transformed into anxiety, which turned into psoriasis carving deep pits into the skin of his jaw and neck. This condition was badly camouflaged by a white sunscreen, which actually betrayed him by giving him a shiny, sickly look. His crowning attempt to cover up his marked-up face also backfired; his canvas hat, especially at night, only made him creepier standing there just outside of the Gucci Store by Nammos Club.

Manos balked at the sight of him. He needed his laptop - but only had his phone. He wanted the protection of the weapon Bellas had given him - but only had Chrisanthos. And he needed Mei... but it was Lena by his side. No margin for error tonight. But errors were all he'd brought.

＇

"He's going to buy a chain," said Lena, as if reading his thoughts.
"Wha-?"

"He's going to buy that chain. From the shop," she said with confidence. "You'll have to run your algorithms again, Mr. Zuckerberg."

Leo A. was at the register. Chrisanthos ran to peek through the window, but the necklace was so flashy they could have seen it from across the street. The sales girl had it in her hands: a heavy chain with two interlocking letter Gs.

"That's what he was Googling when your system found him," said Lena. "I don't blame the man! That chain goes for about a thousand. I was thinking about it myself, but tough luck," she added with a smile. "No one offered to buy it for me."

"Stop," Manos hissed. "You know our system is much more sophisticated."

"Maybe," smirked Lena. "Still, a guy who's buying a chain like that for his wife or girlfriend doesn't seem like the type to run different chains through a person's ass. But that's just me..."

Chrisanthos didn't know what to do. He looked first at Manos, then at Lena. Officially, he was to wait for Bellas, who was staying overnight at the office waiting for information on their Big Six. Once that came in, he would start a cycle of phone calls to the hotels and rented rooms for reservation names and passport numbers. The order would be simple: *Bust their door down! Search for the crime scene!* But for the moment they weren't busting anything down. They were watching a middle-aged man buy some jewelry, and meet a woman at the entrance, exchanging a little peck.

"Here's the lucky lady," said Lena.

It's not him. Manos could feel it in every bone of his body. But Chrisanthos made to move, thinking the woman was in danger. Manos shook his head no. Not our man. Tough luck, as Lena would say. The couple now went to the restaurant next door and took a table. The man placed the gift bag before the woman, who accepted it neither as lover nor wife. They were father and daughter.

But no data should go to waste. Manos took out his Interpol phone, focused the camera and snapped a shot. He sent it to Mei over Signal, adding: @leonardan8 with daughter - right? He knew she would run everything again specifically for him, with some slight parameter changes, to find someone who had not only a dog but a daughter as well. Remove him from their list. The guy might not be a murderer, but he was no angel. Should they notify any agency about him? Was it his duty to speak to the daughter about her father's dark traits, which they had found based on his profile, his interests, his online interactions? No - people are who they are. Better off letting him enjoy this fleeting summertime dinner with family.

"I got another one," said Chrisanthos, ending a call. He understood the dynamics now.

"Another one?" asked Manos.

"Caribou6."

"What's Caribou up to?"

"Went out for a good steak."

55.

At the world-renowned Nusr-Et steakhouse, above Boni windmill, festivities were under way. Manos arrived with Chrisanthos and Lena to see James' bachelor buddies, lined up like cheerleaders, pelting the bridegroom with flowers. A table of Greek women, untouched by any financial crisis, flirted heavily with the famous Turkish chef as he served them coarse salt and slabs of fatty, succulent meat; another pack of gorgeous girls from the Gulf were fawning over him too, fueling their secular soirée with one margarita after another. And dinner was just a foretaste, the night promising to get much more savory. Most of the possibly two hundred people in the place were strung out on booze and drugs.

"Here's my MAN!" James, wearing a white button-down shirt open to reveal strands of colorful beads, looked like a totally wasted young Gaddafi.

"Some stag party, man!" Manos wondered if he should tell James anything. *So, like, there just happens to be a psycho at your party who, drugs people and turns them into trendy jewelry using a half-sunken buoy...* He kept quiet. Why blow a perfect cover? He had to tell Chrisanthos and Lena what to expect.

"Sorry we're late," Manos said.

"Manly-MAN!" James sloshed. "Come meet our pretty new friends!"

Two girls who looked like supermodels and Sandy Voss, the only socialite in the bride's circle up for a threesome. Behind them, James' gang were enjoying some good, clean fun. Frederick for example; next to his T-bone platter was a broad line of coke which he snorted right off the table with the concentration of a biologist over a microscope. What would dear Liz Will make of all this? Manos wondered.

"My friends are ...having a little party," he explained to Chrisanthos and Lena, who introduced themselves awkwardly.

"And my friends have been following you for a few days, to see how you catch this murderer," Chrisanthos whispered into Manos' ear. He nodded towards the end of the bar, where two plain-clothes guys from Athens Homicide greeted him with a slight lift of their glasses. Manos nodded back with a smile.

He had an idea.

Tugging Chrisanthos' attention back, he asked, "Notice our friend?"

"Let me take a little walk. I'll be right back," he said.

Manos and Lena took their places at James' table; Lena had to listen to their admiring praise. *In the force, too? You knew Man's a policeman, right?... Got yourself a sweet little lady cop here, Man-Man!... Yo, better brush all this snow off the table! These people are going to cuff us!... I'd cuff her, my friend - keep an eye on this doll!* But rather than keeping an eye on Lena, Manos was very busy chatting up the most strung out - and most beautiful - girl at the table. He needed to set up his game with the commander-in-chief of young ladies and copious drugs, who in this case also happened to be the best man.

"Stefan!" cried Manos, lashing an arm around him. Lena watched from the corner of her eye.

Before long, Stefan, Manos, and the spaced-out model - a sweetie named Erika - were in an intimate tête-à-tête over the boneless chops and overturned shot glasses. Chrisanthos joined them a minute later. Manos got up, whisking away with him Erika, who had just a second to grab her little clutch bag containing the required materials. *I should update Lena*, he thought, but Erika was high as kite, spilling forward on her next step. *No time to talk.* At the bar, all alone, Caribou6 sat slowly sipping his cocktail. He looked exactly like his profile picture, and Manos felt a familiar shudder, realizing how much people uploaded online and how much of their lives was right there in public view.

Erika took over. Obviously, no stranger to hustling, she sat right next to him and started playing with her phone. Manos moved to avoid being noticed, but just then he got a juicy slap on the back.

"Mr. Manu! How are you?"

It was the two Greek plain-clothes cops. This type always traveled in pairs: if the first one spoke, the other backed him up; if the other took a few steps, his partner shadowed him. Their role here wasn't very clear, except for one thing they had clearly decided: this computer geek from Interpol was some bigmouth!

"Having a good time, I see!" said one.

"Again," said the other. "Tsardis, Athens Homicide. We've met."

"Sure," said Manos, angling them away so Caribou6 wouldn't see them.

But this manoeuvre landed them in front of the stag table, as though he were about to introduce them. James was standing there, his no-name beach babe flicking wine at him; Frederick, using his steak knife to cut a fresh line, was licking the serrated blade like a pirate. The best man, a respected partner in one of the Valley's biggest VC firms, was glued to Sandy Voss. Sandy, a naughty gleam in her eye, surveyed the available candidates; she found them all perfectly suitable.

But Lena didn't. Lena was gone. *Lena? What the fuck!*

He'd explain it later. For now, he couldn't shake off these two little Greeks.

"Have your models predicted the next murder?" They asked.

Manos turned, vaguely glimpsing the bar. Erika was slowly, tenderly stroking Caribou6 on the temples.

"Working on it," Manos answered absently. "Excuse me."

He went for his cell phone, but it was 6:30 in the morning in Singapore. Mei would be sleeping another half hour. The MANU had given its all. Time for human chemistry to work its wonders. Erika had drifted to the restrooms to rendezvous with the suspect; Chrisanthos trailed them, shooting a look of panic at Manos. When Manos gave him a discreet nod, he turned back to the restrooms to keep watch over the happy couple.

Within twenty minutes, Caribou6 was at their table.

56.

Manos was witnessing his parameters in the flesh for the first time, his model brought to life in the thoughts and words of a real person. Caribou introduced himself as Noah from New Zealand, a film editor based in Sydney. As he began sharing his reasons for leaving his native city of Christchurch, Manos detected a high correlation for the target criterion of egoism, amounting to nothing more than self-centeredness. He was also a dominant type. Manos knew he needed to adjust the weighting of certain criteria, such as aggressiveness, impulsivity and perspective-taking, keeping in mind the generous serving of cocaine Erika had graciously cut for him in the bathroom. Observing the drug's effect on him - he grew more talkative, more open, carefree and sincere - Manos let Erika persuade Noah that he had finally found truly kindred spirits. Not the people who had hurt him so deeply in Christchurch and Sydney. Not the ones who'd promised him work in London, or who'd left him to drink himself blind in Mykonos. Not his past. Or his wives. Here, over the chef's signature chops, Noah found a safe zone; he could say anything. It was that kind of Mykonos night, encrypting their conversation like a secure app where only a select few could bury their truth - and forget it.

Manos took Erika's place, who was now clearly relieved to be off duty. She sat down next to Caribou-Noah without a word, though she maintained her caring gaze. So did Manos, who had a question for him.
"So, are you free?"
"Sure - have a seat," said Noah.
"No..., I mean, do you have... free will?"

The man gave a scoff as if to say, *Who does?* But then something like a shadow passed over his face, a shadow centered completely on himself.

Silent, he seemed to be simultaneously wondering *'Why the question? Does this guy want something from me?'* and *'Well, do I?'* He broke into a smile, as though just realizing within himself that indeed, he really had made the effort to live with as much freedom as anyone possibly could. Yet with a shrug of his shoulders, he just said the first words that came to mind:

"Is anybody really free these days?"

Manos knew he wasn't their man. From six, they were down to three suspects. He noticed the officers from homicide across the place suddenly on the move. Chrisanthos was at his side a second later.

"Manos, got a second?"

Manos let himself be led away, saying almost to himself, "No, not him either."

"Got a message from Bellas," said Chrisanthos. "We have another body. Out in front of Caprice. Little Venice. The roads are blocked. People are terrified."

Manos looked over at the two Homicide cops. Officer Tsardis, slowly raising his hand as if accusing Manos, held his index, middle and ring fingers close together.

Three.

57.

Willa Kendall's corpse was lifted to the water's surface before dozens of frightened tourists directly in front of Caprice Bar. Under the pressure of so many fresh witnesses, the police decided to be organized this time. Willa's friend Kevin was confined at an interrogation room, his phone confiscated in exchange for a flimsy receipt with a sticker so he could pick it up later. Jenna's was sent to Athens for examination by Digital Forensics, but Billy Casey's phone had yet to be found. Lieutenant Petro Xagoraris had instructed Stella and George to enter the details of each crime into the Athens-based case management software, only just installed, so as not to seem a laggard to Interpol. Greek keywords - 'angira", "anchor,' for example - could be used to find prior searches, provided they had been run. *Your search has 0 results. Please try again.* The staff retrieving the body had arranged to close off the site before putting on gloves to investigate the surrounding areas; they had even succeeded in collecting unrelated objects, which they placed in small plastic bags for evidence. The Mykonos Police Station, the sleepy outpost where drunken tourists snored off their buzz before getting behind the wheel, was abuzz tonight, like a startup on the eve of a major release. Those cops without evidence or information to provide busied themselves at the three or four working computers. Everyone else, enjoying a cigarette outside, discreetly leaked information to the mayor and the central office. The two homicide cops, arms folded, waited for orders to take matters into their own hands.

"Our colleagues in Athens are clever, but you can't blame them," Bellas rationalized with a yawn. "They're sent here to get information for the homicides in Mykonos in the dead of summer when really all they want is to spend time with their families. They get here, and what do they find? Mavrudis has it in for them. Local police are understaffed. Central

office orders them to wait on their guru from Interpol to share his wisdom, but the guru's a social butterfly, drifting from bar to bar with his
rich friends and the former police chief's daughter."

"This whole island is a club," Manos answered, unconcerned.

Lounge music was pouring from the speakers in the police station itself, but Bellas wasn't going to take the bait.

"Listen, I've made I don't know how many requests for a coroner.
They've sent officers but no doctor. We're still hanging onto poor Stevis.
I'm trying to search the yachts, but then I get calls from the Ministry
itself telling me to take it easy. Then I have all the bloggers, requesting I
make a statement about the investigation's progress - preferably in goddamn French!"

"You might not be able to publicize it, but you have your list, Officer," groaned Manos. "No one has ever been handed a list like this," he
added, not sure Bellas understood the significance.

"I saw it. Four people. Want to know what I think?"

"Absolutely."

"He's not on that list."

"Oh?"

"I'm not saying I won't look into it. I asked the service providers. The
shift on duty might send them any minute now. I'll give orders to find
where they're staying. But I'm telling you - he's not on that list."

Manos understood. Too much at stake. One way or another, the end-
game was near. With Athens breathing down his neck and Interpol leading him by the hand, Officer Bellas wanted to regain control of the investigation. Regain control of Mykonos, before it changed beyond recognition.

"Want to come to the autopsy?" Bellas said as a sort of compromise,
heading for the door.

Singapore was sleeping. Athens wouldn't budge till morning. Manos hadn't the slightest inclination to visit the morgue. Nothing more to see there.

"Officer, you know my role is only advisory. You may have x, y or z theory. Even as an Incident Response Team, Interpol has no concrete jurisdiction."

This worked. Bellas stopped just at the threshold. "Right," he said curtly. "You don't."

Manos went for it. "But the protection of the sixteen potential victims we identified is still your job. Willa Kendall was your job."

Bellas hung his head. If he had followed the directives, Willa Kendall would still be alive. It made no sense for Manos to continue, but he did:

"There are another fifteen out there. Three of them are my friend and his parents. The other twelve are innocent people who will find themselves in the crosshairs of a killer because their name has the word 'will' in it somehow. Are they being protected?"

Bellas threw up his hands, playing the helpless martyr. *Look what I'm working with here!* The lounge music was even louder, the police staff bustling not unlike a bunch of teenage girls staging their next TikTok. But then Bellas changed tactics, clearly not wanting to show weakness.

"Mr. Manu," he said, "you're toying with untried methods, with people who need it the least."

"How so?"

"Because this force might not know about data, but they know crime."

"But they don't - they've never even had to."

"It's not that you haven't helped us. What I'm saying is -"

"Do you happen to have a list?"

"Me, a list?" Bellas was wide eyed with surprise. "No!"

"Then you know you can find me the rest of the night."

"Where?"

"Drifting from club to club," Manos said with a smile. Then he lifted the front corner of his shirt, adding, "Oh, and good thing you gave me my entry pass."

The butt of the gun he'd been issued the day before gleamed in the dull fluorescent light.

58.

James' parents were the first stop. Though sleeping soundly in their room at Santa Marina, Manos insisted on waking them just to be sure. He left his card with the Singapore number at the reception desk to be reaching if anything suspicious happened in the night. On his way out, he ran into Liz, the bride-to-be.

"Everything ok?" she asked nervously.

"Just going to catch up with James," he answered quickly, giving her a hug.

"Yes, I know it's your big night," she said, with a hint of sarcasm. Wanting more details without asking for them.

"Liz, James loves you very much," he said, suddenly. "Don't forget that."

It was the reassurance she needed. She hugged him again; Manos felt the tension in her light, willowy frame, as if she were silently asking for a promise: *Take care of him.*

Damn right, he would!

But where was James now? He tried his cell. Nothing. Tried Stefan. Nothing. Then a call came in from Chrisanthos, who sounded anxious.

"A message came in earlier from Cosmote, the Greek cell carrier. About Angel ...er, Angel--"

"Angelof," Manos cut in. "Did they send anyone?"

"His name's Brochman, something like that. No, they have someone at the office calling the hotels. But we have his most recent location."

For a second Chrisanthos was silent, his attention drawn away a moment.

"Listen Manos . . ." he said.

"I know, you have your own list," said Manos into his airpod mikes.

Chrisanthos lowered his voice. Manos could picture him blushing to the roots of his hair. He didn't like Bellas lying to him, but the world was full of guys like him.

"We got some leads from Jenna Will's phone," said Chrisanthos. "And Bellas found some names from the boat rentals."

"You won't get anything from those devices!" Manos blurted in frustration. "The murderer is not stupid! He didn't call and ask them out on a date. He didn't rent the boat himself. But it's worth a look - the boat had to come from somewhere."

"One of those guys who take people fishing, you know, under the table - missing too."

"Might be his. Have Bellas check it out."

"You think he killed him?"

"You know what I think! Our killer is too methodical to be caught by any regular police hunt. Look at the time he takes to perfectly thread each chain through the victims."

"Listen, I trust your list," Chrisanthos said apologetically. "Bellas can tell, that's why he gave me Angel."

"So what's his location?"

"On the road to Ftelia. Cosmote reported an hour ago. I'm sending you his cell and a picture. There's a concert at Alemagou. It's like a beach bar, everybody goes."

Well, that's a fact ...thought Manos, who saw a WhatsApp message banner descend onto his screen just then: *Manna! Where are you?...* They were at the same place.

The "concert" was Armin, an aged Dutch DJ superstar playing electronica. The bar was transformed into a seaside bash with thousands of people dancing on the sands. *Well, Manos Manu?* he asked himself. *How will you remember this sight, years from now? As a bureaucratic joker like Novak, fiddling with Java scripts, or alive like this, dancing with the whole world?* Without a moment more for contemplation, he felt an arm wind around him, moist lips kissing him, and a sweet little tongue slipping into his mouth. *Who is this?* He ran his hands over her body, pulling her closer. For identification.

"Oh, I've wanted to do that for a long time..." It was Alexandra Atkinson.

Wild applause came from a nearby table. James, Stefan, Frederich and Sandy - all joyously wasted - were enjoying the scene. Manos had spoken with James at the steakhouse, making sure he realized he was a target. He'd told Stefan not to leave him alone for an instant, even for the bathroom. He seemed safe with so many friends around him. Not far off, Lena Sideris was with her professor friend from the conference. She was looking at him, not at all surprised. Dancing, she made a little show: *Got my arms up in the air, dancing like I just don't care!*

And I, thought Manos, have no time for bullshit like this.

He left Alexandra, wading into the water up to his knees, trying to hear Mei in his airpods.

"Got your messages," she said. "I'm running the Key West data. Also running the two you want taken off the suspect list. You're at another party?"

"Good morning."

"Good morning," she answered. It sounded like she was already at the office, but not at her desk. He pictured her in the cafeteria as she spoke. "You do know that Novak's freaking out about the breach, right?"

"Which one?" he asked.

"Manos," she lowered her voice, speaking carefully. "Watch out. He pulled Zao into this game, and probably regrets it. He'd like nothing more than to drop the Mykonos case and get you on the first plane back."

"I know. Did the ISPs send anything?"

"Not yet."

"Not to us, no. But they're starting to contact Greek Police directly. Listen, I need a real-time UDID for one of our friends here. I'm sending his cell number."

It would be impossible to spot the suspect on this beach from some uploaded picture. The Unique Device Identification was a distinct number for every existing device. They were expecting it from the local carrier, but he could also use social media. Once Brochman logged into any service from his device, Mei could send his precise current location.

"Ok. I'll start streaming his coordinates once I get it."

"Hold on..."

Chrisanthos was calling. Manos switched apps.

"He's right behind you," he said.

"Who?"

But he understood and hung up. From the water's edge, Chrisanthos was looking past Manos, who turned, looking right into the man's eyes. Brochman realized it, looking back with an affronted air. Alexandra Atkinson, egged on by Sandy Voss, saved the day by coming back to finish what she'd started. Manos grabbed her and kissed her like he was about to fuck her right there on the sand for everyone to see. When he looked up again, Brochman had turned away, staring into the pumping dance of the crowd. Manos left Alexandra, trying to trail him. But then he remembered. The table. The cheers were louder now, and Lena Sideris had turned her back. *Is she leaving? Have to talk to her.*

"Hey, Manna-man! You ok?" Alexandra was blind drunk.

"No - Yes! Sorry, Alex, I'm... working."

"I can see that," she said, to his surprise. "Listen, I don't know if Stef's told you, but Jeremy Ong's here, on his boat."

Ong was a well-known and ultra-rich former developer, Head of Product at one of the giants. Perfectly natural for him to know Stefan the best man; perfectly natural for him to not know Manos the cop. Alexandra was making a friendly attempt to bring Manos down to earth, where people didn't chase after paranoid maniacs for almost no money. Much better to get paid a great deal of money to start a family and enroll your children in the most exclusive schools.

"He'll be at the wedding tomorrow. Maybe he can help you. You know, with whatever you're doing."

"Right," said Manos, taking this in. "Thank you, Alexandra."

And he meant it. Chrisanthos was staring at him, eyebrows raised, to get his attention. Brochman was heading to James' table. As if planning to stop by and say hello.

59.

Dr. Stevis had smoked a pack of Camels in two hours. He'd come to Mykonos for a family vacation, and now here he was - gutting a third new corpse. Of course, it was his duty; in the face of such crimes, he would do his utmost. But he couldn't go on, especially alone. And he was desperate for another smoke. When the young woman with the criminologist handed him a fresh pack, he thanked them with all his heart.

"Really," he sighed, utterly drained. "Thanks..."

Officer Yanis Bellas ushered Lena Sideris and her companion into the operating room, which, otherwise unneeded, had been converted into a morgue.

Bellas lifted the cover, saying, "Here - this is what we're facing. I need your help."

Willa Kendall's body lay face up on the surgical bed, exactly like Billy Casey and Jenna Will. The same heavy chain ran through her body with the same white buoy sprayed in red paint:

FREE

It was too much for Lena. A wild cry broke from her, and she sobbed, unable to catch her breath. Never again in her life would she be free of this sight, this angelic form, completely ravaged. Grasping somewhere to steady herself, she leaned on the man she thought she'd left behind. The events of the last few hours had shown her that he, her mentor, Franz Hansen, was the only one she could really trust. "I need Lena's help, as an expert - and yours, professor. To find the bastard behind these murders."

Hansen looked as if he admired this statement. *What science brings to light! Did anyone need science? She does!* And... Illumination! Bellas' flick of the wrist seemed like a magician's as he covered the body again, leaving only the anchor and buoy to be seen. *Ah, sublime!* It was as though Bellas, in another corner of the room, was going to remove a different green cover with a dramatic flourish, revealing a living Willa, who would step forward and take a bow. But Bellas did not; he took each of them by the arm, leading them into the corridor to talk. *No matter... Perhaps next time.*

Dr. Stevis seemed already in need of more cigarettes.

60.

Brochman wasn't alone.

Two tables past James' crew, a couple came and gave him a warm hug. Thirtyish. Chrisanthos questioned Manos with a look. Not him? But Manos knew serial killers look like everyone else; the most pragmatic seek to be also the most ordinary, to avoid notice. Death, so unexpected, is twice as thrilling, a garment of light wrapped around them. And the high is much higher for the invisible type, a finer cocktail of adrenalin, serotonin, and dopamine.

To trail Brochman, Manos and Chrisanthos circled back to the frenzied Stanford party. Frederick, Stefan, Erika with some no-name friend of hers, Sandy Voss, Alexandra Atkinson along with a dozen or so guys from other spheres of James' life. Manos didn't know them. Sprawled on the plush outdoor sofas, the whole bunch were getting freshly hammered, pouring out punch served in huge pitchers.

Manos tried to look busy to avoid staring at Brochman. Parched, he downed two tall glasses of fruit punch. The guys were dancing, though looking more like athletes warming up for a marathon; the girls had grooved their way back from the dancefloor, arms laced around each other, exchanging sweet little kisses. Chrisanthos kept his eye on their suspect while Manos, worried about security in all this fun, got James in a headlock, explaining again about being a prime target. James did listen, but thought Manos might be showing off. James was also worried about Frederick, who hadn't stopped snorting coke all night. *I'd rather not get arrested the night before my wedding...*

Chrisanthos, after chatting a few minutes with one of the Greek waiters, came up to Manos.

"Don't drink any more of that," he said. "The guy just told me someone passing by slipped something into it."

What? Who?

But it was too late. Slowly, strangely, Manos' head started whirling. Colors became brighter, sounds tingling in his ears. He fixed his eyes on Brochman, who was reaching to the sky with his friends, elated, as if crossing the finish line without having to run the race. The thousands of party people across the sands at Ftelia rode the same high wave tonight.

But they had a murderer to find.

Who spiked the booze?

Chrisanthos got a call from the station. Speaking, he glanced at Manos, then ended the call and turned to him with a guilty look. As if he'd killed someone.

"Athens sent the information," he said. "I think already Bellas had it. They searched three rooms, but didn't find anything. The tenants want to file a complaint."

"What about Brochman?"

"No word yet. They're looking, but he's probably clean."

Manos couldn't take more suspense. "And the fourth guy?"

This is it. The end of the road.

Manos had his phone out, ready to call Mei.

"The fourth one can't be located."

"Meaning...?"
"Meaning he probably has a fake account. We have to -"

Meaning real professionals have to deal with this! Manos put in his airpods, but Mei couldn't understand him. He went back in the water, up to his knees.

The end is near...

Mei spoke directly. "Philip Brochman is not my man."
"You mean our man."
"I mean his phone's squeaky clean."
"So what?" Manos shrieked.
"His geolocation's been on, recording for days."

Little by little, the colors around Manos transformed. Everything, so intense... Reality had slipped down a tunnel, a cosmic hole brimming with colors.
"Manos," Mei was saying. "Brochman has never been to Faro Armenisti -"
"He wouldn't bring his phone."
"- or Caprice Bar or Ornos Beach..."
"Makes sense. When he gets rid of the bodies, he doesn't carry his device."
"We ran a confusion matrix. And just correlated the times of the abductions, Manos! The guy spends every minute either at a restaurant or at home, with his friends," Mei explained. "Emilia Mayer and..."

They were plotting against him, surrounding him. Conspiracy!
Chrisanthos came, up to his knees in the water, a look of pity in his eyes.
"They searched Brochman's too," he said.

Hearing this, Mei said, "They won't find anything."
Manos heard it in his airpods as Chrisanthos said, "They didn't find anything..."

The work. Two hundred and fifty thousand lines of code.

Just an account.

A fake account.

Nothing more.

Chrisanthos was tugging him by the hand. It appeared that Manos Manu, the notorious boy-wonder from Singapore with his sophisticated algorithms, was not well. Not at all well. Chrisanthos spoke slowly and carefully. "I have to go back. There's a press conference in the morning, at the station. I have to get some sleep."

A press conference. I'm not being asked... thought Manos. *Real colors ...and these strobe lights... Brochman!*
"I get it," he said.
"Can I take you back to town?" asked Chrisanthos.
"No, I have to... stay. Have to... to think." Manos was down on the sand, trying to dig into it with his palms.

Chrisanthos stared down at him, aghast. *Think about what, my friend?* He leaned towards Manos, hand hovering over his back, unsure about leaving him down there. *What the hell is he doing?* But all he dared say before leaving was, "You did everything you could, man." Manos was utterly engrossed. The colors were flowing from the sand now. But something in his pants was bothering him. Something festering in his pocket. He wrestled it out - it was the weapon from Bellas.

Violence, he thought. *Really an excellent mathematical accelerator.*

Then he heard voices, people taking pictures of him. He tried to get up, to collapse... *I can do this right...* onto someone else's outdoor sofa.

THE MACHINE MURDERS

VIII. Online – Offline

61.

Half the office was gathered around Yan's computer screen watching a video; Mykonos police was giving a press conference on the murders. Brianna, a lanky administrator from Norway who had finally found clothes her size in Asia, had her phone out for the WeChat translator app. At intervals Yan stopped the video and they listened to the rendered message.

"We are making every effort with our criminologist colleagues to face the challenge of this unprecedented... horror. The monster perpetrating these crimes on the most beautiful island of the Mediterranean should know that his hours are numbered. We have recruited the finest minds. We are leveraging the professionalism of Mykonos police with modern technology and we will soon see results. I give the floor to our research team..."

A beautiful young woman sat before the microphone.

"Good day, I am Lena Sideris, professor of criminology. We are working with the police within the framework on our recent symposium here on the island. These killings have shocked us all. We have already compiled a profile of... the criminal. We are dealing with a very sick individual. To him, we say that it's only a matter of time until he is apprehended."

Yan groaned. "Stupid! Typical cops-and-robbers crap!"

"Happy New Year! It's 1920!" said another voice.

Mei arrived, her inquisitive look on her face. She looked carefully at Lena Sideris on Yan's monitor as it summed it up for her. She felt no jealousy but still, it wasn't right. *Oh, Manos...* She tapped the call button on Signal. Twenty past three, Singapore time; Greece was five hours back. Still no answer. It was like the earth had swallowed him up.

"You have a profile of the criminal?" asked a member of the press audience.

"Profiling is one aspect of the process, yes," answered Lena Sideris.

Profiling! The Singapore team scoffed.

"Using what?" asked Yan.

"They burn branches and watch the smoke as it rises. And writing reports," said Brianna.

"They read goat entrails," said another.

Everyone laughed. Except Mei. Beside Ms. Sideris on the screen was a man somewhere in his fifties with a perfectly sculpted goatee. Brianna was fiddling with her translator app; everyone was glued to her screen.

Lena continued. "It takes people to understand a person."

A slew of further questions was ready to burst forth from the audience. Mei had seen enough. Ahmad, a rather humorless Malaysian from Yan's team, took her off to the side.

"Dr. Novak would like to see you in his office," he told her.

Daniel Novak was glazed over, staring at the Greek blogs. He looked like he was hiding behind his huge iMac when Mei walked in.

"Ms. Ni," he said gravely.

Mei stood there. She didn't know what to expect, but she sensed it was a time of reckoning. Time to take the lead.

"Our first results were for sixteen suspects," she said. "After we reconfigured based on the idea that the killer is making a political statement -"

"Targeting Wills and Willas! What makes you so sure? Three victims with the same name - that does not rule out a coincidence!"

"Especially for a name shared by thirty million Americans, right. But we've run a basic OSINT for each suspect." Open Source INTelligence. Meaning that for each one they had googled all the public information and metadata possible, using some specialized software tools available to every police service in the world.

"So it's not..." Novak sighed, "a coincidence."

"We ran the possibility of a coincidence. It's a hair above one ten-thousandth. We can expect the next victim, if there is one, to have that name, with probability -"

"Right, understood."

"That's how we realized that "FREE" on the buoys is political. These configurations led to eight suspects with a probability of ninety-six per-cent. It's never been higher, even in simulations."

"But your team are the only ones who care, Mei."

"True," Mei conceded. "People want results."

"Bull!" barked Daniel Novak. "Nobody cares about results. They only want to look like they're getting results. Posers! And can you picture the most recent pose of Interpol's Global Complex for Innovation?"

Novak shifted his screen for Mei to see. She could just make out a tourist who'd fallen over, clothes drenched, lying in the sand. What was it? Leaning in, she realized the tourist was staring at an exposed weapon he held in his hands - as though puzzled about what to do with it. Manos Manu.

"Dr. Novak! Daniel... I - I don't know what to say."

"Central office in Lyons sent the article," said Novak with sincere sympathy. "Some local rag, The Mykonian. But that's what people read nowadays, not The Wall Street Journal or the New York Times. Any joker can write on a five-dollar WordPress template! It gets shared thousands of times. Tens of thousands of shares!"

He showed her the number on the article's widget: 50k. *What the fuck, Manos!*

"And now you're telling me you have 96 percent probability. Look at this -" he said, showing her the article again. "One hundred percent probability I am a jackass!"

"There's no such thing as one hundred percent prob-"

"Mei Ni!"

"I understand, Dr. Novak. But this is a deep fake! And if not, it is out-of-context! A random snapshot. I spoke with Manos this morning. He was fully operational, tracing the target. Let me finish -"

"No."

But she did.

"With the list of eight suspects, we asked Dr. Zhong for help."

"Without my permission! You were only permitted to show him the system, not to take your pants off!"

Mei pretended not to hear. Gaze steady, she made sure he was just using... a figure of speech.

"It was a... technical issue," she said, with some dignity.

But this very phrase brought Novak to the breaking point. The possibility that he might explode was palpable beyond the office walls. Everyone turned from Yan's monitor and the press conference, skulking shamefaced to their workstations.

"You giving the local builds from our partners to the Chinese government is a technical issue?"

"Dr. Novak, we work with the Chinese government." If the Czech's hair wasn't bristle-cut, he would have torn it out. Mei rushed to give what she called reason number four - which from the day before had leapfrogged to number two: "Those builds contain nothing they themselves can't buy today, if they want it, from the Dark Web for five Ether," she pleaded, using the jargon for local codes run by the social platforms, "They might even have it already..."

She paused, looking guilty.

To her surprise, Novak calmed down. No one in the global intelligence community had forgotten Operation Aurora, a Chinese hacking of the source code for Google, Yahoo and many others. These leaks were commonly known to be directly related to the source code running locally for many, many services. Novak crossed his arms on his desk as though someone were about to hand him a bill.

"You're right," he said. "We never had this discussion."

"No! We never did. And any meetings I had with Professor Zhong were strictly personal. But it's exactly such meetings that allow us to go from eight suspects at ninety-six percent probability - to six, at ninety-nine percent! Nothing like this has ever been achieved in the history of law enforcement - nowhere in the world. An achievement made possible under your leadership!"

"Uh-oh! Code - red! Bullshit - alert!" he said in a digital voice, pretending to grab his cell phone.

Mei sighed, toying with her bangs. *How would he like it if I took off to get a haircut?*

"Ever since yesterday, Manos has gotten close to these suspects with the help of the Greeks," she said, ready to flounce away.

"Making personal contact..."

"Yes, manually, with backup from the police. And he eliminated two of them."

"How?" asked Novak. Finally, something was coming to light.

"He just asked them."

For the first time since she'd stepped into his office, Novak cracked a smile. The tension gave way a little. If they were silent a moment longer they would have heard the familiar tap-tap of typing from the open offices outside.

"From one million, three hundred thousand suspects, we got it down to four individuals," Novak said, thinking aloud. "So why are the Greeks throwing us under the bus?"

"They're doing what they have to do," said Mei. "They simply don't understand what we have here. They have no faith in our models. I don't think they've ever worked with predictive models."

"They certainly haven't. If they had, they wouldn't be so damn surprised every time they go bankrupt."

Mei smiled. It's so easy to set Europeans against each other...

"But they did what we said," she added. "Three hours ago they searched the rooms of two of them. But they didn't even find a trace of the victims' DNA, or anything else."

"Are they working with Integen? Or waiting on regular laboratories?"

"No, they go directly."

A traditional DNA test took days, if not weeks. Interpol had furnished a number of its members with mobile units that gave results within an hour, at most ninety minutes.

"And now?" he asked.

"We're down to the last two suspects. A German tourist Manos was tailing a few hours ago - and an unknown number."

"And so we have..."

"The German showed open geolocation. We ran comparisons with the times the killer was active. So he's ruled out. Manos knows."

"So, we are left with the fake account."

Mei took a breath before uttering the sentence:
"So, we are left with a fake account."

Novak took a deep breath too. He felt like each of his feet was planted on two sides of a fault line that was going to grow wider and wider with the years. He understood why the Greeks had given that morning's press conference. To an extent, he had to agree with them. They had sifted through seventeen possible killers. Why should they believe the murderer would be the very last one they checked, an eighteenth candidate? They felt that Interpol had betrayed their trust, left them to themselves - with three bodies on ice! They might even assume Interpol had dropped them intentionally. *Whatever Mykonos lost, Ibiza would gladly take over.* He'd have to contact Lyons and have them call the Greek ministry. But first he had to restore respect for his own department.

"What now?" He sounded helpless.

"What else?" Mei said. "We work the passwords. We run on-off correlations."

Novak didn't remember how anyone managed to find the owner of a fake account. All he cared about was that they could.

"How much time does this piece of scum have left?" he asked her.

"The murderer? You mean if none of us got any sleep at all?"

"How long?"

"Gee, you mean this gifted, underrated, underpaid team with the bad reputation? The ones I have running correlations as we speak?"

"Mei Ni!"

"And given that all the majors will collaborate quite quickly?"

"How long?"

"Well," said the young lady, "I'd give that motherfucker less than twenty-four hours."

In another life, Novak thought, I would grab you and smother you with kisses. But in this life he would have to owe some serious favors before Manos Manu could be wiped from the timelines.

And he had to call the Greeks. To tell them they were doing a wonderful job.

62.

The hunt for @55godlessgod was underway. But neither "Godless God" nor "55" meant anything. But this code - when they found it - would save lives. People are not defined by usernames, but by their choice of passwords. The murderer had used an anonymous browser, Tor; the information behind his Facebook page and internet activity was very well hidden from global law enforcement authorities - or so he thought. For all activity related to the murders, he used the Android now referred to as Cellphone One. This included web searches on types of paint, purchasing buoys, the best way to find boats and anchors - and of course to read his victims' posts. But for his everyday life, including Facebook and Google profiles, phone contacts and maps use, the suspect used Cellphone Two, which would yield real, or at least traceable data and Internet Protocols for the creation of real datasets.

Thanks to his UIID matching up, they were able to locate him among the service providers. From this they could confirm the existence of @55godlessgod and his extremely high correlation with the MANU parameters. But unless they had his account and a trace on Cellphone Two, how could they locate and identify him?

This was a question for Michaela Saab and her unit.

"The only specific information we have on the perpetrator is what we can infer from his username," she said, standing next to her PowerPoint slides in the crowded meeting room off the main hall.

"And the password," Novak concluded, predictably.

"And the password," affirmed Michaela, whose Italian accent never failed to make her listeners smile. "Whatever Facebook knows, we know. Same with Google."

"Except they're driving us crazy," added Novak.

"When we have to wait for them, yes...," said Michaela, knowing that the department could get codes saved directly on browsers, though in the case of Tor, this was not certain.

"We'll get them," said Novak firmly.

Mei, listening carefully, wasn't so sure. She had sent @godlessgod to Menlo Park six hours ago. Manos' contact there, clearly tiring of them, was stalling. *Sure, I'll see, gimme a day or two ...Sure, it's a matter of hours, not days, I get it.* If they went through official channels, it would take at least a week. Their only choice was to trust Manos' source - and hope all the majors would be on board when asked for cooperation through other channels.

"The password then has to be traced throughout the entire internet," Michaela explained. "The odds of it being a single-use password - meaning once the user has created it, he doesn't use it for anything else - are quite slim. Sixty percent of all people use the same password everywhere, across devices and across services. Among those, nine out of ten use a password they just have in their head. Of those, a further nine out of ten have entered it at least once with a typo for an online service with a recognizable IP. We need that password. We need everyone to look for it. Because finding it means finding Cellphone Two. Then we'd have the perpetrator in our hands.

"And if that doesn't work?" asked an audience member. "Or if one of the platforms won't respond?"

"Your second question, I can't answer," said Michaela, gathering up her files. "As for your first..." she trailed off, nodding towards Mei.

"We'll be running Manos' solution at the same time," said Mei. "On-off correlations."

She realized all eyes were now on her. Manos Manu being absent, Mei Ni, who was practically his shadow, naturally assumed leadership of the Data Science Unit. Unhurried, she got up and took her place below the projector screen. Never in her life had she made a PowerPoint, and she wasn't about to start now. On the rare occasions when anyone dared ask for one, she conveniently used Manos' stock refusal: "I'm not in the movie business."

"Could you explain this solution in a few words, Ms. Ni?" Novak asked, not without some insistence.

"Online - Offline. Our team came up with a little script on Lisp using _-"

"Mei, in English, please."

Mei was baffled. "This is... English."

But she noticed the array of administrators staring at her, cross-eyed. It got so quiet they could hear the fluorescent lights humming. *Damn! If we don't even know what the hell we're doing, how the fuck do we expect an ordinary cop to trust us?* She backtracked.

"Michaela explained the two devices. One user, two profiles. Two profiles, two sets of data. And our reference profile, which emerged from the first sixteen Unique Interaction IDs. It's a silly thing," she smiled apologetically. "We run correlations for both profiles with the reference profile. What we don't have are the regular online interactions. It's like a puzzle with three pieces. One consists of GodlessGod's actions on Cellphone One, the second is the reference profile generated by the system created for these murders. We're missing the interactions of Cellphone Two, which is why we are asking our providers to send us scatter diagrams and bubbles having one hundred percent correlation with what we've sent them - it would be providing us with that missing piece.

It was starting to make sense to them.

"In the words of Manos Manu," she said, "You can try to hide from the internet, but you'll never escape data."

Now everyone seemed to get it. Magic.

63.

Manos had not slept at all. He'd spent the night plodding from hotel to hotel seeking every Will, William, Billy and Willy on his list. He found no prey, and not a hint of the predator. If he went to bed now, he'd be out for days - but James' wedding was only hours away. A dive in the hotel pool helped revive him. He saw Mei's multiple messages but ignored them, watching Lena Sideris' police interview. *What the fuck is she thinking? I just don't know...*

The excitement of wedding preparations filled the air; tables were moved and golf carts bobbed along, delivering flowers. The band was setting up speakers. Waiters were taste-testing hors d'oeuvres. The wild caravan was arriving at its final destination, after a week of delirious parties - and three sunken corpses.

"You're a friend of James Will, aren't you?" A tranquil voice came from the hotel bar. Manos recognized the slim man, but couldn't place him. "I'm Jeremy. I was just reading about you - the murders."

"It's not my best side...," Manos said gruffly.

Jeremy Ong. First a programmer, then a founder, in turn acquired by a major where he was Head of Product. Good friends with the best man, Alexandra and James, he spent his free time expounding on the future of artificial intelligence.

As for me, thought Manos, *even after my little swim, I can barely stand upright.*

"I see what you're doing," Jeremy said enthusiastically. "Amazing, what you've built. Self-supervised machine learning with police data. Ground-breaking!"

"A lot of features don't work properly," Manos admitted.

"Still, it's revolutionary!"

Jeremy had already ordered. Manos asked the barman for an orange juice.

"There's no revolution, Jeremy. Everyone yesses you to death, but no one takes action. Remember 'Old School'? With Will Ferrell?" Manos adopted a comic voice, clutching an invisible microphone: "We're going streaking!"

Jeremy laughed. Perhaps all their input datasets were quite similar.

"Another 'Will,' right?" he said. "Your guy plunges Wills into the deep and hangs his sign on them. Drowning freedom!"

Jeremy Ong sipped his beer. He seemed to have spent a much easier night than Manos. Lots of easy nights, in fact. And lots of easy days.

"Every act has its natural cause, correct?" he asked Manos.

"Sure."

"The same is true from a tech standpoint." Manos, setting his juice on the bar, shot a look of curiosity at Jeremy, who continued. "I mean, if you don't believe in free will... Or, on the other hand, if you don't believe our actions are induced by data we're exposed to, then what kind of data scientist are you?"

"Honestly I'd like to kill the guy. That's the kind of data scientist I am."

Jeremy Ong couldn't help but smile. A moment later, a man appeared on the stairs leading down to the pier where the dinghies were tied up. He made a signal to Jeremy, who left with him.

Manos took out his phone; sending just two words to Mei: "Password. OnOff."

Her answer was almost immediate:

"Think we waited for you?"

Then she sent another:
"B3n3d1ctusd3Sp1n0za"

Followed by a third:
"Manos, we found him."

64.

When Manos' pal at Menlo Park finally sent @55Godlessgod's code, Mei flooded his Slack account with gratitude. The team had established communication with eighty to ninety percent of the globe's internet. Had the code ever been used as an Apple ID? They would find it. Anyone ever typed it in by accident on a Google account? They would find it. Had the password *B3n3d1ctusd3Sp1n0za* been used with Microsoft, Amazon, Alibaba, WeChat, Yahoo, Go Daddy, Shopify, Uber, Tinder, JustEat - or any of the tens of thousands of microservices lodged within the servers of Amazon, Microsoft or Oracle? They were going to find it.

"Spinoza, my man! It's your big comeback!" sang Yan, seeing his inbox flooded with messages wanting to know the deal with Interpol's crazy query.

Mei, Brianna, Ahmad and Michaela stared at him, faces blank. Yan Googled it for confirmation.

"Spinoza, guys! The Dutch philosopher? Look."

"Ok, so?" ask Mei.

Yan copy/pasted @55godlessgod's password into a text editor: B3n3d1ctusd3Sp1n0za

Then they saw it. The murderer, using 3 in place of e, 1 in place of i and zero in place of o, had met alphanumeric user code requirements - and transformed Benedictus de Spinoza into B3n3d1ctusd3Sp1n0za. This was the Latin variant he used, according to Wikipedia, for his writings in Latin. The team read the same information at the same instant, each on a different screen. Brianna, with her undergraduate degree in classical literature, turned to Ethics first. Ahmad rather pragmatically Googled spinoza:free will...

"It's him!" he declared.

The search revealed that the Dutch thinker had spent his entire life arguing against the concept of free will. In his own way, the killer was trying to convey the same thing. A wave of euphoria flowed from one workstation to another; the puzzle pieces were coming together! Mei updated Manos on Signal; MANU works! We found our man! From half a million candidates, down to one: Baruch Spinoza!

"We continue as before," she said in the firm voice of Dr. Mei Ni, not wanting to betray the pride she felt. "We run online-offline correlations for both profiles with our reference. Yan...?"

"Running!" he called, his voice choked up.

Then Mei ran to hide in the ladies' room, bursting into tears of joy, grateful no one had come with her. She wasn't one for big speeches, but a new day had dawned for law enforcement. As if he could feel it across the ocean, after so much struggle and millions of lines of code, Manos Manu sent her a single, simple emoji.

Only they knew just how much it meant.

65.

Manos wished they could say they were done. That they had reached the point where their findings had convinced the police, setting them into immediate action. But no. This was another ten or twenty years off. For now he was bound to warn them that @55godlessgod was in fact the killer and wait for the confirmation of the on-off correlations - and the police. But the police had other priorities. Officer Bellas was not answering Manos' calls, except with an automatic message saying he would respond later. Manos, as head of the Incident Response Team, was to have undertaken the entire investigation, but he sensed things had taken a different turn in his absence. Whether he'd told them the killer was @55godlessgod, @amazingvic008, or @kingstonbay768, the Mykonos Police Department would do the same thing: absolutely nothing.

Chrisanthos had referred to leads from Jenna Will's phone, but the perpetrator would never have set up his abductions by phone contact. Bellas nursed hopes of clues from the coast guard and boat rentals - as well as anything from Stevis, the coroner. Had they found the suspect's DNA using devices provided by Interpol - and just conveniently forgotten to mention it? To find out, he called Dr. Stevis and asked about the fragment of line they had found in Jenna's body. Stevis sounded confused by the question; assuming everyone reported to Manos, he was surprised his results were not known.

"As I told Officer Bellas," he said, "it is unfortunately very difficult to get a sample from a thread."

"That's what I thought."

"Especially one so fine."

"Understood."

"But the officer has apparently matched the type of thread. Turns out we've helped quite a bit."

Manos could read between the lines. Officially, he had no jurisdiction there. Jenna's family was flying from the U.S. to collect the body. While they could file a complaint against him for desecration of the corpse - he had opened her chest - it was rare that family members wanted to see the entire corpse. The glassy look in their beloved's eyes would be enough to make them sign anything. But it would help Stevis if his contribution was considered valuable to the case. Manos couldn't resist toying with him a little.

"Did they say they've found the supplier? Or are we just left with an open body?"

"No! They found it, for sure - not the actual end of the thread, just the same type, you see."

Fantastic! What a joke! "Where's it from?" he asked.

"Piraeus, some shop up there."

They had nothing! But they were going to hunt down some poor guy who'd bought the wrong thing at the wrong place.

"Thank you, doctor," said Manos before hanging up. "You've really done a lot for the investigation."

Gotta work the Will angle... If the murderer continued his political statements, he need only pinpoint the potential victims. Jeremy's words came to mind: Our legal system is based on free will. He couldn't do anything about free will, but he could put pressure on the system. He sent a message, the same one, to Bellas and Chrisanthos and Mayor Mavrudis.

Are the people with Will in their name being protected? Is Mykonos Police protecting everyone on the list sent by the IRT? Manos.

Who knew if they would even answer? James' parents were just coming out from the suite where the groom was getting ready. They'd taken one last glimpse of their son as a bachelor. Inside were the best man and few of the old crowd.

"James! Mrs. Will, Mr. Will!"

"Hey, Manna-Boy! My favorite investigator!" cried James. "Mom, did you know we've got a detective at this wedding?"

Manos said, "Congratulations on your son's wedding. Not many grooms are as lucky!"

"Oh, thank you! Is everything all right with... the man you're looking for?"

"Yes, but please, please be careful," he urged them. "Don't go off alone."

"No worries, my friend!" said James. "The police have notified us, and just to make sure I invited a couple of cops to the wedding. They're at your table."

"Really?" Manos asked. "Who?"

"How should I know?" James shrugged his shoulders. "Whoever they send."

Behind them, Stefan and Frederick's entourage were snickering. Manos tried to insist. Three of the original sixteen Wills were right here. Another had died. Two had left only hours earlier. There had been no new arrivals. Three out of thirteen meant a twenty percent probability they would be the next victim. But the wedding was three hours away. The groom must get ready. Rumors had brought the bride to the brink of hysteria. So very many things could go wrong at a wedding. What if the cake hadn't set properly? Or someone slipped on the steps? And if the confetti streamer machine malfunctioned? What if, at the wrong time, the balloons set themselves... free?

No one wanted to compute probabilities right now.

66.

When Mei, Novak and Yan had run comparisons for the eight Unique Interaction IDs with similar types on the network, two additional suspects had surfaced, though neither with any connection to the Mykonos murders. One was in Singapore, another in the United States. Having secured the man Yan called Spinoza, Mei wanted to revisit the issue. They obviously had one murderer, not three. And they'd found him. Who were the other two? How had they gotten shuffled into their results?

Mei recalled the article Manos had forwarded a few days earlier, about a similar murder in Key West, Florida. She used her credit card for a monthly subscription to Keynews.com to get through the paywall. The article stated the body had been found off the waters at Dog Beach. With a chain running through it. Leading to a buoy. She decided to use Novak's login credentials to get into the FBI's ViCAP database. Nothing was easier. Like everyone of his generation, d.novak used the same password for everything and had once shared his password for an internal site via Slack. It was as though he'd given the green light for his programmers to get into anything they wanted: d.novak for this, d.novak for that. Only his ebanking had been spared.

Mei used it now to run keyword searches on the incident, which came up immediately: July 16th, ten days prior. She downloaded all the documents into her computer. Any search the FBI might run would indicate "Chinese hackers." *Great,* she thought. *I am Chinese.* She opened up each of the .pdf files and started reading. Less than ten minutes into the reports, she'd found everything she was looking for.

The buoy had been marked with spray paint...

Someone had written on it before immersing the body.

...With a single word.

"GOT HIM!" she heard someone shout.

It was a triumphant cry. They had finalized the online/offline correlations. @55godlessgod was their man. Mei wanted to run to the team, to hug them, to supervise the team's next steps even before getting the awaited answers for "B3n3d1ctusd3Sp1n0za." She wanted to update Manos: "On-off ok - he's ours!" Then they would hit up the Greek internet service providers for the killer's geolocation. And local police for the arrest. But Mei could not get up so fast. What she'd read on her screen was pulling her down, deep into her seat. The murderer in Key West had written one word on the buoy holding his victim upright in the water's current:

FREE

Mei minimized her browser window and gave a wave to say she understood. *Yes, got him...* She had to make a call, which everyone assumed was to Manos. But she'd already looked up the corresponding murder suspect that had shown in Singapore. Finding an accessible, detailed profile, she picked up the phone to speak with the Commissioner of Singapore Police. She knew the Director of Police from his numerous presentations at the Global Complex, but the cell number he'd given out was little better than a glorified 800-number, which repeatedly redirected the call. With a little luck, you get someone who knew just a little more than the last person. Reaching the Commissioner himself was a full-scale miracle. Mei was overjoyed to get his assistant, a man named Hoong Wee.

She explained her discovery: there were indications that a serial killer was already operating within the city limits.

"So what I need," she concluded, "is a police escort for me to interrogate him regarding serial murders in other parts of the world."

"Impossible!" Wee scoffed as if he'd just been told a great joke.

"But why? The individual is called Guo, Guo Long. After questioning, he can go back under the city's jurisdiction."

"This isn't Hong Kong, Mei. We can't just arrest people on fabricated accusations! Forget it!"

"They are not fabricated! We're not even talking accusations."

"That's the point. What are we supposed to say? Interpol's algorithms generated a suspect? There's isn't even a crime!"

"We have Missing Persons," Mei insisted through gritted teeth.

"Missing Persons? Mei, this is a democracy!"

"Fine," she snapped, her face burning. "I'll go by myself!"

"Go where? Interpol has no authority to arrest citizens!" bellowed Hoong Wee as if he were telling off his boss.

"I'll speak with Dr. Novak," she said, like a spoiled child who wasn't getting her way. Beet red, she slammed the phone down.

The whole office was staring at her. Afraid. Without a word, their faces asked, *But didn't we just confirm the identity of a killer 5,600 miles away?*

She answered her colleagues with no more than a look. *We also have to find the ones right next door.*

67.

It was 10 p.m. Daniel Novak wanted to go home. But here he was with Mei. The last thing he wanted to do was upset her, but as usual she took the initiative and did it herself.

"Absolutely not, Mei! It's not our job to pick on every weirdo in the world!"

"He's not just weird, he is in the same dataset. And it's not the world, it's here in Singapore!"

"In Mykonos they have bodies. Here, we just have public parks. And forgetful banks."

"Mykonos had bodies because we found them. By chance!"

"Find me a body here, and then we'll discuss your Singapore murderer," said Novak, heading for the door.

"I need backup."

"You need a doctor!" was his arrogant reply, walking out.

Mei grabbed her phone, checked the time and went back to her computer. Most of the team wondered if it weren't time to go home. Some were already dozing on folded arms right at their desks. Mei went into the system, looking up information on the owner of the UIID from Key West. Then she used an anonymous browser to send an encrypted message to the local Key West police in Florida. It was a link leading to the Facebook profile of a man named Larry Wozinsky.

Then she went back into the FBI database for the coroner's report on the sunken corpse from Dog Beach. The registered time of death was just eight hours after that of Billy Casey. Could a copycat killer see that so quickly? She'd have to verify the exact time Happy-Hari posted the pictures. But she was almost certain it was a good twelve hours after the fact. Even if the American coroner was off by ten hours, it didn't explain the timeframe. The most direct flight from Miami to Athens took over fifteen hours. Doesn't add up.

There was always the possibility of a coincidence. But she had to find Guo Long. With Daniel Novak home sweet home with the wife and the Singapore Police refusing to work with her, choices were few. Zao Zhong sounded genuinely happy to hear from her.

"Mei! That broken heart mended?"

"It was easy," she answered on WeChat. "I used legacy sorting algorithms for all my feelings."

Zhong laughed. "How can I help you?"

"Sorry to call so late. I need to locate someone local. Someone possibly connected to the buoy murders."

"No help from the ISPs, I bet."

"Not at this time, definitely not at this hour."

"I am more on the scientific side of these things, you know."

Mei didn't like the sound of this.

He thought a minute, then said, "Send me his details. And upload the application I'm sending you. I'll send the credentials separately."

"Thank you, professor," she said as sweetly as she could, knowing there were others listening in. "Will I also be able to see his user history?"

"Only if he is a person of interest."

"Thank you, Zao."

Person of interest. Meaning a person who had attracted the notice of the Chinese government at some point. A foreign official, for instance, or a troublesome student organizing rallies in Hong Kong. Mei doubted Guo was in this category. She uploaded Zao's app and entered the credentials she'd received in another WeChat. Her person of interest turned up on an embedded page of Baidu Maps. A flashing dot was pulsating at alarming speed along the south pier at Marina Bay. With an open profile and fully accessible details, the Chinese were able to locate him very easily - unlike the Mykonos murderer. Mei put on her sweater, grabbed her backpack and called to Yan, who was half asleep.

"Call me when Spinoza's located!"

It was 11:30 when Mei reached the humid city. Guo's dot was moving west along the number 6 metro line. Had she waited for B3n3d1ctusd3Sp1n0za's identity, the suspense would have driven her crazy. She had to find where his Singaporean partner lived. Perhaps he would reveal something. She remembered what she'd said to Manos the day before: *Jesus, Manos! You're no cop!* What the hell was she doing? But she knew data doesn't lie. Guo must be a horrible man. Maybe he'd done something no police force in the world had seen. Yet.

And no one seemed to care. Yet.

Their technology was working. Validated. Secure. Unstoppable. Mei wanted to take the next step. Even if she was alone, with no protection. For an instant, just exiting the Global Complex she'd hesitated, ready to drop everything and go back inside. But Guo Long's dot had stopped moving. Right at the Harbor Front station. From there, he would leave metro line 6 and take the Sentosa Express. What was the probability a man like him was staying on Sentosa Island, Singapore's little Disney-land? Or Sentosa Cove? What were the chances of him starting a work shift there at this time of night? Night watchman? Mei looked at his pro-file again. It can't be! She turned on her engine and headed that way.

Has he gone hunting?

She called Manos on Signal. She heard a sound - applause - but no reply. Was it the bride arriving at the church? What the hell time is it in Mykonos? The call dropped. And the dot showed Guo, arriving at the Waterfront station.

Have to hurry.

Her mind was spinning. And the electric SAIC she'd managed to wear out in a year was zipping eighty miles an hour down Queensway Road. A driver swerved out of her way to avoid getting mown over. The car slid for a split second, steadying itself thanks to a nearby sidewalk. Slow down! A call to Hoong Wee will get me nowhere with Traffic Patrol in this country...

Manos returned her call.
"I hope you're wearing a suit," Mei said.
"I did. Dressed up to hear your news," he quipped.
"The on-off's final. Baruch Spinoza's a perfect match. Manos..."
"Yes, I know," he said.

It wasn't an answer. It was a zero, a placeholder, a phrase that said it all. What a moment for the two of them! A time of victory and celebration. Gratitude. And commitment - to each other. He missed Mei Ni. And she missed him.

Yes, I know.

"Just need the password," she said. "It won't be long, possibly a matter of minutes. An hour, two at the most. If it was entered even once, we will find him."
"Are you going to bed?" He realized she was driving.

"I'm actually following up on that lead. The other two candidates."

A shadow loomed over the victory. Was there a mistake? If so, was Spinoza also an error?

"The two mirror UIIDs. Did you go step by step?"

"Yes," she said. "With Yan. And the body at Key West, that article you sent."

The call was breaking up, but she heard Manos ask, "Copycat?"

"Maybe. Can't know for sure. So I'm going to check out his Singapore partner."

"You've located him?"

"Yes."

"They give you backup?"

"No."

"Mei!"

"Yes, I know."

Not an answer. Just a placeholder.

In the background she could hear all the sounds of the long-awaited event. Guests were arriving at the church at Santa Marina in brilliant summer attire, exchanging air kisses. Gorgeous attendants were serving apéritifs from silver trays before the ceremony began in the traditional little white church. The sun was slowly setting on a sandy Greek beach. He seemed farther away than ever.

She had arrived at Sentosa Cove.

She left her car in the parking lot of a bar and got onto a bank-sponsored timeshare bike. Handlebars in one hand, phone in the other. Her screen showed Guo on one of the boats off the pier. She set it up so as to pass in front on him, as if looking her own boat, or one where she was staying. Most of them were closed up, but from some of them music was playing.

The dot showed Guo on the third dock of the wooden pier. When she got there, she shoved her phone back into her pocket, looking closely at a white, thirty-foot speedboat. The only one with a light on. She could see the back of a wiry man somewhere in his sixties, lugging fishing gear to the bow.

"Excuse me," she called.

The man turned, clearly taken aback, as if he'd banged his forehead somewhere and was trying to recover. But he stood still, looking at her.

"Could you tell me where to find Eagle Wings?" asked Mei cheerfully.

"One or Two?" asked Long.

She was not prepared for this. She had seen Eagle Wings quite crowded as she passed on the bike. I guess Eagle Wings has a partner, too.

"Gee, I'm not really sure!" She smiled. Guo looked at her gravely, the bag of fishing equipment in his unsteady hands. Then he nodded back to the pier she'd just passed.

"Over there. Where they're making all that racket."

"Racket! Right! Thanks!"

Mei got back onto the bike, turning back clumsily. But she didn't turn in time and almost crashed into a bollard.

"Need help?" asked Guo, taking a step towards her.

"No!... Thanks!"

She was in a daze. Like she'd seen a killer or something.

IX. We Have Our Man

68.

As delighted sponsors, the parents of James and Liza spared no expense: the band, the luscious menu, charming balloons, even custom lighting and decorations for the church - and of course, the arrival of the bride in the back seat of an electric passenger drone operated by the groom. Not until the show-off landing manoeuvres were just over their heads did anyone realize there were people aboard; not until they saw Liz's wedding gown spilling from the open pod did they realize who it was. On cue, the church bells started their exultant ringing. Bold, futuristic and completely gratuitous.

"Isn't that dangerous?" Alexandra asked Manos. She was clutching his sleeve so tightly, she had stretched it out.

When the couple emerged safe and sound, wild enthusiasm broke out. They waved in greeting, triggering a cannonade of confetti and streamers thick as boa constrictors. The photographers rushed to immortalize the happy pair. With a smile, Manos let himself forget the murders for a while. He was happy for his friend. Happy to see him married, happy he'd learned to pilot a drone, and so content to be among these friends. James, Stefan, Alexandra, Sandy, even good old Frederick - and so many others. His festive mood wasn't even tainted when he saw Officer Bellas, looking on from a distance with a distracted grimace. Bet he wants to slap the groom with a traffic fine.

Manos went over to him. The officer spoke first.
"We have our man."
"Really?" said Manos, uncertain.
"I'll say this much, we are very pleased with Interpol's cooperation."

His suit was typical of any civil servant working the islands. But what a tie! thought Manos. It was a masterpiece of color and quality. Ferragamo, I bet, or Gucci or Hermès. *What a man of contradictions.*

"I watched the press conference, with Lena. The criminologists..."

"Tonight," was Bellas' reply, "we'll have him."

"How do you know it's him?"

Enchanted, the guests watched the couple exchange their vows. The priest waved his hands around their protestant heads as if shielding them from mosquitoes.

"Remember the winch Xagoraris found in that hotel?"

"It was for a boat."

"Right," said Bellas. "No connection. But we kept looking, since it's the only thing strong enough to pull a chain through a body. Traced all the winches on the island."

"And?" Manos was intrigued.

"The thread Stevis found in the girl's body matches a kind that goes on a particular kind of spool."

"Wow! What a longshot! And you located it..."

"And we located it."

"Congratulations!" said Manos.

"Athens Homicide helped too. The killer's Greek, rented a boat here about a week ago."

"Very interesting," said Manos.

"No signs of violence on the boat, no identification - forensics checked it out. But we believe -"

"This guy you found..." interrupted Manos.

"...he's around twenty."

"Twenty years old?"

"He drugs the victims and winds them up tight. Then moves them without a trace."

"Has he gone to college?" Manos asked.

Bellas was not expecting this question.

Manos probed further. "If so, what was his major?"

"No," said the officer, glancing uneasily at Manos. "The criminologists will sort out all that."

"No college?"

"No."

"He's not your man," said Manos.

Their system distinctly indicated a highly educated suspect, not Greek, male, somewhere around fifty. Research by Mykonos Police pointed to a Greek male, very young, with no college degree. Two parallel investigations. Two different methods. Two different worlds. Manos wondered if he could have handled things differently, but Bellas had made his decision. *He can just taste this victory! So scared someone's going to snatch it away...*

"Manos, you failed," said Bellas tersely. "It's time you faced it."

"Actually, it's not."

"You tried fifteen individuals, not one of them right. Your research lead nowhere. I'm not saying you didn't try. I'll cover for you, I'll say you did what you could. But for police work - for everything - you need people. All you had was numbers. Numbers!"

He spoke the words just at the moment the priest said, *You may kiss the bride.* A new life promised - in words. Not numbers.

"You know, Officer," said Manos. "We have very different ideas about people. You think they are created by something very, very big. I believe they are made up of pieces that are very, very small."

The wedding guests were clapping and cheering with jubilation. Rice was scattered. A golf cart drove up for the newlyweds. Bellas shook an admonishing finger at Manos. "You must renew your faith, young man!"

"Yanis," Manos said urgently, "it's not him."

"Yes, you and your theories! Oh, and I'd like..." Bellas made a motion toward Manos' pockets.

The gun... that's why he came.

Manos was used to having it now; he preferred to keep it, but couldn't refuse. Turning away from the gathering, he discreetly reached under his suit jacket and gave back the gun in its case.

"The Mykonos Police Force thanks you once again!" chimed Bellas. "Good luck back in Singapore, or wherever you go..." Bellas had spotted Mayor Mavrudis and Chrisanthos, who was in full uniform, ready to pick up his boss. Manos greeted them with a nod, which they returned with guilty faces, looking away.

69.

The guests were conveyed to the seaside bar for drinks and music before dinner. Manos came down the steps, got a drink and stood alone in a corner. In Singapore, it was 1:30 in the morning, and Mei was driving back to the office. Her voice gushed through his airpods, "Benedictusdespinoza was saved as a Chrome password, in numericals. Once. On a single IP in a British internet café!"

"And the browsing history?"

"Not much, unfortunately," she replied. Hearing the faint roar of her engine, he pictured her at the wheel. "Just that it was accidentally typed in at Researchgate. The guy reads a lot of scholarly articles."

"Matches the psychographics."

"Matches everything! Thing is, Researchgate is a German site based in Berlin. We've sicked Novak on them, hoping to find out what IPs he's used to connect. @godlessgod is not joking around. But they demanded a warrant."

"Anything we can do in the meantime?"

"You know them, Manos. It lands on the desk of some whining little clerk - *No personal data!* Novak's moving heaven and earth, and I think he's close... How's the wedding?"

Manos' eyes swept the guests, the wait staff threading through them.

"Mei, he could strike today. I'm worried about James. His parents too. Anything's possible."

"Not with all that protection around, though Godless is certainly the type to try. But you do have backup?"

Manos had no idea which officers were to be James' guests; he didn't mention his recent conversation with Bellas. *No, Mei. No one believes us anymore.* Then he recalled that Mei was heading back to the office.

"How are our copycats? Did you pinpoint the times?"

"I sent one off to Florida police - anonymously, to avoid problems. I'm just coming from the second one now."

It hit him; she'd been in danger. But she stuck to the work at hand. Did the time of death on the Key West coroner's report line up with the deaths of Casey, Willa and Jenna? Was this the same murderer? If so, why the same UIID in Singapore? What part did Guo Long play?

"I'm not sure everything started in Mykonos," ventured Mei.

"Something in the data-"

"No, there's no overfitting," she broke in. "Neural worked just fine."

"No, not that. Maybe it's not a copycat. The probability of having two UIIDs -"

"Is astronomically low, yes. What, then?"

"I don't know... let's verify the times first. Think you met a serial killer down there today?" asked Manos.

"On his boat in Sentosa Cove, the hottest spot in Southeast Asia. Try not to meet one there tonight, ok?" He heard the note of fear in her voice.

"I'll call you back," he said, hanging up.

Just opposite, Lena Sideris and the guy Manos recognized from the symposium were getting drinks. She was absolutely dazzling. Seeing Manos from the bar, Lena stepped away from her companion and approached him with a completely professional air, as if wishing introducing herself for the first time. Ready to teach him a lesson. *Hello, don't think we've met...*

"Good evening, Lena," said Manos coolly.

"Your friend invited us - Franz and me." *To look after him.*

"No better protection than the presence of criminologists."

She answered this sarcasm with an easy gaze. *Manos Manu! The Zuckerberg of crime!* His rumpled suit jacket and messy black hair. It had only taken a night or two to get over him, and she was determined to let him know it.

"Manos, I'm sorry." *Sorry? For whom, exactly?* Her smile a bit haughty, she continued. "I know you did all you could, but the police here have very precise methods. Don't underestimate them. They're experts -"

"We don't do the same work..."

"- and data science, for them, is just one lead among dozens. Same thing for us, the profilers, the psychologists. Just another lead. They evaluate what we have to offer, all of us."

"They have no idea what they're facing. Neither do you."

Her eyes narrowed. He had seen them that way peering at the former suspect in Gucci Boutique. "This is your issue, Manos!" she said briskly. "You find everyone inferior, driven by forces they don't understand."

"Those forces exist."

"And you alone understand them. Have you any idea how idiotic this is?"

Somewhere at the edge of the gathering, a lighter flashed. *Do people still smoke? Amazing.*

"Tell me about you and your friend," Manos asked.

She had issues of her own to explain. Pretending to moral superiority would win her nothing. Franz was twenty years her senior; she had just left him, only to return the next day. Manos read her expression. People are just... people.

"We're friends. For a time, it was more. I once loved him. When I was studying, Franz was a demigod to me. For the work I was doing, what I wanted so much to become."

Manos saw Franz approaching with a fresh drink for Lena.

"Mr. Manu," he said. "We never had a chance to talk after the conference."

"Hi."

"But we can chat tonight. I just saw we've been seated together."

Them? Mykonos Police sent them to protect James?

"Wonderful," said Manos icily. If Manos were seething under the rivalry, Hansen was no different.

"We'll catch up later," Hansen said, retreating with a faint smile and blending smoothly into the crowd.

When they were alone again, Lena went on. "In senior year of undergrad, when you're just about to start your Master's, you really believe in it all."

"And you believed in ...?"

"What Franz and I both knew to be true. He'd written so much about social-process criminology, meaning -"

"People commit crimes because of their surroundings."

"Yes. But for them to receive government support instead of being crammed into jail cells, we needed to demonstrate that help really works. That people could rise up, change their lives - even give back to their communities. That's what I wanted, what Franz and I both wanted. Here, in the UK, in the US – everywhere. To help legislation get passed and ensure help for struggling families, or secure housing for young people on the streets who knew only a life of crime. Not just research, academic papers. We wanted to show this very help directly leads to people improving every aspect of their lives through their own efforts, regardless of circumstances - that appealed to conservatives."

"So what happened?"

"We got some NHS programs subsidized," she sighed. "Thanks to Franz's work, certain infrastructures were put in place. And I made my modest contribution."

"Then why split up?"

Lena laughed nervously, as if he'd just found her most ticklish spot.

"Well, Franz started to believe less and less. In the power of humanity, people's ability to change at any point. It weighed him down. It was even seeping into his writings."

"But you still believe people can truly do what they desire."

"Always. That's why I liked you."

"But I don't believe they can."

"I noticed," she laughed. "That's why I dropped you."

"You can do whatever you think best."

"But of course, Man-Man! I have free will."

70.

The lavishly decorated balconies of Santa Marina's Buddha Bar now welcomed the wedding guests for the reception. Girls, lovely as young celebrities, discreetly poured champagne; rare, sumptuous delicacies were offered by young men who would have been eunuchs in ancient Athens. The musicians unfurled their seasoned talents with taste and style. The temperature was perfect for shedding one's suit and tie and cooling off in a shower of ice. A perfect evening to simply be.

"Is it possible to overcome oneself?" Franz Hansen was asking the table of guests. They were seated together after all, with a few others they didn't know. After preliminary introductions, the conversation centered on the Greek police, particularly their quaint way of ignoring the experts. They disregarded Professor Hansen's profile findings just as they had dismissed Manos' work.

They had their own methods.

"The killer is educated, undoubtedly," Hansen insisted. "We said so in our report."

"Just yesterday," Lena added.

"The Greeks believe what they want to believe, period. They can't change."

"Do you think they'll catch him?"

The question came from a young woman who was deeply shocked by the murders. If the murderer wasn't caught, she didn't plan on coming back to Mykonos next year. Or the year after. Hansen's eye was fixed on Manos.

"Mr. Manos, you are, as Shakespeare put it, 'more matter and less art'. Tell us. Will they get him?"

"Very soon," Manos answered.

Hansen was quick. "How soon?"

"No longer than it takes to read Spinoza's Ethics."

"No longer than - Spinoza's Ethics?" asked Lena.

"Oh, I've read that! I think...," said another of their tablemates, and odd bird who, having eagerly introduced himself, quickly left them - then just as quickly settled back down again in his chair to introduce himself again.

Franz Hansen sat silent, possibly contemplating Ethics. The young woman spoke again. "Well, these crimes are unethical. That's what you mean, right?" Manos didn't have a chance to answer. He felt a message from Signal on his phone.

From Mei.

A name.

Ari Fischer.

Just then, James Will stepped to the microphone set up by the bridal table. A hushed silence fell.

"Dear friends," he began. "Thank you for coming from all over the world to share our blessed day, on this blessed island."

Applause. A few hundred people now hung on his every word.

"My closest friends can attest to how I've mocked lofty speeches, how ridiculous I considered commitment. Now, making the biggest possible commitment, I only have lofty words to say. So, I've done all I can to change - and yet here I am!

Ari Fischer. Where is he?

Lena noticed something was up. So did Hansen. They watched as Manos tucked his phone away and filled his wine glass. *No news...!*

"We really think we chart our own course," James expounded, keeping back just a bit from the mike to avoid feedback. "We pick a field, select a university, go on interviews to embark on the path of our own choosing. Even if others don't agree - isn't that right, Manos?"

Heads turned towards him, a few merely from polite curiosity.

"My friend who joined the police - he's protecting us tonight from the bad guys!"

James, cut it out, thought Manos. He sensed Lena beside him, enjoying this immensely. Thankfully, James moved on to Stefan.

"Others, like my best man here, chose a life of crime. I mean - he's a venture fund manager!"

Laughter.

"What I'm saying is, we make our choices. Based on what we want. Except for one thing..."

Someone called out, "Except for love!"

"Except for love," James agreed warmly.

The guests erupted into applause and cheers.

Ari Fischer.

Manos tried calling Officer Bellas. No answer.

The wedding guests ambled down to one of the hotel's wooden piers extending over the heavenly blue water. The bride and groom carefully cut a piece from a towering cake; as they exchanged their first bites, hundreds of balloons rose into the air, and everyone clapped again. But not Manos.

Ari Fischer.

The request to the Greek internet service providers was pending. If they accessed the suspect's geolocation on his device, it would be sent to Manos via Signal within seconds.

Am I ready?

His hand went for his weapon, but it wasn't there anymore. He watched the newlyweds dancing, gazing into each other's eyes.

His blood froze.

There was a new target. As of three hours ago.

Mrs. Liz Will.

71.

Remezzo bar, restaurant and club. Open since the 1960s and commanding a spectacular view of Mykonos Town across the water, Remezzo was like a historical monument, their steeple of San Marco's, their Empire State Building, Trocadéro and Trafalgar. It was a place of gatherings, of elegant excess, and of last resorts. And never had so many people hovered, ready to bust their way in, as tonight.

Their target was twenty-five, a Greek waiter the police had nicknamed 'Jerry.' Petro Xagoraris had joked one day, *Hey, we're Tom, and he's Jerry! Get it? He's the mouse...* The mouse sniffed something in the air. He let his boss know tonight was his last shift; he was leaving for Athens early next morning. Bellas didn't take his eye off Jerry, knowing everyone else had their eye on him and his force. Jerry's arrest wasn't going to be like the Saroglu ferry debacle.

Time to take action. Order at table four. Check for table twelve. Jerry scurries here and there. On his last day.

Upon the news that the killer had been located, reinforcements for the two Athens Homicide cops were secretly flown in from Special Operations that afternoon. About twelve agents in khaki uniforms, tactical boots, gas masks and service weapons. Officer Bellas knew his local team could take Jerry without help, but after the embarrassment of involving himself with Interpol, he wanted to maintain excellent relations with Athens. And Athens wanted a perpetrator.

The take was set for eleven o'clock. Bellas, fully in charge and picturing a blitzkrieg invasion of Remezzo, changed the time to midnight.

Jerry was on duty till 1:00 a.m. No sense letting the mouse dash away early into the back alleys! *Can't let him disappear...*

But disappear he did.

Twenty minutes to midnight, Chrisanthos and Stella took a table in the restaurant. Happy customers. They noticed Jerry was late bringing out an order. Word had gotten out the police were planning a raid. In the kitchen, the rumor spread like flames in a flambé pan. Men and women from the Mykonos Police Department, Athens Homicide and the Operations Commission waited outside Remezzo, weapons drawn. They filled the little seaside path and stopped traffic on the coastal road to Neo Limani. But it was Jerry's last day. He'd taken his stuff and left, skirting Agia Anna beach and reaching the marble bust of Manto Mavrogenous. Just at the entrance of the town. The town now flooded with thousands of tourists looking for a place to drink, dance and have the time of their lives. The officer stood with a few others in front of Agia Kyriaki church, his wireless radio raised, as if invoking a blessing. He had just sent a small group to the suspect's house and another to surround the rented boat.

"Groups of three!" he bellowed furiously over the radio. "North to south! Every café, every bar, every restaurant!"

This was their night. Their man.

72.

Of all Berlin's pretty suburbs, Julia Thornston preferred Grunewald. It was near the city, only a half-hour commute to Researchgate on the green line. Yet she was close to the lakes, just at the edge of Westlicher Düppeler forest. So peaceful at night. In winter, she loved to listen to the wind rustling in the trees, and in summer, she could hear wild ducks splashing on the water. Tonight, however, she heard a voice. A voice in her own house.

"Ms. Thornston, this is Dr. Daniel Novak. I know it's late..."

It was well past eleven. She fumbled for her phone to see how the speakerphone had been activated. But she'd turned it off before going to bed. The man's voice was not coming through her phone. It sounded like the security system in her own house.

"Ms. Thornston, this is Dr. Novak. I am the director of Interpol, calling from Singapore. I sent you an email with my contact information and a meeting link for a video conference. I understand it's late and quite illegal to have my team reach you through your home security system, but we haven't been able to contact you by phone, and human lives are at stake at this moment if you don't take my call."

Julia was certain the voice was coming from her intercom. Unthinkingly, she pressed its little white button.

"Ms. Thornston, we are not at your door. I am speaking to you from Singapore!"

She tried to concentrate. What was it? An email? Oh, yes, the email! Could this man enter her house through the security system? Goodness, anything is possible! She turned on her iPhone and waited for it to boot up.

On the other end of the line, Michaela Saab and her team surrounded Novak, hoping with baited breath he could persuade this researchgate.net administrator to give them access to usernames associated with Ari Fischer's account. She was the only one who could. Novak now spoke into the camera on Yan's laptop. "We believe that Mr. Fischer has committed a series of crimes. If you do not give us the search history and the IP addresses he used when connecting to your platform, we cannot verify his real identity."

"I trust you are familiar with the laws protecting personal information-" This administrator spoke with the tone of many years' experience, but the Czech was ready for her.

"Ms. Thornston - may I call you Julia? We are a global organization, and you will find a warrant for this inquiry in an email... tomorrow."

"So let's talk then!" she snapped, and hung up.

Panic. Novak motioned to Michaela to connect again.

Mei stepped back from the drama. She'd come back to GCI taking Napier Road and was sitting at a nearby workstation, glued to Zao's app. Guo Long's location dot had been motionless for some time. But not at his boat at Sentosa Cove pier. He was off the shores of Palawan Island, at the southernmost tip of mainland Asia. *What the hell is he doing there?*

"Julia, the man we are looking for has already killed four people," Novak was saying into the camera, his voice steady this time. "Young people. If we wait until tomorrow, he will kill again today. Now."

Julia was silent. Thinking. Then, clearing her throat, she said, "I hung up to get dressed." She spoke a brusque English. "To go to the office."

"The office?"

"I don't have home access. When I get to the office, you have to tell me which IPs, and who you -"

"Fischer! Ari Fischer!" Novak repeated, clinging desperately to this good fortune.

"...Mr. Fischer. I will send you his details once I arrive."

When they hung up, the office was exalted, whooping as if they had won the World Cup. In another half hour, Julia would be turning on her computer. Day was just beginning to dawn in Singapore.

I've got thirty minutes, Mei calculated. The streets of Berlin are empty. But the time it will take for her to get there, to park, to speak with Novak... Mei made a sign to Michaela. *Send everything to Manos the second you get it.* Michaela understood, nodding. They were all exhausted. And Mei had very little time.

Half an hour, forty-five minutes at most.

In that time, she would be able to see where Guo was. And come right back.

73.

The sunrise over Singapore was pregnant with heavy clouds threatening to bring forth a violent storm. But Mei had no time to check the weather on her phone. Only to make sure the dot was still there. On the open waters off Palawan Beach, but not too far out. She'd see the boat from the pier. If Guo had dropped anchor here or threw something else overboard, she would see it. If the weather broke loose, and he put the engines forward to fight the current, she would watch him. If he realized she was onto him and simply threw his phone into the sea, she would know.

She'd swum here before - but never so early, and never when it threatened screaming rain.

If she didn't pursue him, the sleepless nights would overpower her. Manos was on the other side of the world, chasing real criminals. When he came back, she didn't want him to see her as just a system operator. He should see her passion, her heart teeming like the waters of this heart-shaped beach. She parked in the hotel lot of Capella Singapore. At the shop, she got a diving mask and a coffee to go.

"Early-morning dip, huh?" The cheerful sales girl took her for a hotel guest.

"Might as well. Weather's going to spoil."

Mei checked the dot on Zao's app and reached the path, across from where the dot indicated Guo Long would be, expecting to see his boat. Expecting to see him watching her, hands on his hips.

But there was nothing. Just the water.

She double-checked the location on her screen. A hundred meters off shore. In her bathing suit, she descended the boulders of the manmade waterfront. Grasping her mask, the warm water seemed a kaleidoscope of pale-colored vortices whipped up by countless whisks. The moment she stepped in, she wanted to get out.

Strong current...

But she kept going. What had seemed like sunken buoys were actually huge clusters of seaweed. Dense as trees, rolling in the jostling waves, they were impossibly tangled by the stormy wind. She adjusted her mask and dove. In the sudden silence, she could see the giant tendrils of kelp whirling up from the deep like slow-motion tornadoes.

She couldn't believe her eyes.

She had seen seaweed like this at Singapore Straits. She thought it was the effect of ships passing, thousands upon thousands. The filth, the inevitable waste arising from world trade. Now that she was swimming in it, she saw it was something else completely. A living, towering underwater forest, robust and magnificent as the forest of Zhangjiajie. Completely alert, her drowsiness was vanquished. But not her fear. To overcome it, she swam out with long, deep dives, coming up to the surface only to fill her lungs with air and plunge again into the deep-water forest. Underwater for minutes at a time. Losing herself in the brown branches of seaweed.

Far down, it was easy to confuse the surface with the depths. Until she could discern the dim daylight above, she sought the canopies of the swaying seaweed to climb to the surface.

This was not the Singapore she knew. This was the other coast. Indonesia. Nowhere in Singapore were these sea forests of kelp. It was such a surprise that for a moment she forgot what she was doing there, at this hour. Forgot the Mykonos murders. Forgot Guo Long.

But she recollected the buoys. Just ahead, among the giant branches she saw two white jerry cans bobbing towards the surface. And new, clean chains, free of algae, holding them down. Two swim strokes further, the forest was replaced with sunken forms.

The forms of human bodies.

Bodies held underwater by chains.

Two.

Three.

Four of them. Five.

A whole forest of sunken bodies and white, marked buoys.

She was swimming among them.

Among their faces. Their joyous expressions.

Open mouths. With chains in them.

Running through their guts.

Leading down to an anchor. Abandoned at sea.

Mei let the water into her lungs like a cold arctic wind. It was lovely to breathe, and for a time she felt refreshed. Until she realized she was drowning and she, too, raised her arms high, instinctively, like the bodies all around her. With an unexpected burst, she surfaced. Her cough, tearing through her, saved her life. But terror was not her reaction now.

No. There was something else, more like love for these bodies in the ocean. They had shared a secret with her. A hundred meters from shore, they had welcomed her to their sea forest, playing hide and seek with her. They played so well, who could ever find them?

No one but her.

74.

Chrisanthos had the killer just behind the door. He took out his weapon, shouting: "Freeze! Open the door! Slowly! Don't move! You are surrounded!"

Jerry.

The commotion of the escape attempt had drawn clusters of onlookers. Here and there in the club, cries of panic. The target had raced to hide in the bathroom with a few others. No hope of getting away. Most people didn't wait to find out why so many police agents were suddenly the scene; they ran helter skelter in all directions. The Special Operations team brought up the rear, screaming and using their clubs to evacuate the last stragglers.

A matter of time.

Stella and George ran to back up Chrisanthos; Tsardis came, flanked by two more from the Athens force. Once apprehended, Jerry was covered with a black hood covering him to his waist. He was paraded down to the middle of the port like a jihad terrorist. Tourists were posting pictures and videos nonstop.

They had their murderer!

Not until they had taken him to the airport police annex, untied his hands, taken off the hood, and placed him squarely in front of Bellas did they understand that they hadn't captured someone who drugged men and women to run chains through their entrails. They had captured a market clerk.

"L - Lulis wanted it! Th-that's why I -! Lulis asked me t-to bring it from P-Piraeus!"

Mini Market Mykonos, which had started out as a tumbledown grocery was now a very chic, very pricey supermarket with all the most fashionable delicacies, despite keeping its distasteful name. Its founder, Lulis, was very often to be seen, freshly coked up, cheerfully handing out slices of feta cheese to passers-by. Somewhere in his sixties, rumor had it he was in love with Mavrudis. "Mini Market" was their new target. Lulis had sent Jerry to get the custom aluminum accessory for the Smittybit winch. The one that matched the thread found in Jenna Will's body. Longshot, Manos would say. Officer Bellas knew it was sound, methodical police work.

The twelve armed men - in uniforms, tactical boots, and gas masks - descended upon the elegant establishment, ignoring Mavrudis' protests.
"Someone is making a mistake!" The mayor spat amidst the confusion. "They will pay for this!"
The situation was out of control. He didn't like it. It was far too late for Officer Bellas to turn back. On his phone he saw ten missed calls from Manos Manu. Three from the Athens team. Six from officers on his own force. Each of them on the edge, testing his character: *you're making a mistake; backtrack now; stay still!*

But Bellas had never been wired for stillness or backtracking, much less mistakes. The police bashed through the doors; Lulis was hiding behind his feta counter. Shoppers getting groceries at two in the morning ran out in terror; wheels of gourmet cheeses fell from the shelves. But the questions flowed from Bellas quietly, in the polite conversational tones normally heard on the shores of a Swiss lake.

"Why did you order a mechanical winch?"

"It wasn't for me! I don't buy for myself!"

"For who, then?"

"A customer!"

"What customer?"

"A foreigner! For... I don't remember - Ari? Was it Ari? German...?"

"Ari German?"

"German, from Germany! Doesn't speak Greek. He wanted it for fishing. The winch is German, too."

Bellas took his cell phone from the middle pocket of his uniform.

But he didn't call anyone.

75.

Mei was trembling.

She turned to swim back.

But she wasn't alone. On the edge of Palawan Island stood a silhouette.

She lurched back to hide. But where?

The silhouette was immobile, only pivoting slowly towards her. Mei screamed with all her might.

Guo Long was waiting for her.

There he was, before her. Mei had nowhere to go.

Except towards him.

But she'd gone completely numb.

The current was carrying her in, and Long stood on the rocks, waiting. Five dead bodies two meters down.

The tropical storm broke. She struggled to keep her head above water - but couldn't. She forced her mask into place and let her body sink into the canopy of the sunken forest, struggling to take a breath. Twenty meters ahead, she saw the outlines of the buoys and took heart - she was not close enough for her legs to get tangled in them. She didn't need to see them to know what was written on them.

FREE

What if it isn't him? Mei lifted her mask, squinting at the shore. *I'll show him I'm not afraid...* She make a few strokes in his direction, and

Guo Long - it was him beyond any doubt - started in surprise. But then his hand reached into his back pocket and reappeared.

She saw the blade of a knife in his grip.

Mei screamed and wailed with all her remaining strength. But who could hear her?

Who would ever hear her again?

Palawan Island was still asleep, the storm raging on. In the black, cascading rain, it was like dawn and nightfall had come together over their heads.

Mei Ni was trapped. The sea swelled. The only way to steady herself was to remember the victims. A man, somewhere around thirty. A woman... two women. One with short, black hair - or was it a man too?

With her last shreds of courage, she shouted, "The police are on their way! Commissioner Hoong Wee!"

Guo didn't seem to understand. As though perplexed to find her there. As though another day to meet would have suited him better. But nothing mattered. Except that she was there. And he was guilty. She knew his secret. She had to be killed.

On the waterfront, another man appeared.

Mei screamed, her voice deafening in her own ears. The man, probably from hotel maintenance, saw something was going on. Saw the knife in Guo's hand. He started to run, but Guo chased him.

"RUN!" cried Mei. But the man crashed into a trash can along the path. He was down. Guo rushed up and, plunging his knife once, then twice, left him there covered in blood.

He turned back to Mei.

People had heard the screams. They came running.

Pounding steps. Voices, shouting. Guo didn't lift his eyes from Mei.

A shot rang out.

She was safe.

Come and get me. I'm behind the buoys.
Bastard.
Come save yourself.
Set yourself free.

76.

Julia Thornston stepped into a Vital Spätkauf in Schöneberg for some nachos and a soda. She was surprised to find it a bit busy and got in line behind two young Goths. Must be coming from a party, she thought, giving them a smile. When her phone went off, they gave her a disapproving look over their shoulder. *Who is calling at this hour?*

Covering her mouth, she whispered into the phone. "Thornston!"

"Julia! Dr. Novak."

"Doctor?"

The Goths lost interest in her. Just a nurse.

"Dr. Daniel Novak. Singapore..."

"Yes," said Julia with a hint of guilt. "On my way."

She exited the Spätkauf in a daze. Who were these people? How dare they call again and again - and so late? What if they weren't who they claimed to be? After all, they could be hackers. They'd hacked right into her home alarm system!

It was a warm night. Completely awake at this point, she considered turning off her phone, going home to Grunewald, disabling her security system and going to bed. Let them send their warrant to her director. Tomorrow! Then he could request anything they wanted. That was the protocol. And that was exactly what she would have done - if only she knew how to disable her intercom. She sat down on a bench to think, opening up a bag of chips. She could tell they were perfectly capable of calling her all night long. On her phone, she Googled Daniel Novak; he was in fact director of some Interpol Lab in Singapore. The man in the photo resembled the one she had seen earlier on FaceTime. He was also on LinkedIn. Still using the browser on her phone, she opened up a tab to access the Researchgate administrator panel, logging in right there. She would tell them she'd just remembered she had access - rather than admitting what a creature of habit she really was. It was true she much preferred the wide screen at her office. But why go running across Berlin at one in the morning if she didn't have to? She typed in a search for Fischer's username.

Ari Fischer.

Member since 2011.

He wasn't exactly a power user. His file indicated he only uploaded private articles. No public files. Only drafts, which he shared.

With one person.

Always the same one.

Was it his mentor or something?

Julia had reached the bottom seam of her nachos bag. She decided it best to go back home. Before she looked any further.

77.

No expense has been spared! The dome of black sky over Mykonos Bay suddenly filled with fireworks from above. Fascinated onlookers, crooning their acclaim, filled it from below. Even as far away as Ornos Beach, Manos knew anyone seeing this would feel the same as these pampered guests: *Awestruck.* The newlyweds ended their bridal dance with a kiss for the photographers - and then dance party music filled the air. Instantly resonating with its rhythm and passion, the younger ones leapt to the dancefloor, and the older ones picked up the vibe. Liz was glowing, James blissfully lost in the prevailing abandon. His parents were dancing nearby, their friends all gathered together.

But Manos kept his eyes on the wallflowers. Among these was Frederick, lugging cocktail pitchers like a busboy from the back room.
"Freddo!" someone called. "We've got people for that!"
"Not for this we don't!"
"Are you slipping something in there?" Manos asked, grabbing Frederick's bicep. Frederick gave a guilty little smile, like a kid caught in the act. But Manos was ready to deck him - the psychedelics in last night's punch at the concert in Ftelia had cost him the last shred of credibility he had with the Greek police.
"It's nothing! Everyone's going to be just five percent happier!"

Party quant.

"So you spiked the booze last night?"
"At Alemagou? No! Didn't you see him? It was your buddy."
"My buddy?" Manos shouted to be heard over the music and merry-making.

"The psy-chol-ogist!"

It was impossible to hold on to him. A train of dancers shuttled by, grabbing Frederick for a caboose. *What psychologist?* Manos left the dancefloor and asked for the bathroom. He went through a group of guests just drunk enough to look forward to getting really smashed. Manos hadn't taken so much as a sip. *Tonight. Tonight is everything.* At the oversized marble hand sink a man had just come out of a stall and was washing his hands. Manos' question was instantly answered.

This psychologist.

Moral detachment. *The Greeks believe what they want to believe, period. They can't change.*

Machiavellianism. *I've worked this crowd for years, you know...*

Psychopathy. *I say whatever it takes to get what I want.*

Egoism. *Is it possible to surpass oneself?*

But how was the man in front of him connected to Ari Fischer?

Through the mirror, Franz Hansen saw Manos approaching. Cool detachment immediately set in. Hansen stopped washing his hands, the water still flowing.
"Alone?" asked Manos, turning on the next faucet.
The babble of the water neutralized the pumping of the music outside.
"Lena is in the ladies room."
"You've found each other," Manos smiled. "Again."

"Yes." A trace of triumph played on Hansen's lips, but they quickly formed a crooked smile.

Manos said, "Because Lena believes in the power of people to change."

"Lena does believe."

"And you?" Their eyes met in an icy silence.

"Does it matter, what I think?" His voice was rough, hoarse, as if someone else were speaking. "Everyone knows they can change," he said. "Civilization is based on the idea of change."

"The idea of free will…" Manos whispered.

"…a myth." Hansen picked up a linen towel and started wiping his hands. "We won't be able to deny the lie for long. Did you know that two hundred fifty neurons predict an individual's decision seven hundred milliseconds before it's made? What do you think, Mr. Manu?"

"Call me Manos."

"Well, Manos? Do we have free will?"

"We have life."

"And what is life without freedom?"

Manos shut the tap off to hear him better. But it wasn't completely turned, and the drops fell onto the marble in counterpoint to the dance music. Hansen seemed to be expecting Manos to contradict him.

But Manos said nothing. Franz Hansen lay the towel back down.

Manos did nothing. Franz Hansen smiled at him.

Manos remained still. Franz Hansen walked past him.

Manos let him go.

His phone went off in his pocket. Ignoring all calls and messages, Manos called Officer Bellas. It went to voicemail. Manos stayed put. He looked over the earlier calls. Nothing from Mei. No Signal messages either. But there were four missed calls from a different number. From Singapore. He went into one of the stalls, ringing the number back. Then, as if from another world, another planet, came the familiar, stately tone of Daniel Novak.

"Manos! Mei isn't picking up. I'm calling you. We heard back from the Germans. The suspect's name is Ari Fischer."

"Yes, I know," said Manos dully.

"He uses his account to upload lots of drafts, all kinds of papers. He hasn't published anything, but there is a coauthor for all of them."

"Franz Hansen," said Manos. The line went so quiet it sounded like the call dropped. Manos' voice was stuck in his throat; he waited for Novak to speak.

When he did, Manos felt his voice like a hot iron plunged through his heart.

"How did you know?" Novak asked.

78.

At Cambridge University, Franz Hansen had a birds' eye view over the role of consciousness. Could people truly change? From where do people's decisions arise? The daily bread of philosophers was now the deep concern of data scientists.

But not Manos Manu. His only concern right now was Mei. Coming out of the bathroom, he called her again, then sent her a simple text: Hansen. He tried Officer Bellas again, pressing the phone to his ear to hear over the music and woop-woop of the dancers.

"It's Franz Hansen!" he blurted the second Bellas picked up.

"You just hate him...," said Bellas.

"He matches everything!"

"Well, you've got one thing right and one thing wrong."

Right? Wrong? What the hell is he saying?

Bellas went on gravely, "He's not Greek. But it's not Hansen."

"Who then?" Manos shouted.

"His name is Ari Fischer," Bellas said importantly, as though winning a debate.

"Ari Fischer is Franz Hansen! They're the same person!"

Bellas groaned. The line went dead.

The dance party was heating up. Friends and family formed a ring around the happy couple on the dancefloor; the music was heard so far and wide it was as if the whole bay of Mykonos was attending the wedding. Manos scanned the faces for Hansen. *Is he gone?* He searched for Lena. *Nowhere...*

All of a sudden Alexandra Atkinson grabbed him by the waist and tried to drag him to the dancefloor. Manos tensed up and pushed her. "Not now!" She lost her balance and fell. Mortified, Manos tried to lift her back onto her feet. A push from behind knocked him off balance - it was Sandy. Then Stefan and Frederick. In a frenzy, they pulled him up by the arms, dragging him off to dance. Manos struggled, wild-eyed.
"Not now! Guys! NO!"
What's the deal? Mannio takes himself so seriously! He found himself in the middle of the dancers. Was that Lena's silhouette? Was she dancing? He thought he saw her staggering. Was she leaving? But the light was blinding, the walls of music closing in on him. It wasn't her. He had no time to lose. He had to keep weaving through the throng.

Franz Hansen was nowhere to be seen.

Conference leader. Lena's lover. Letting her come and go and come back again. The MANU system had identified him days ago as the Mykonos murderer. He'd devoted his life to proving that criminals could change. As Ari Fischer, he uploaded papers to *Research Gate* before putting his real name to them. Humans were rational beings. They change. Such was his conviction. But he'd also seen criminals slide back into a life of crime, unable to transform themselves. Who's to blame? The datasets of each lifetime? But that would eradicate the possibility of free will - making punishment impossible. How could anyone be punished if they couldn't erase the datasets of their past? If they literally can't start over?

He called Lena's cell. Her abandoned phone, lighting up, was visible on the table where they'd just had dinner. He started asking anyone who'd listen to him.

"Have you seen the professor? Hansen? He has a little goatee... Or Lena? Did you see a young woman? Lena Sideris? She's in a white dress. No, beige...!"

"MA-NOS!"

His phone call to Bellas hadn't gone wasted. Before him was Captain Panagiotis, Lena's father, his face anguished. He stared into Manos' eyes, desperately seeking the result of a program running its course on the other side of the globe. They didn't need to say a word. Where was the perpetrator? Where had he taken his daughter? He holed up in a corner, talking on his phone. Very soon, half the Mykonos police department would be here. The parking lot was three hundred meters away. Manos left the Captain to run and meet them. But he ran into James. "Are you ok?" he asked Manos.

"I think so. James - you have to watch out for them."

"Is... is he here?" gulped James, realizing his friend was trembling. Manos nodded. James' mother swept up, beaming, unaware.

"James! Where's Liz? Must have a dance with my Liza!" James' face drained of all color. In a flash, he was on the dance floor, pushing through everyone.

"Liz! Liz! LIZ!"

Manos watched. Any second now, she would emerge smiling from the crowd in her dazzling white gown and give James' cheeks a pinch. Tell him to calm down. Teasing, dancing with him.

Wait! The bathroom! But the best man and James' father had just checked; Manos saw them coming back out, distraught. He heard the clamor of a group arriving in the parking lot. The music pounded on, louder than ever.

Liz Will had disappeared.

79.

Hanging up from Manos' call, Bellas suddenly felt a hundred years old.

Franz Hansen...! During any contact with the police, he'd raised suspicions about Interpol's work. Suspicions he himself was all too inclined to take up, in turn provoking Manos. That's not difficult, though....

And Lena, his protegée!

The first call he made was to her father, who was five minutes from Ornos. The second was to direct Tsardis and his homicide agents directly to the hotel in Houlakia and arrest Hansen on sight. The third was to Chrisanthos, to send people to the wedding. He left the special operations crew out of it. Their only strength seemed to be terrifying the populace.

"What about Ari Fischer?" Chrisanthos asked.

"They're the same person."

There was a pause. Bellas could hear Chrisanthos trying to take this in.

"Something happens," said Bellas. "You chop it up with numbers, and you serve it."

After the calls, Bellas felt the silence settle around him. Nothing more to do. For years, he had tried to quit smoking. Perfect moment to drop the effort. He lit up and drew the smoke into his lungs to full capacity, feeling utterly refreshed. His phone rang. He clutched it to his chest as if the call was from someone for whom he had a burning, secret passion. But it was Captain Panagiotis. And Bellas immediately knew the news was terrible. He braced himself.

"Yes...." he said.
"He took Lena...," said the Captain.

Bellas had no words.

"And the bride is missing."

80.

The music stopped. The lights came on. Some people didn't even notice, as if partying were such a deep commitment that music, flashing lights and cocktails were extraneous details. James grabbed the microphone, calling out for Liz; most people saw there was an emergency, but not everyone; someone shouted, "She's fed up with you! She took off with a waiter!" Laughter here and there. But it was plain on James' face: *If only that were all! Just tell me where she is NOW!* People had checked her room, her parents' room, and the newlywed suite. Nothing. Her father and James searched through all the bathrooms.

Manos' battery was practically spent talking on the phone with Singapore. It would take hours to locate Hansen by his device - if they could even find which SDK he'd loaded onto his phone with third-party apps. If they came up against local internet providers like Cosmote or Vodafone, they would need a prosecutor's warrant. There was "fingerprinting," enabling them to locate his phone from an algorithmic combination of device type, screen size and even brightness. But even that would take hours. Hours that Liz didn't have. Or Lena. But at the other end of the world, Yan had an idea:

"Teehee! The guy never thought we'd find him! He posted a shot of the beach!"

"Facebook? Instagram?"

"Whatever!"

"Any comments?"

"The sea. Whatever!"

It was Yan's Boolean expression when he thought anything close to this level of irrelevance was fit for the trash can. He sounded like a sportscaster in Manos' airpods, and Manos pictured him sprawled out on his adjustable armchair, with Novak hovering. *Whatever.*

"Can you run--"

"Cyber's already on it."

"Tensor -"

"Tensor Flow, keras - they already downloaded the Google Earth set. Give us ten!"

With MANU, they discovered @godlessgod55 on the network as a mere username. They uncovered Ari Fischer with this user's *B3n3d1ctusd3Sp1n0za* password. Researchgate.net confirmed it was Hansen's. Now they needed to use Hansen's regular social media account to run image recognition on a photo uploaded a week ago. It must have been taken on his cell phone, and from what Manos could gather it was mostly of the sea and just a sliver of land. The edge of a cove, half a hillside. Nothing that could reveal the location even to someone who had spent time there, looking at the same cove, seeing the same hillside.

But image recognition can make you *really* see things.

Manos was proud of his team.

Meanwhile, James was on the phone with Mykonos police, who informed him an operation was in place at Hansen's hotel in Houlakia. In no time at all, he had taken and drugged two women, driving off from the parking lot like a man on vacation.

But there wasn't one chance in a thousand he went to the hotel. He went to where he took all his victims. On the edge of a cove. Along half a hill.

"Where's Mei?" Manos asked, tense.

"She's safe with Singapore police," said Yan. "She found corpses just like yours over there..." Manos could breathe again.

Mei's safe. More murderers. The system worked! But what was happening?

Jeremy Ong - impeccable as a groom himself, with a breathtaking girl hanging off his arm - nodded at him, full of concern. Manos nodded back.

"I noticed something," said Jeremy. "Come to the boat tomorrow, ok?"

Manos was on fire. "What's up?"

"Nothing important right now."

The tumult grew louder. James had grabbed Stefan and came over, cheeks drawn and white, his eyes uncertain in their sockets like bubble levels.

"We're taking the drone to go find her," said James.

He wasn't joking.

"We don't know where she is," reasoned Manos.

"The hotel, of course! I just talked to the police! That's where he took them!"

"James, the whole Singapore team is working it. They found an image! They're trying to... match it with Mykonos image datasets... satellite images... they've written... it's image recognition, to find the place. It's our only sample -"

"Are you crazy? What the fuck are you saying? They have Liz!"

"Can you do ass recognition too?" asked Stefan, who gave his own a little spank as they stalked off.

Someone had the nerve to put the music back on. The lights stayed bright. A few people hadn't grasped what was going on and started dancing again. Everyone else was frozen, bewildered by the surreal whisperings about a murderer. A double-abduction. *Inconceivable!* And something about a drunken pilot, who apparently attempted to take off in a drone with the equally plastered Stefan, trying to get to Franz Hansen's hotel to kill him.

But it was no go. Six feet off the ground, the drone faltered as if hungover, rolling sideways. James tried to keep it upright, but could only veer to the right, then swerved to avoid hitting anyone and landed on a cocktail table. It immediately collapsed with a crash. James turned off the engine and sat there, on the verge of tears. People came to see if they were all right - and in their right mind.

Frederick, seeing the wreck, told Manos, "I have a better way." Without a word, they marched to the parking lot. The attendants were beside themselves. They'd seen Hansen with a girl. She was out cold; they thought it was the booze. They helped him get her into the car.
"See the bride too?"
"Not the bride! I told Mr. Will!" one of them said; thirty-something, he was covered in tattoos and crying like a baby. "Just the girl!"
"Beige dress?" asked Manos.
"Yes! Long black hair!"

Lena. Drugged.

"Do you know where they went?"
They pointed towards the far end of the island. Far from Ornos. Far from Mykonos Town. Far away.

On the edge of a cove. Along a hillside.

He put his airpods back in and called Yan via Slack.
"Anything?"
"Working. Had a convolution issue, but we're on it. Gigantic sets!"
"Tell me the second you know!"
What else was there to ask? If Mei were there, she'd be in charge. If only she were there.
"Let's go!" It was Frederick. Manos was sure he'd drunk half the bar. He was on a wacky, multicolored guruna bike. There wasn't another one like it on the island. On any island. On earth.
Frederick saw Manos hesitate. "Just trust me! I told you, I'm a models guy!"

Manos let him drive, but he didn't know where. Just driving. After a while, Manos asked Frederick to turn back, but he wouldn't. Leaving Ornos and Santa Marina, they crossed half the island in the dead of night. They reached Ano Mera. It was soon clear Frederick had no idea where they were. He looked at Manos, defeated. *I tried...! Really...*

Manos' device lit up with a Slack notification. It was a location, shared by Yan, then a number: 88. It was the probability. Touching the link, he saw it was on the northeast end of the island.
"To Profitis Ilias! At Lagada!" he called to Frederick.

Manos had just the time to grab Frederick's heavy body as he accelerated. In his other hand, his screen lit up. Another link. Another location on Maps. His battery died before he could open it. He didn't catch a glimpse of its corresponding probability either. Yan was probably sending a whole list, but couldn't see it. He'd have to call.

"Let me have your phone!" he called to Frederick, who was racing through the narrow black streets of the island as if they were motocross tracks.

"I don't have it!"

"Your phone? You don't have your phone?" Manos was horrified.

Frederick could only shrug his shoulders and flash him a look full of shame.

But it didn't matter. There was a sign. Vathia Lagada. He tried to recall the location of the first link that came in.

This was it. The ground was rocky and dry.

Here.

A perfectly white house glowed on the cliff of a hill. A bit further down, another house overlooked a small beach. Manos got off the hog and motioned to Frederick to go back.

Get help. All the help you can find.

As fast as you can.

81.

The burning night winds of the Aegean were muted just before dawn. Like a silencer, thought Manos, recalling the gun he'd carried until yesterday and wishing he had it. He trudged along the dirt path leading to the hill. Not a soul.

He headed down towards the beach. There was one more house. The very last one.

What am I doing here?

It would take time for Frederick to get back with anyone, critical time Manos would spend here, forgotten on the other side of the island.

A vehicle. A little Smart. Parked outside the last house. The neurons in his skull emitted a dark chord of electrical signals. *Hansen.*

Over the low notes of the wind, an animal was bleating. A hit and run left on the road. He approached the house carefully. A tranquil splashing of water on tile. A pool. The bleating on the road.

The house was fenced in by a stone wall, about a man's height. Decorative olive trees in huge ceramic planters stood at the entryway gate, which was of fine teak with a metal frame, studs and lock. Perfect view of the stony beach. Manos thought how wild it must be in winter, the high waves breaking, washing the rocks in salty foam. Not even a cactus could grow to any height in this wind. He thought of winter because the silence was fearful. Climbing onto an arbor, he scaled the fence and sprang over it.

What am I doing here? Hunting down a murderer.

What will I do when I find him? No idea.

Not thinking, he grabbed his phone to call for help, pressing every button and swiping the screen again and again until he had to accept it. Just like Hansen's victims. *Dead. Dead. Dead.* But there were signs of life. A mummy was rolling in a corner near the pool, trying to escape its bindings and return to the world of the living. Trying to breathe. Bleating... Manos stepped closer; the bindings were actually a long, winding fishing net. Within, something like an angel's robes. Or a wedding dress. He tugged the net from Liz's mouth. She was crying, her azure eyes crystalline as Arctic lakes.

"Ma... nos..." She could barely form the sounds. The net so tight around her chest. Manos tried, but couldn't unwind the net. He turned her body carefully beside the pool, but if she fell in, she would drown. If he took too long, she would be killed. If she spoke, they would both die. He had to find a knife, anything. She couldn't get away on her own. *Drugged.* She lost consciousness again in his arms, still completely bound.

The veranda doors stood open. There was only the swishing of the water in the pool. The muffled winding Cycladic winds. Faint roar of the sea.

Daybreak.

The border around the pool was smooth, polished cement. The outside patio beneath the trellis was the same. Manos stole inside. The whole house. Polished cement, sleek as tiles. *Of course, that's why he chose it.* Even in the living room next to the open kitchen. Much easier to mop it all up. It would take time, of course, with so much blood. But the pool was right there. Easy to go back and forth with buckets until there was nothing left the pale floor. Even the owners wouldn't be able to tell. Forensics could, but until a short while ago, Franz Hansen didn't even exist for them.

And now he was invisible.

There was only blood.

Dripping. From the marble table placed before the circular couch, which was also polished concrete. No cushions to get dirty. Blood, dripping from the mouth of a head that was thrown back; emptying from a naked body, lying face down.

Lena.

Manos kept his distance. Franz Hansen was not far. Behind the side door? Behind the curtains? Upstairs? Manos entered the kitchen. No knife in sight. But he had to find one. Their lives depended on him getting his hands on some kind of blade.

What was he doing here? He had to escape!

In the kitchen, he opened a drawer as quietly as he could. Dish towels. No... A pair of scissors was hanging on a wooden rack on the counter. He stepped towards it. Lena's blood, redder than anything red he had ever seen, was flowing closer to where the rack stood. He advanced slowly, silently, arms slightly open for balance. He took one step through the blood. Two. Faintest squish of it. Sticky. But he got the scissors.

Done. Better than perfect.

No time to waste. Nothing could be done for Lena, but he could try and save Liz. If he didn't hurry, his bloody footprints would lead Hansen right to him.

He was out.

The wind had changed, caressing his face. It gave him hope. He crouched down to cut through the net with shaking hands, barely knowing what he was doing. Cutting and cursing, tearing her bridal gown. She stirred. Opened her eyes. Remembered. Manos placed a palm over her mouth. Liz panicked, then realized. He felt her breath easing. She tried to get up, but couldn't. Manos lifted her on his back. *Light as a feather...* They got to the gate; he tugged the handle. It betrayed them with a noise. Creak...! But it didn't open.

He settled Liz against the stone wall and made a sign, asking if she could walk. She nodded and tried to stand upright, her hand pressing into the wall. *Not possible.* She grabbed his hand, not letting him go. Manos considered trying to get her over the fence, as he'd come in. Then he remembered: in the kitchen near the rack with the scissors, he'd seen a set of keys. Hansen must have tossed them there when he'd returned. One of them had to be the key to the gate.

He decided to go back to the kitchen for them. He put the scissors in his pocket.

It would take time to clean his bloody footprints from the polished concrete floor. However this night ended, forensics would have the house shut up for days. It was so remote it probably wouldn't be let for the rest of the summer. But this was Mykonos; the house would find its way back onto Airbnb next summer.

He crept to the kitchen. The keys lay directly opposite. And beside them stood a well-dressed man in a suit, his white shirt stained with blood.

Franz Hansen looked at him without a word.

He seemed to be expecting someone else, as though now trying hard to remember who Manos was.

Manos heard himself stuttering. "It's-s o-over. They'll be here in a few seconds."

He wanted to sound casual. Just passing through. To delete himself and Liz from the murderer's mind. *It's over. Nothing else mattered.* But Hansen's tone was much more serene, deliberate.

"Really? How many?" But the tone conveyed a different message: *I am going to kill you. You and the girl.*

Manos calculated his next move. He had the scissors in his pocket; Hansen had his bare hands. The ring of keys was on the counter, about ten of them. If he remembered right, the lock on the gate took an ordinary serrated key. The set on the counter had three double-bit keys, the rest serrated. More than five possibilities. One of them would turn the lock. Twenty percent chance. He would have to lay them out to choose; if he was fast enough he'd have at most the time to try one, perhaps two. If he were able to eyeball the difference between keys, he could increase his chances to fifty or sixty percent of picking the right one. And have enough time to get Liz on his shoulder and get her out.

Hansen could choose to simply sit and watch him, letting him leave. He could pursue him and stop him at the first key - unless the first choice was a lucky one. And he could get Liz out.

But Hansen did neither. He was caressing Lena's hair, his mouth pressed into a smile of farewell. Then he disappeared through a nearby door.

Manos lost at least two whole seconds to sheer shock.

Can it be that easy...?

He grabbed the keys on the counter and sped to the gate. Liz was struggling, trying to climb the arbor. She kept slipping. Setting the keys on the ground, Manos peered at the lock and made yet another choice. Wrong key. And another...

Hansen appeared. It looked like he was carrying a broom, but it was a spear gun. The weapon didn't frighten Manos - it was the long chain hanging around Hansen's neck.
"Manos!" Liz's face was livid. "Run!"

Where?

He pulled Liz down from the arbor and tried another key. The door opened. He pushed her. She fell to safety at the last second.
"R-Run!"
He had to force the word out of his mouth.
Because something very hard was caught in his calf, like the sting of a huge wasp. There was no pain yet. Manos let the door swing closed behind him and locked it again. Then he took the keys and pitched them with force right into the pool. He stood, staring. Made it... Pool's twenty yards away...

Liz was safe. He was locked in with the murderer.
"Really?" Hansen laughed. But there was no message now.
The pain set in. It was like a transfusion, millions of minuscule drummers drumming on his hip and the arteries of his leg with red-hot little hammers.

"What do you owe anybody?" asked Hansen. "You only care about data."

"Data brought me here."

He took off his tie and squeezed it around his hip, uselessly. It would probably cause more bleeding somewhere else before it could stem the blood already flowing. Hansen was taking aim again. Determined to kill him. Right here, at the stone fence. Makes sense, statistically. Many people have been executed against a stone wall...

"Psychology brought you here," murmured Hansen. "I brought you here..."

The pain crawled through Manos' leg, becoming intolerable. He made to run, but fell, narrowly escaping Hansen's next shot. This time, the spear was attached to a thread. The same thread he'd seen in Jenna Will's body.

He was going to die. Murdered, here and now. In seconds. *Really? How many?*

This time, Hansen needed time to reload. Manos ran back to the living room. He needed a weapon. A phone. Or anything to shield himself. He found nothing but congealing blood. He slipped suddenly and fell hard onto Lena's body. He tried to get up. *I'm weak.*

A chain.

In her mouth.

He tried to get up. *So weak.*

Then another. Around his neck. His own neck.

He was choking.

Hansen had dropped his weapon, strangling him. Not strangling - transporting. Strangling, for him to transcend. Manos heard the winch activate. He was dragged to the other side of the table, slammed like a fish breathing his last on the railing of a fishing boat. The chain was shifted down from his neck, winding around him, compressing his chest. Pain surged through his body. The smell of blood filled his nostrils; the strands of Hansen's blood soaked goatee dug into the nape of his neck. The adventure is only beginning, their prickling seemed to hiss into his skin. The pain only starting.

"Not... your fault!" Manos spluttered. "You're... not alone."

Hansen heard him, but had every right not to listen. He decided these weren't words. Merely a distant sound.

"The murders..." Manos panted, "...happening... other places too. You're... a team! You don't... each other... think you're alone, but... ha- ...hackers on the same pr-project... different places. Same... murders and... chains. The winch - same. Same... buoys. Same... message. Three!... Three places... You're p-puppets! They'll... see your... time-lines. We don't... not correlations. We read... read algori - these are... deep... murders..."

The open wound was searing his leg. His lungs felt ready to collapse under the chain's tight grasp. Pain flooded his whole body, digging deep into his brain. *No one can hear me.* He squeezed his eyes shut, choking on the reek of pain, his mind reaching for something else, anything else, to process.

He didn't want to live his last moments in fear.

Mei's face glimmered in the darkness.

82.

If you can turn freedom into slavery, then surely you can create a simulation for love. Right? Some, you make criminals. Others, you declare innocent. Convert the serious into the ridiculous. Truth into lies. Lies into reality. So it is with love. To make it look present where it is absent, unravelling it wherever it exists. Like a hologram, appearing and disappearing before our eyes at the click of a mouse. And yet, you can't.

Because I am here. With my love. The one I fell in love with even before I understood how the world works. The one I've come to know so well. In the icy landscapes. On the sea... Her body. Her laughter. The one who made me rethink everything, who restored my faith. She's here on the boat. We're slicing the waters at forty miles an hour. Somewhere beyond the horizon, where the sun is rising, lies Turkey. Beautiful Turkey! Our Honeymoon.

But that was not meant to happen.

Franz Hansen set out to do what no criminal ever does: Start over. At the beginning. Not to forget their crimes, but forget themselves.

Now, three miles back, he could already see them: two coast guard speedboats with their grey hulls and a helicopter, rising from the island and gaining on him. *Run! Run and search our timelines! You'll see how it all happened.*

Before escaping the island, he had left Manos Manu half-unconscious, half-delirious. He'd heard the wheels of a car grinding along the dirt road. And another from the opposite direction. No time to finish. He left the winch running. To do the work of suffocating Manos. *No time to clean up.* No longer any reason to. No time to dive into the pool and get the keys to go find Liz Will. Nothing to get from upstairs.

Time only for a perfect departure.

There was a smaller doorway in the fence. The back door, giving right onto the cove. He lifted Lena's body onto his back, taking her buoy and another one - his last. He went down to the beach. Turned on the boat's engine. Tied the buoy to himself. Then he sped out onto the open waters. Above, people were breaking down the gate to the house.

He had time. All the time in the world.

Him. Her.

He gripped the boat's steering wheel and looked back. Where Bill Casey, Jenna Will and Willa Kendall had lain, Lena Sideris lay, naked. Dead. A chain running through her corpse.

Things had gone terribly wrong. Or perhaps, perfectly well. They could not start over from the beginning. But at least they could finish at the start.
"Police! Doctor Hansen! Turn off the engine! Stop the boat! Now!"

A megaphone, high overhead. The deafening whirr of the helicopter. He looped the boat in a circle.

And stopped.

The sea was calm as a pool of blood. Hansen dragged Lena's body to the boat rail.

"Freeze! Don't do ANYTHING!"

He raised his arms. The chop-chop-chop of the helicopter bearing down on him. With a jerk, he pushed Lena's body overboard. Then the anchor. He watched the chain unroll, then go taut, sucking her whole body down. Almost immediately, her beautiful face vanished into the depths.

It didn't shock him.

He lifted his arms again, as if saying, *I'm here. I've really made it.* The officers at the chopper didn't know what to do. Shoot him? Could they? *Really?*

Then, as though he'd forgotten it, he threw another anchor overboard. Its chain was attached to a rope, tied in a bowline knot around his ankle. The rope now uncoiled, seemingly endless. On the other end, his buoy. He climbed onto the railing, looking ready to turn himself in. Then he plunged into the water. The falling rope tugged him down by the leg.

Sinking swiftly. *So deep...* He could not see the bottom. So very blue... It seemed to surge from below and within. As if straight from the center of the earth. Open. Sparkling. He breathed in this blue with all his might.

He saw the eyes of his victims. They did not seek mercy, but freedom. It was his legacy. He was glad. And then, the blue darkening fast, he saw the bottom. How ordinary it was. Two boulders. Seaweed. Endless sand. He needed nothing more. In the ordinary, he could begin again.

His chest was throbbing hard. He looked up. His rope was more than ample. Far above, the buoy floated. White. Bearing its short message:

FREE

83.

Somewhere, children were playing.

Manos couldn't tell what game it was, but from their voices, he knew it was serious. Someone was winning, but the losers wouldn't let up. He tried to open his eyes, but someone else was leaning on him. "Mr. Manu!" they were saying. "Manos!"

Is this hide-and-seek? Am I it? Even though the light hurt his eyes, he had to come out.

Time's up!

"Manos!"

But who was there? Frederick? Was that Chrisanthos? Bellas?

More voices outside.
"Let me in! That's my friend!"
"Calm down, guys! He's ok!"

I'm alive?

An unbearable weight on his ribcage. Hansen's winch, left running... Such pain in his chest, every breath cost him. But the worst was his leg. He managed to see it; there was a hole on both sides. Fantastic. The spear had gone clean through.
"Ha-Hansen..."
"Hansen's swimming with the fishes!"
"Take a breath."

With the fishes...
"Dead!" called Chrisanthos. "He drowned!"
Lena... she was just here. And Liz!
"Liz is ok!" cried Frederick.
"Manos..."
"Does it hurt? We're getting you out of here."
"Help me with these chains!" yelled one of the police officers. Voices he didn't recognize. Trying to figure out how the winch operated. They were unwinding him, just as he had tried to untangle Liz. Shaking pretty badly...
"Call a doctor! Get help!"
It was all he could remember. Struggling with the net. Lena... *Who's going to tell her father?* He was about to cry, but no one noticed. He drew himself a bit straighter. *Hansen...* He wanted to tell them where to find the keys to the gate. *Check the pool! We have to get out! There's no other way...*

He fell asleep.

When he awoke, the sparkle of daybreak had given way to the glow of sunset. Completely exhausted, Manos didn't know the difference. Thinking he'd only nodded off a few minutes, he'd been fast asleep for thirty hours.

He was in Mykonos Hospital. He could hear the woosh of cars outside, heading to and from the beaches. Cicadas. Reaching through the pain, he searched for his phone.

On Signal, one 💟 from Mei. On Slack, a .pdf from Novak: airline tickets. *I'm leaving... is this...when?* On WhatsApp, Jeremy Ong sent an invitation to visit on his boat along with get-well wishes. Viber was flooded. Dozens and dozens more on Messenger. The story of Hansen's arrest was public. Two more on Telegram. He didn't dare check Twitter.

"You can go in now . . ."

He didn't see the nurse, but she was letting someone through. It was James. Without sleep for two days, his beard was overgrown, he looked like he could use some hospital time too.

"Thank you," he said. "For saving my wife."

"She ok?"

"They gave her something to calm her - and to counter the ketamine. She's right next door here."

"Some wedding, huh?"

"Some wedding!"

There was so much left to say, but it would wait till another time. The day was waning; people were on their way back from the beaches, getting ready for their night out. James looked more anxious and exhausted than ever.

"Does it hurt bad?" he asked.

"I just... have to get something off my chest."

They laughed.

Then Manos said, "James, I'm ok, really."

James gave his hand a squeeze.

"Then let's get out here, right?"

He was discharged in no time, more thanks to Officer Bellas than the doctors. If Mr. Manu wished to leave, then of course - by all means. If Mr. Manu wanted a doctor, then only the very best! If Mr. Manu wanted a massage, they would bring Mykonos' top masseur. A crutch for Mr. Manu, quickly!

But Mr. Manu only wanted to say goodbye.

Manos and Bellas stood just outside the hospital's main entrance waiting for Chrisanthos to bring the patrol car around; he and James were going to bring Manos down to the port. The bride would be discharged later in the day. For these murders, Bellas had done his best with the information he had. But a new world was emerging, one he didn't comprehend, eager for hacks and math. A world devoid of what had brought him to law enforcement in the first place. And Lena Sideris was no longer there to explain it all to him.

"It's torn our hearts out." He did sound like his heart was gone, adding, "I knew her when she was a baby, when her father ran the department."

"Chrisanthos told me she was... brought back."

"Yes, she wasn't so far down. They got her first, then him. She was buried in the afternoon."

"What about the funeral?" asked Manos.

"It's over. It's what the family wanted," said Bellas, his voice trembling. "And of course the new guy came! The coroner from Athens! Right on time..." He laughed bitterly.

Manos said nothing. *Where the hell is Chrisanthos?*

"But why...?" It was all Bellas could say.

"No one knows," said Manos.

"I mean, she didn't have will in her name, right?"

"Lena told me they were writing a book together. That's probably why she went back to him."

"Ok, but why kill her? Why so... brutal?"

Manos felt a shiver run through him. Half pain, half something else.
"I don't know," he said. "All I have is… numbers…" Then his own voice was shaky too, as he said, "Please give my regards to her father."
"I will," said Bellas. "You always have the right answer."
"Not always," mumbled Manos. "Not this time."

The patrol car rolled up. Chrisanthos got out of the driver's seat to open the rear door, ready to help Manos into the back. James got out and stood waiting for Manos, as if these were standard bureaucratic formalities. Bellas put his hand on Manos' shoulder, holding him back a minute.
"I'm sorry," he said, with tears in his eyes. "And thank you."

Manos let go of the crutch.
"You did what you could," he said, aware that whatever he said would be etched in this man's mind forever. "You almost got him yourself."

Bellas' face suddenly brightened, even for a second. It was as if he was counting probabilities, for the first time. And doing so, made him briefly a friend to himself.
"Almost," he said finally, before letting go of his hand.

84.

"Manos! Our new superstar!"

Jeremy Ong greeted Manos with a big hug. Seeing Manos' bandaged leg and the protective gauze dressing wrapped around his chest, he took a slight step back but no injury was going to dampen his enthusiasm.
"Welcome aboard the Hayken!"

Manos and James had just climbed the stairs onto Ong's 150-feet boat, which was moored in the port of Mykonos Town. Manos had never been on such a big, luxurious yacht before; in spite of his pain, his own triumph and his relative indifference for such things, Manos couldn't hide a faint sense of awe over the way some people lived.
"Would you like someone to give you a tour of the boat?"
"I'm good, thanks."

The bow alone had four tiers, each as large as a good-sized apartment. The stairs had led them to the second of these, which featured outdoor sofas, a broad mahogany dining table, and a bar complete with high wicker armchairs. Members of the crew in white *Hayken* t-shirts - three men and two women - came and went, discreetly anticipating their employer's every desire.

Ong's was a charmed life. He had created a small universe of his own, placing himself at its center. As for Manos, he was thankful to be alive.

James, perfectly at home in this environment, led Manos to a couch and asked a crewmember for some drinks. He had changed. There was something different in his whole demeanor. Almost losing Liz had shaken him. His having invited Hansen to the wedding weighed on him heavily, and Lena's death left a little crack in his pearly newlywed soul. The world was a tougher and a less predictable place than he'd ever imagined. He showed more appreciation and respect for Manos. Not only because he'd rescued Liz, but for choosing to enter law enforcement in such a world. New mysteries had carved out caverns beneath the surface of this wedding, a secret moat of blood and fleeting chances. The friendship mattered more to him than ever.

"You and Hansen are all over the internet," Ong was saying. "The psychologist and the data scientist! The rationalist versus the empiricist! Aristotle meets Plato! Spinoza against Locke!"

"The internet has no idea who Locke is," said Manos. "I barely know myself."

"Oh, sure! You know nothing of philosophy," Ong laughed. "I know what you've been through, but still - very intriguing!"

"What?"

"Hansen and his theories, struggling to find the root cause of crime. Total fail. And you, trusting only data. I mean, both of you took it really far."

"Jeremy," said James firmly, standing by Manos, "the man put his life in danger."

"Yes, but look at him now! He's fine." Ong stood back, as if pointing to a statue. "He's the first person ever to find a criminal strictly using data science. He's changed police investigation forever. Tomorrow, everybody will be doing it."

"They already are. Today," said Manos.

"They're not going this far!" Ong insisted.

A man brought over a tray of drinks. The doctors had advised Manos to avoid alcohol for a few days, but that didn't seem likely.

Jeremy Ong knew exactly what Interpol had made public. He knew what Manos had presented. Even his presentation to Hansen's Conference was online. Did he know it all? Certainly not. Essential pieces were missing. The core of the MANU methodology. Its sources. And of course, their sheer luck. But for a mind like Ong's, understanding the result meant understanding everything that mattered. Not the flaws of the system or the inaccurate weighting. Not the bugs, or that they still had to beg for data or process it manually. Not even the fact that Yan himself didn't always understand exactly how some of their mathematical models worked. What mattered were results. One man - not all of the Greek police force - discovered the murderer. One man had located him at the critical moment. And this man was sitting right in front of him. A perfect example of proof of concept.

"Every police force in the world will want to lay hands on this system. I think you have a multibillion-dollar market at your disposal, Manos," Ong declared. "You will have to decide what you want to do with it."

So this was what he'd wanted to tell him.

James looked at him. Good for you, Man-Man. He seemed to be saying. You were right. You pursued what you wanted. You didn't become a VC partner like Stefan. You didn't go down to Wall Street. You became a cop. Everyone laughed at you - even me. But you did it. You stood apart from the crowd and did it all yourself. Great! And yet it was as if Ong had crossed a line. James got up without speaking and went to the railing, looking out.

James Will had changed.

"You know, I'm a cop." Manos was suddenly dizzy from the combination of sugar and alcohol. "If it weren't for cops, there would be no order. Without order, there is no information. No way of understanding people. Of understanding ourselves."

"You're a Police Philosopher!" said Ong.

"In the service of Interpol," said Manos, wrapping up the discussion.

"To serve and protect, is it?"

"To upload and run!"

They chuckled over this, and the atmosphere lightened.

But Jeremy was still interested. "So - case closed?"

The question gave Manos a pain in his chest he couldn't hide. *Should I hide it?* He wondered.

"Of course not," was his answer.

"We still have the other murders, right?" asked Jeremy.

This got James' attention. Jeremy Ong and Manos Manu knew something he didn't. Jeremy swept both of them into an enclosed lounge with two huge OLED screens behind the bar. But they weren't showing soccer games or local channels. They were connected to a huge office space. Three people were looking at them from a webcam.

"I told the boys to take a look at what was going on with these murders."

The 'boys' in question were there on the screen. In spite of the slippers and t-shirt, Manos recalled that he wasn't talking with just any tech genius. This was product manager at one of the giants.

"They found press coverage yesterday," said Ong. "Five victims in Singapore. Another in Florida. No mention of their being linked, of course. Nobody's made the connection. That would require skills."

"They never will connect them," said Manos bluntly.

Ong nodded in agreement. "Yesterday, they caught Guo Long in Singapore. His victims had been killed within the last five days. With a spear gun. Passing chains of increasing gauge through them. And he put them in the water with a white buoy for each of them. And all labelled with the same word."

James now spoke. "Free...?"

"Ding-ding! Shan, the Confucian equivalent. Same thing for the guy in Florida, Larry Wozinsky. They tried to find a connection, but they found nothing. So the question the boys were asking -"

"How is it possible..?" James asked. He was pale as a ghost from lack of sleep, but Ong's insinuation was inconceivable.

"How on earth can three men who have no documented communication between them, all in different parts of the world, have exactly the same idea for murders which they execute at exactly the same time in precisely the same way? What's the probability of that, Manos?"

Manos was now concerned that Jeremy's next step would be extortion. Forcing him to leave Interpol, bringing MANU with him, to package it for the police and sell it to the private sector. For billions. But he had miscalculated Jeremy Ong. He wasn't talking about money. He was talking about possibilities.

"In the millions," Manos answered.

"Exactly!" Ong agreed. He was on fire. "With MANU, Manos actually reverse-engineered a whole other system..."

A new world! A new era!

"Christopher, are you online?" This was the coordinator for the video call, managing the sound and any time lag on the call from behind his Mac. Ong continued, "I am with Mr. Manu, from Interpol. He's the one who found them here!"

"Good evening - evening for you, Mr. Manu," said Christopher through the screen. "Congratulations, and we hope you feel better very soon. It's an honor to meet you."

Everything about Ong's outfit breathed sobriety and discipline. Manos put his drink down on the counter.

"Should we treat them to Operation Shawl?" asked Ong. "I feel like showing off a little."

"Coming right up, Jeremy," said Christopher, turning to his own team. The video call was muted on both sides.

"We like to toy with social engineering, too," said Ong excitedly. "You know, for fun, on the weekends. But what the guys did with those murders is way out of our league!"

"What the guys did with those murders?" James asked.

Manos went to a nearby railing. Jeremy gave him a significant look. "Manos, what happens on the Hayken stays on the Hayken. And trust me, there's been a lot!"

James looked like he wanted no part of this pleasantry, but Manos explained.

"Jeremy's right. Our system found three murderers with the exact same characteristics. Among the trillions of interactions occurring online, this is actually impossible. For something like that to happen, their basic characteristics would have to be identical. This is especially true for the inputs."

James was lost.

"Hel-lo!" chimed Ong. "Someone hacked their timelines!"

This was no help to James.

"Our system looks for people with certain basic characteristics - mostly what we call dark traits, as outlined in psychological studies. Egoism, Machiavellianism, moral detachment, narcissism, psychopathy, sadism - you get the picture. These can be measured for anyone online by their actions. Think of it as a credit score for psychopaths. We know who these people are, or we can find them if need be. The issue is -"

"How anyone else can find them!" Ong cut in.

"How others can find them, yes," nodded Manos.

"The way I'm about to find out which women like red scarves," said Ong. He now had them both at the railing, gazing at the port. Thousands were strolling in the later afternoon sun. The restaurants were full. "Who wants to bet that in the next hour, we'll see at least five red scarves out there?" asked Ong.

"Me!" laughed James.

Manos said nothing. *I want to see how he does it,* he thought.

"It'll cost me a couple thousand, but when it comes to progress, money is no object." Ong was cheerful. "So! How many red scarves do you see out there? Check out the whole port."

James looked carefully. "None," he said.

"None!" repeated Ong dramatically.

Just then, a girl wearing a Hayken t-shirt, her hair in a smooth pony-tail, came into view.

"Dinner is ready, Jeremy," she said.

"Dinner is ready!" repeated Ong gleefully.

He sounded rather like a winner himself.

They went one deck below to an extravagantly laid dinner table commanding a scenic view of the port. And a surprise: Stefan, Frederick, Sandy and Alexandra, along with another friend or two, were waiting to welcome them. It took neither genius nor intuition to spot the guest of honor; the center seat awaited Manos Manu, who, handing his crutch to a crewmember, put his arms around Frederick. He owed him his life.

Jeremy Ong raised his glass.

"Friends, we were invited here for a wedding. But we met with so much more. In James, a witness, attesting to his love with marriage. A fighter - Liz - who will be with us shortly. And a hero. Manos, who caught the murderer!"

"With Freddo's help!" said James.

"A models guy and another models guy!" said Alexandra.

Applause and cheers all around.

Alexandra's hug had been slightly awkward; she and Frederick were finally an official item. It was the best news of the day; Manos had no room in his life for Ms. Atkinson. As it was, he was being whisked off the next morning to Mykonos airport for his Athens flight. From there, he'd have barely enough time to catch the flight for Singapore via Dubai. Now that's murder! But he'd already survived once; seemed like he would survive plenty more in the future. Ong had invited him to stay overnight, offering to take him to the airport in the morning. He was eager to hear as much as he could about MANU directly from its creator. The internet was glutted with leaks from Greek law enforcement about Interpol's assistance and their 'digital weapons'.

Manos declined. "Perhaps another time..."

Ong devoted the evening to his demonstration of the internet's vulnerability. During dinner, his team ran targeted advertising, purchasing location data and calibrating it with psyops on the population currently at the port. MANU-manoeuvering for shawls! as he quipped. Days earlier, his crew had placed high-end luxury shawls on stands in every boutique, priced so low that not a single merchant turned them down. All red.

"We could have gone directly into Google's Ad Manager or Facebook," Jeremy explained. "Just like the Chinese in '09 - everybody does it! I imagine the buoy hackers did just that. But why raise any red flags, eh? Pardon the pun...!"

Then his eyes lit up like a schoolboy, a mischievous smile spreading across his face. Sandy was the first to turn and follow his gaze, scanning the people walking and lounging along the pier. A woman in a red shawl appeared.

"Ooh, I want one of those!" she said.

Music was now coming from the deck speakers. James Will stood up and went to the railing, as if something was missing. Something his life depended on. But Jeremy Ong also wore a look of concern, rising from the table to descend the stairs leading to the dock. They thought he was completely absorbed with his experiment, but he reappeared with Liz beside him, delicate and lovely as ever.

"Liz!"

They sprang forward to hug her, not without some tears of relief and joy. As if she had washed ashore in Homer's nets, cast upon the dark-wine sea. She thanked Manos with a warm kiss and sank down next to James. Wrapping her arms around him, she gently kissed his lips. The two of them beamed brighter than the pure whitewashed houses of Mykonos in the moonlight, sharing their glow with Alexandra and Frederick, Stefan and Sandy.

Manos set aside both crutches and leaned over the railing. There were now red shawls everywhere, freshly purchased and billowing in the night air, draped over dozens of tanned shoulders.

"You realize this is a paradigm shift," said Ong, leaning beside him, perfectly content. "Not murders. We're talking viruses."

"And what's a cop supposed to do?" Manos asked, his voice hushed. "Catch the murderers - or the programmers?"

"Both!" said Ong with a smile. "One after the other!" The music was more and more enticing, but Manos Manu was without a dance partner. He couldn't breathe so well just yet, and every time he took a real step without his crutches, a needle of pain shot through his leg.

"One after the other," Manos said, with resolution.

X. Deep Murders

CJ ABAZIS

85.

Interpol had only one way of expressing thanks, and they used it sparingly. He stretched his legs comfortably in the first class for the Athens - Singapore flight. He slept all the way to Dubai, but his body clamored for more rest. When they landed, his mouth was dry and his bones ached. He wished the flight could just keep going all the way home to New York; he'd sleep the whole way over the Pacific and not wake up until the plane circled down over JFK. But the Pacific would have to wait.

The day was hazy and hot over the island of Tekong and Changi Airport. The Emirates flight attendants notified him a golf cart had been ordered and politely ignored Manos' protests that he didn't need one. Not wanting to make too much fuss, he accepted, letting himself be wheeled to the exit. They took a different walkway; Manos saw barely any other travelers. Along the way, he asked to get down and walk, but the attendant wouldn't let him. She steered him along a corridor leading not to another exit but to another boarding gate.

"Sir," she said, "someone wishes to see you."

"I can get there myself," Manos was almost whining at this point.

"From this point, yes," said the attendant, bringing him to the edge of a different embarkation walkway. Manos saw that it led to another airplane.

Air China.

"Here?" He asked her.

She nodded with a smile.

A small airport security team was watching from a discreet distance. Manos stood up; he regretted it almost immediately, but, grasping the cane he'd bought at Duty Free in Dubai, he shrugged off the attendant who'd come to his aid. He advanced the length of the airway and, after a sign from a security agent at the door, entered the plane.

It was empty.

He was about to turn back and say something, but the man at the door motioned for him to continue. He reached business class, where, in the space between business and economy, someone spoke.

"Dr. Manu. Dr. Manos Manu..."

He turned. Standing there - quite tall, somewhere near fifty, and rather handsome - was a man who needed no introduction. Anyone involved with machine learning knew exactly who he was.

"Dr. Zhong," said Manos.

"Zao, please. I hope you will forgive me for this unexpected meeting. But I've come a bit early for my flight, and I understood you were passing through. I am very glad to meet you," continued the professor. He stepped forward, shaking hands.

"The pleasure is all mine," said Manos, with sincerity. He was hooked now, not a trace of jet lag. Ready to get as much insight as he could.

"You might not realize it, but we too have been following the buoy murder cases very closely."

Who is 'we'? thought Manos. Then he said, "My colleague told me you and she had a very good... rapport." *Diplomatic indeed!* The same thought ran through both of them. The same longing. "And," he continued quickly, "you helped us. Thank you, really."

Zao gave him a smile, clearly taking a liking to him. After a pause, he said, "Yes. The case is of particular interest, from an investigative stand-point." He let this sentence hang in the air a while; it was a technique Manos knew well, designed to induce him to divulge what he knew.

"So - this virus is your little game?" he asked, unable to stop himself. Zao took a deep breath, as if he needed more oxygen to fuel the thoughts he was about to unveil.

"It may have been us," he began. "It may have been someone else. It may very have been no one at all - or you yourself!"

"You really don't know?" asked Manos.

"Dr. Manu. Over four billion people are contributing as we speak to research on AI and machine learning."

"Someone should let them know it."

Zao motioned for Manos to follow him to where the flight crew prepped the in-flight meals. He opened a cabinet or two, fished out some coffee, and poured a cup for each of them.

"Right... or perhaps not. Does it matter?" Zao said, taking a cautious sip. He wasn't a fan of airplane coffee, especially this late - it was nine o'clock. But it was a courtesy for Manos after his long-haul flight.

"The virus... the program... it isn't necessarily malware. What matters is why it was created."

"My question exactly," said Manos. "A dozen people were murdered. Five of them here. Their bodies were desecrated, in the worst way. Why? If you don't know, Professor Zhong, who does?"

"It could be anything! A lone gunman, or someone just doing AI re-search in his room."

"But you don't believe that."

Zao took another sip of coffee.

"Think about it, Manos. In our work, the money is controlled by people who most fear the weaponization of AI. They're terrified. That's why we're here. Don't forget incentive wrapping within an AI's framework, the system's ability to reward people - contributors - for its success."

"That could indicate a lone gunman."

"It could."

"Someone is creating algorithms that will make future artificial intelligence systems richer. They manipulate strategies and validate them in the real world... with real actions... and extreme, antisocial... high-risk behaviors..." Manos felt a sudden wave of envy for any such programmer.

"It's... pure gold!" said Zao.

"He fully expects the system to reward him."

"Hey," chimed Zao. "Let's change sides! Smarter to be in with whoever's up-and-coming."

"So it's people, not governments."

Zao set his coffee down on the little table.

"I'm not here to tell you how I know it, Manos," he said, "but I do congratulate you. While you were away, I got an overview of the modules you built. You are the first one to prove something like this is even feasible."

"Thanks -" began Manos, but Zao was quick to continue: "I want you to know we could get better results working together."

Manos froze. *Is this an offer? A threat? From who?*

"Why don't we let the politicians decide that?" said Manos.

"All the politicians will want is help getting elected. The rest is up to us, Manos. The truth is, you have problems with your data, and you know it."

"No problems - just need a serious debugging."

"Manos..."

"Change some weights. Adjust endpoints."

"Ma-nos."

Quiet. Zao had the upper hand.

"I know your difficulty in procuring quality data. In the end, they'll give you nothing - even pull the plug on you. Is there anything worse than being forbidden to dream?"

Manos considered a moment.

"Yes," he answered. "Having your dreams dictated to you."

Dr. Zhong decided he'd gone far enough. He didn't want to risk burning any bridges with this team. The time would come when they would indeed work together. He gave him a soft smile, nodding in the direction of the airplane entrance.

"Whoops! It looks like we'll be taking you to Beijing!"

Two or three people, shuffling about as if boarding, came and glanced their way. After making a show of putting a few items in their seats, they left. Manos smiled and gripped his cane.

"Some other time," he said.

Zao Zhong gave him a firm handshake. Then he took out his business card and gave it to him.

"Take care of that girl of yours."

A current of electricity ran through Manos. He knew exactly whom he meant. He'd sent her loads of messages before leaving Greece. Another upon landing. No answer.

"She's quite out there." Zao smiled, a genuine grin Manos had seen in many photographs. "You're made for each other."

They both laughed.

It would be a while until the Air China craft took off. But Dr. Manu was expected elsewhere.

86.

Next morning, IGCI's central hall was packed, mostly with people Manos didn't even know. Beside Daniel Novak stood Michaela, Brianna and other members from Cyber. He saw Ahmad and others from their own team, but other faces were completely new to him. *Was there a hiring spree when I was gone?* In fact, Manos never fully appreciated how many people worked at Interpol's Innovation Center. From the start, he'd narrowed his world to the few individuals coming and going from Novak's office, including Yan and the math team, who were as critical to the system builds as electricity to a computer. Now, as he made his way through the entrance of the hall, leaning on his cane like Gregory House, Manos was applauded by dozens of people.

They did it. They'd really succeeded.

But Mei was nowhere to be found.

He shook hands with each of them. Project managers congratulated him, wishing him a speedy recovery. Tech managers gushed about system upgrades. In his office, someone had put up a posterboard: "J0hnL0ck3" Now that's cute... Seeing Novak motioning him into his office, Manos pulled Yan aside and asked for a quick favor before going in.

Once the door was closed behind them, Novak said, "The guys ran correlations between Guo Long, Larry Wozinsky and Franz Hansen. Web, social, blogs running alongside searches, news - the works. This thing goes back three or four years."

Manos said nothing, letting Novak spill everything first.

"Very often, the same sources. Articles appearing only to them. GANs, clearly." Generative Adversarial Networks, a machine learning technique making it possible to rapidly create compelling images of non-existent people. Combined with other techniques, the networks could fabricate millions of profiles on social media within seconds. By the time social media algorithms could parse them out, the damage was done: an adversarial AI had picked out, among billions of people, those who shared the fundamental characteristics of a serial killer. And created millions of other fake profiles. Thousands of fake news items. And every time the possible candidates of the system connected to the internet, they were automatically steered towards creating a plan for their own "redemption," seen by no one - or so they thought. "The triggers are what you would expect," continued Novak. "An article on the mechanization of research. Another on the importance of the individual within society. Ads for winches. Articles about murderers who'd made their victims swallow objects. Hints suggesting the use of buoys to send political messages." He took a breath. "They were driven to it, Manos. Driven to it step by step."

"And among the millions, it came down to three," said Manos.

"A numbers game, yes."

"Where's Mei?"

"She's with the chief of Singapore Police. Giving a statement."

"But why not you? You're her director."

"They seemed to think she'd give better tech insight. Crazy, I know." Both men laughed. Then Novak said, his tone more grave: "Manos, we're trying to keep this quiet."

Manos understood; Novak wasn't looking to keep the murders quiet - it was the correlations he wanted under wraps. This was the real reason Mei was debriefing Singapore Police. It was important to convince the local authorities that the sovereign city-state of Singapore would benefit most from downplaying the whole affair. Mei was perfect for the job.

"There is no reason to connect these murders to any official file," said Novak.

"Mykonos never connects anything," Manos muttered.

"Oh, Mykonos makes connections. But not the connections Singapore makes. And Singapore won't make the connections Key West makes. As far as we are concerned, these events are unrelated. There are no machine murders. Only machine solutions."

"Understood."

"But we can't control everything, damn it!" Novak said, laughing. "Some people will sniff it out. And someone already has found out - about you. You're the official Guru of machine crime, my boy! I've already gotten an order to send you home."

"Home?"

"The FBI has requested a meeting. Their Behavioral Science Unit would like a briefing about our department - and our system. Pittsburgh awaits!"

Manos couldn't suppress a smile. He did miss the States.

"I'd need a few extra days," he said.

"Fine. But listen, don't even dream you're getting away from Interpol!" said Novak. "Once you're back, we need to create a strategy for all this."

"Oh, but we already have one," Manos was beaming now.

"We do?"

"We catch the murderers. And the programmers."

"How do we do that?"

"One after the other," said Manos, opening the door to Novak's office.

"And if it's governments, Manos?"

Manos stood in the doorway.

"One after the other," he repeated.

87.

Piece of cake! Yan had promised.

Mei already had Interpol apps on her phone. On his way out the doors of ICGI, Manos received Yan's link through their official Slack; he drove straight to the Botanical Gardens on Marina Bay and stood in line with the tourists to buy a ticket. Entirely enclosed beneath an enormous glass dome, the gardens featured a towering man-made cliff covered with plant life, complete with caves to discover and scenic overlooks. Cascades of water rushed down from various heights; by the tallest of these Manos singled out the elegant lines of her back.

"I knew it," she said when she saw him.

"Knew what?"

"That you would make Yan find me. I just thought I'd check."

She was clearly struggling to keep a smile from spreading across her face, scanning his injuries instead. His chest seemed healed beneath his t-shirt, and the bandage on his leg was small. *He's ok...*

Manos took her in also; she seemed just as fearless and stubborn as ever.

"You realize we need to upload a new build, don't you?" he asked.

"For MANU?"

"Nope. For MEI-NU. Our other project." He meant a new version of some software they had written on their breaks. Just for fun. They each put their own weights on a search for the perfect partner, crawling the profiles of every available dating site. This gave them much more specific results than the individual host sites could. A love menu, their own personal dating aggregator service - but it hadn't gotten them far.

"Oh, I already have."

"Really!" said Manos.

"While you were away. I found I'm much more of a data slut than I thought."

"Data slut?"

"Yup. I'll do anything for just a little more input."

"So your ideal partner is someone with access to data..."

She shook her head. "My ideal partner is someone who can tolerate it."

Manos laughed. "But it's not such a bad thing!"

They strolled to an overlook to avoid being splashed.

"I also tweaked a few of your details," said Mei.

"Such as...?"

Mei held back at first, but then she said, "You demonstrate more of an inclination for the Mediterranean type than I foresaw."

"You need some high parameter tuning, I see."

"No need. I've got good ol' linear regression."

"You're way off! I told you, I like Sun Li."

"Full-on Mediterranean..."

"I think you should validate your data, Mei."

He took her hand.

They hovered a long moment over their clasped hands, their eyes streaming information.

Mei leaned forward to validate.

The End

The Machine Murders: Island Buoys was printed on black and white interior with cream paper with a trim size 6 x 9 inches (15.24 x 22.86 cm) with Matte cover and is offered by KDP Editions on behalf of Publisto Ltd (2021). For enquiries about the book and information about its author, please visit: www.themachinemurders.com.

 Publisto

Made in the USA
Columbia, SC
07 August 2021